The Minority Report

The Minority Report

Silenced by Religion

Loren Fisher

Fisher Publications

Willits, Ca

To order additional copies of this book, contact:
Xlibris Corporation
1-888-795-4274
www.Xlibris.com
Orders@Xlibris.com
24217

Contents

For Betty,

Who seeks no reward for her extended hand.

Other Books by Loren Fisher
from Fisher Publications
and available at Xlibris.com:

Genesis, A Royal Epic
Introduction, Translation, and Notes

Who Hears the Cries of the Innocent?
Introductions, Translations, and Notes for Job I & II

The Jerusalem Academy
A Story of the Production of a Royal Epic

The Story of the Shipwrecked Sailor
Translated from the Egyptian by Loren Fisher
Illustrated by John Fisher

"Profound flashes of insight remain ineffective for centuries, not because they are unknown, but by reason of dominant interests which inhibit reaction to that type of generality."

(From Alfred North Whitehead's *Adventures of Ideas*, [1933], Free Press, 1967, p 171)

Acknowledgements

This is a fictionalized story about real events. It is clear that someone did enter into serious debate with the fundamentalists whom we meet in the traditions of the Hebrew Bible. We may never know exactly when this happened or who turned against these fundamentalists, but it did happen. I have put some fictionalized flesh on factual bones in order to allow Keziah to tell her story.

Most of the minority opinions expressed in this book, I have encountered in the literature of the Ancient Mediterranean World. When it is possible I look at the actual text, and at the end of the translation or discussion, I will indicate where the text can be found, or the reader can find such information in the "Afterword." Sometimes I have depended upon the translations of other scholars. For some Sumerian texts, I have used Thorkild Jacobsen's *The Harps that Once . . .* (New Haven: Yale University Press, 1987) and for some Egyptian texts Miriam Lichtheim's *Ancient Egyptian Literature* (Berkeley: University of California Press, 1973). In Chapter VIII, I have translated *The Story of the Shipwrecked Sailor* from Egyptian, and Lichtheim's translation was helpful and informative. However I wanted to make available for my readers a few more options within the translation. James B. Pritchard's *Ancient Near Eastern Texts,* Second Edition, is also helpful for these materials (Princeton: Princeton University Press, 1955).

The portrait on the cover of an Egyptian scribe was painted by John Fisher and also appears in our illustrated book, *The Story of the Shipwrecked Sailor.*

I want to thank Daniel Fisher and Stan Rummel for their comments and two presenters from the Mendocino Coast Writers Conference. They are Valerie Miner (2002) and Jean Hegland (2003). Their suggestions concerning this book were helpful and encouraging. My editor, Suzanne Byerley, has helped me for several years. She has had to put up with a lot from my old academic habits. Thanks Suzanne.

Prologue

My name is Keziah. I am the daughter of Jael, my loving mother, and of Gad, who was one of David's prophets. My husband, Jonathan, is David's uncle (though they are close in age) and a scribe in the Jerusalem Academy where we live in the school compound. Soon after I met Jonathan he said to me, "I'm usually in the minority on most issues. I would expect such a thing when I 'm talking with anyone at David's table, but it is also true when I try to discuss matters with other scribes whose positions are predictable on most things. Someday I'm going to write a long poem and call it *The Minority Report*."

We soon realized the "long poem" could be a book. Jonathan was busy with the Royal Epic and later with his poem on Job. So I took over the task of trying to keep track of this material. This is a difficult work, and Jonathan has not ordered me to do it; we do not work that way. Rather, I am doing it because I myself want to make these minority opinions known to all.

After I finished my story about our early years at the Jerusalem Academy, I updated my journal and started working once again on *The Minority Report*. Our son, Naam, was thirteen and our daughters, Elissa and Ruth, were nine and six. All of us have contributed to this book, my father, who was killed just over a year ago, the children, Jonathan, and I. We have not confined ourselves to our own views and traditions but have included wisdom from the literature of other countries. Thoughts on many matters spring from the

cosmopolitan character of our school and our history. For
example, a majority of Egyptians believe that humans are
immortal. Death is a mere door to walk through to a better
life in the West. But there are a few Egyptians who disagree
with this. They understand death as something from which
no one ever returns. We are interested in their opinions.

We do not say that the minority is always right, and a
minority of one is usually wrong. But in our experience it
seems that the minority often has a better chance of being
right than the majority. Often religious, conservative, and
orthodox, the traditions that give the majority its identity
also guard against any change, and those who deny change
deny reality. So why do these minority words remain with
the minority? Some say they are premature, untimely, or
unseasonable; the time is rarely right though we have a
proverb that says, "A word, when timely, how good it is."
(Proverbs 15:23b) Minority opinions can help us as we
attempt to move to an interesting and creative future.

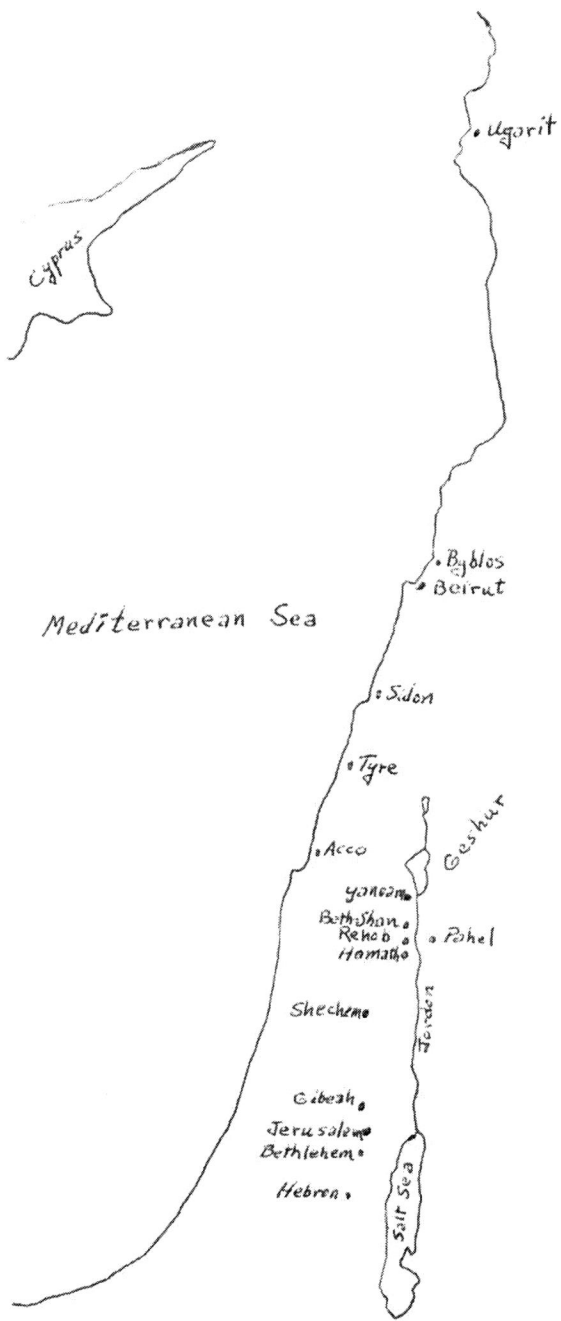

Ugarit

Cyprus

Mediterranean Sea

Byblos
Beirut

Sidon

Tyre

Geshur

Acco

Yoneam
Beth-Shan
Rehob
Hamath

Pehel

Shechem

Jordan

Gibeah
Jerusalem
Bethlehem

Hebron

Salt Sea

Chapter One

Dinner with Khety

On my table there were jars of scrolls containing some of my first drafts, sheets of papyrus, shards, and notes. From this mess I was supposed to bring together *The Minority Report.* It looked like the earth before Elohim established an ordered world: "devastation and desolation," but I was not able to bring any order out of this chaos. I had to stop and get our dinner started, because Jonathan was bringing home an Egyptian scribe by the name of Khety, who may join the faculty here at The Jerusalem Academy. We have had our problems with King David, but he has always wanted to build a great school. That we have liked.

I decided to get the children to help me get things ready. I knew they were up on the roof of our house. It is shady up there in the late afternoon. Our house is made of stone, and it only has four rooms. Thus the roof gives us extra space, which the children need. As I climbed up the ladder, I heard them laughing. Naam was telling the girls a story. I reached the roof and said, "I hate to break in on this happy occasion, but I really need some help."

Both Elissa and Ruth said in one voice, "Not now mother! Naam is just at an exciting place."

"Fine. I'll go down and start the fire for the lamb, but when you see the smoke, all three of you come down. Naam can finish the story after dinner. Soon your father will be here with his guest from Egypt."

I went down to the ground level, and gathered some wood for our outside cooking pit. The lamb was ready to cook. I had two shoulder roasts. There isn't much meat on a shoulder roast, but it is good. The sight of the smoke and the good smell of lamb fat dripping on the coals brought the children down. Naam fetched the bread and the girls the cheese.

Naam had just asked me about our guest when Jonathan and Khety arrived. Khety was a young man, about thirty, tall and dark complected. His Hebrew was not easy to understand, but we managed quite well. He did not have a problem understanding us.

I said, "We are pleased to have you in our home. We are all excited about getting to know you and learning about your country."

"It is an honor for me to be here," he answered.

He looked like a man with confidence and a lot of energy. Jonathan is forty and Magon about fifty, and thus three important members of the faculty would not retire at the same time.

Jonathan said, "We have been asking Khety questions all day, so tonight he wants to ask us some questions about our city, our work and our school. After dinner, Magon and Naomi will join us, and they can help us review our recent past for Khety."

"It sounds as if this is going to be a wonderful evening," I said. "So we should sit down around this table, because the food is ready."

"I would like to ask you a question if that is allowed," said Naam.

"Please," said Khety with a sincere smile.

"If you were having a meal like this for a guest in Egypt, what would you serve?"

"Sometimes we would have lamb as you have tonight, but I would probably serve a *geb,* which is our word for 'goose.'

We feed them until they are nice and fat. I would fill that bird with *hedjou,* 'onions,' and lots of *khizan,* 'garlic.' Then there would be melons, bread, and plenty of beer to drink."

"I would like to sit at your table for a meal like that," Naam said as he licked his lips.

I said, "If you have geese for eating, you must also have a supply of eggs?"

"Yes. We have eggs. Our word for egg is *swkhat.* In writing Egyptian words we place after each word a determinative or a picture of what the word refers to. So after our word for egg, we draw a picture of an egg. In the past, we drew a picture of a goose after this word, because the egg comes from the goose. We found that it was much easier to just draw an egg."

"Now you have made me hungry for goose eggs," I said. "We only have small bird eggs. But you have also given me an appetite for a knowledge of your language."

"And I told Khety that we would answer *his* questions," Jonathan inserted.

Khety said, "I don't mind the questions. Actually I learn a great deal about people by their questions."

I got up from the table to fill the wine cups and pass the lamb around, because the plate was heavy. We could all reach the plates of bread and cheese. One of our great joys was entertaining guests, and I could see that the children were also happy.

Just as we were finishing our meal, Magon, Naomi, and their children arrived. I suggested to Naam that he could take all the children to the roof and tell them some stories. Naam said, "We will also need some raisin cakes."

"And you shall have them."

The children hurried up the ladder, because they liked Naam's stories. Or was it the raisin cakes?

Then I poured some wine for Magon and Naomi, and said to Khety, "Magon has helped Jonathan and me in so many ways. He assisted Jonathan with his work on our royal epic, and he introduced me to his sister with whom I have had an on-going correspondence. Naomi is a friend, who is always ready to do what is needed."

"And so are you," Naomi responded.

Khety held his cup with both hands, "It is wonderful to have such close friends. Magon, is it better in Jerusalem than it was for you in Tyre? Did you teach Babylonian there too?"

"My answer to both questions is 'yes.' I like teaching here. I do miss Tyre and especially the sea, but we have a better chance of building a great school in Jerusalem than would be possible in Tyre. We have had some problems in The Jerusalem Academy, but I don't know of any school without some problems."

"What kind of problems?" Khety asked.

"I'll ask Jonathan to respond. He has been here from the beginning."

Jonathan seemed just a little uneasy. I knew what was going through his mind. He had to be truthful and open, but at the same time he did not want to picture the academy as an unfriendly place. He started with a smile but clenched fists.

"Sheva, who now heads the academy, was a scribe for David, along with Elimelech, Danel, and Noah, when David was still in Ziklag. I joined these four in Hebron, and it was there that David became king of both Judah and Israel. When David made Jerusalem his royal city we moved to Jerusalem. Some of us were acquainted with the personnel of the old Jerusalem scribal school. With David's permission and through discussions with the Old School, we formed The Jerusalem Academy. Ahban was the head of the Old School, which was housed close by, and Sheva led our New School. We added some teachers from both Judah and Israel during our early period. Also we were fortunate to bring Magon here to help us; he gave us a cosmopolitan outlook."

"The Old School has a long history," Magon said. "About three hundred and fifty years ago there were probably some scribes from the Old School who wrote Babylonian letters for 'Abdi-Heba, king of Jerusalem. These letters were sent to your Pharaoh in Amarna, Amen-hotep / Akh-en-Aton. The Old School has some copies of them."

"That is interesting. Perhaps we should go to Amarna and look for the originals," said Khety.

"Yes! Let's. That would be fun," I said.

Jonathan smiled, and said, "It would be a great adventure. It was a sad day when Ahban went to work for David as his counselor. My old friend Zadok became the head of the Old School. Everything was fine until David took Bathsheba for a wife. In order to do this David put her husband, Uriah, on the front lines during a battle, so that he would be killed. Bathsheba was Ahban's granddaughter, and he was grieved, worried, and not interested in continuing his work for David. When David's son, Absalom, led a rebellion against his father, Ahban joined the rebellion. For this act Ahban was declared a traitor. David issued an order to destroy Ahban's writings and to change his name from Ahban, 'brother of intelligence,' to Ahithophel, 'brother of reproach' in any reference to him in our chronicles. Zadok refused to obey such an order, but Sheva went along with it and is a lonely man.

"In addition to all of this, Joab, David's army commander, murdered Ahban, and Zadok left his position and went to Tyre. So Sheva now heads both parts of the academy. At this point you must be thinking that we have had too many problems to ever be a great school. But I want to say that all of Ahban's old friends remember him, and they are dedicated to making this school great in spite of these problems. The fact that we are considering you for a position here is proof that David and Sheva know that we must move ahead. If they can help us grow in this way, there will be a new focus, and we can begin to speak and to plan with them once again. Most of you have heard me say this before: 'plan a great future and live it now.'

"I did not mean to say so much, but I hope this will help."

"It will help me to ask the right questions," Khety said. "However, I want to tell you that similar things have happened in our schools in Egypt. Our best sages usually learn how to endure a change in the regime, and they find a way to plan for a better future."

I got up at this point and poured some more wine. Khety's cup had been empty for some time. I was impressed with his attitude and his understanding. As I sat down beside Naomi she said, "I want to tell you that Sheva is my father. I am sad about these things that have happened, and I cannot speak to my father any more. He should have resisted David's order; others have done so. However my mother, Sarah, tells me my father knows that somehow we must restore communications in the school and in our family. I think this will happen."

I grasped Naomi's hand and said, "We will all help to make it happen."

"According to Egyptian teachings," Khety said, "The fact that you want to make things better is an important part of the solution."

"There are so many things to do that will make the next few years a real adventure," Magon said. "This is not just wishful thinking. This academy has done some great things in the past. Jonathan, Elimelech, and Elishama produced a Royal Epic that brought unity to this kingdom. It was an achievement that will stand for ages."

"Magon forgot to tell you how he helped us at every turn on the epic," Jonathan said.

"I will want to read it," Khety said. "If I come here where would I live? It seems that you do not have an excess of dwellings."

"Ah, but there is room to build another," Jonathan assured him. "There are many things that we can't do, but we can build another house. In fact I am going to ask for *two* new houses. I have been concerned for some time that Magon and Naomi live too far away."

"I know Naomi and the children would rather be here at the school," Magon said.

"Indeed we would," said Naomi as she rose to check on the children. "Naam is probably out of stories by now."

Jonathan said "If you come to our school, Khety, you will help us in so many ways, and this is a good example: we will get a new house for you and one for Magon and Naomi."

Naomi and I found Naam still going strong, so we went back down and brought out some raisin cakes and more wine.

Later as we were going to sleep, I said to Jonathan, "Your suggestion about the house for Magon and Naomi brought tears to my eyes."

Jonathan laughed, "Aren't I a clever fellow?"

He is a clever fellow and my best friend.

Chapter Two

The First Entries

After the children went to school, I began to order my chaos. I knew that hard work would help me in many ways. I was still trying to recover from the death of my father. That bastard Joab not only murdered Ahban but also tried to rape me. Father saved me, but we could not save him from Joab's blade. I knew that writing this book would help me, and I knew that Jonathan has been getting better since he started working on his Job poem again. Father's murder actually helped Jonathan with the central theme of the poem; it confirmed his belief that there is no justice. Some of our best friends here at The Jerusalem Academy have helped us during our period of mourning. Magon and Naomi have supported us, and they always have had time to give when we needed them. Also Elishama, who has been working on Part II of our Royal Epic, and Deborah have taken over the teaching of the children: Magon and Naomi's son, Azriel and their daughter Ahinoam, Elishama and Deborah's three Rachel, Joshua, and Dinah, and our three.

This has happened many times. I started to work; I wanted to work, but I drifted into thinking about other things. I had to move on. The first thing I needed was a list of the minority opinions, but I settled for the ones Jonathan and I have talked about so many times. I knew them by heart:

The Equality of the Human and His Mate
The Question of Prayer
Divine Parents
No Surrogates
The Fear of the Lord
The Word of God
Humans and Beasts

After listing these entries I wanted to remind myself and my readers concerning the nature of minority opinions. I wrote this introduction.

Introduction

Most minority opinions will remain so. Some of them may become important to subsequent generations if they meet the needs of the people and the people can organize to support them. But minority opinions may never be tried or if so only by their believers. We sometimes say that we can live in the future today, but we should not expect others to join us as we try to create a place for these opinions in our lives. For us this has been fun, but we will not always put into practice our opinions because of the chaos it would cause in our daily lives.

One

The Equality of the Human and His Mate

Our Royal Epic contains two creation stories. The first one says little about the humans. In the second, Yahweh-Elohim forms the human or "living being" from the clay of the ground. Then he says, "It is not good for the human to be alone; / I will make for him a helper just like him." (Gen 2:18) So from the ground he formed the rest of the animals or "living beings," and they were brought to the human, who named them. But the human did not find a helper just like him. In order to produce such a being, Yahweh-Elohim had to take some bone and flesh from the human and build that into a woman. Then he brought the woman to the human, and the human said:

> "This one, at last, is bone of my bones
> And flesh of my flesh.
> This one shall be called woman ('*ishshah*),
> For from man ('*ish*) this one was taken."
>
> (Gen 2:23)

In this story the human finally has a mate "just like him." They are equal; they are of the same substance, and this is why "They become one flesh." (Gen 2:24c) This emphasis on the equality of the man and the woman was a minority opinion, and it was never practiced among our people and had no place in our laws and traditions.

We know that this is an important opinion. In Jonathan's poem against the ancient Job, one of the so-called "righteous friends" of Job, Bildad, says, "And how can one born of woman be pure?" (Job 25:4b) This view is typical.

When David's palace was dedicated and our Royal Epic was performed, I was shocked by the story of Lot and the destruction of Sodom. Each evening after the day's performance a discussion group of family and friends met in our home for good food and good talk. On the evening after the story of Lot was performed, the women in our group were angry. We asked why that story was included in our epic. It contained one scene in which a mob gathered outside of Lot's house; the mob wanted to rape the two men who were Lot's guests. According to the rules of hospitality, Lot was obligated to keep his guests from harm. In this situation Lot offered the mob his two virgin daughters to spare his guests. The laws of hospitality, which were also observed by the ancient Job, were more important than Lot's daughters.

"The minstrels say that the people love the story and its sequel about Mrs. Lot, and why she became a pillar of salt," said Jonathan. Elishama was quick to agree with him.

I said, "We know that in an epic you must deal with the people's stories, but with a little more thought on your part concerning your views on the equality of men and women, you could have excluded this story. You should have excluded it even if the minstrels threatened to put it in their performance. After all you have read the second creation story."

And Jonathan answered, "Even when one knows better that knowledge does not always attend the decision-making process. I regret our hurried decision."

The equality of men and women, which we see in the second creation story, is a minority opinion that we live by in our home, but for most this idea does not exist. The majority is conservative and orthodox, and they will guard their opinion and keep women "in their place."

Two

The Question of Prayer

Among our people prayer is thought to be important and helpful. Based on a belief that God is personal, it may be helpful for some people. However as we look around and notice the poor and the homeless, it seems that their prayers are never answered. Jonathan has addressed this problem in one part of his poem on Job:

> From the city the dying groan,
> And a person with wounds cries out,
> Yet Eloah does not pay attention to prayer.
>
> (Job 24:12)

Granted, this is a minority opinion, but we consider it to be valid, born out by observation. Further, we think the poor deserve to be heard.

There is prayer that is hideous in comparison to the cries of the poor. The "righteous" among us, who tell us to pray, exhibit their humility. "We are mere worms and maggots," they say, while at the same time they stress their importance by calling on the creator to pay attention to their personal needs. The "righteous" become the center of the ordered world. We have one suggestion to stop such prayer. Do not speak to God unless he speaks to you.

Note the silence.

Three

Divine Parents

When the human beings began to multiply,
upon the face of the ground,
and daughters were born to them,
the sons of the gods saw that the daughters
of the human beings were beautiful,
they took for themselves wives from any of those they chose.
Yahweh said:
   "My spirit can not be bottled up in human beings forever,
   In as much as, they are flesh.
   Their days will be a hundred and twenty years."
The Nephilim were on earth in those days, and afterwards,
for the sons of the gods did mate with the daughters of the
humans; they bore [children] to them—they were the
heroes of old, the men of renown.

(Gen 6:1-4)

Jonathan and I have always appreciated this text, because it says that even the heroes are mortal. This is also the case with the Babylonian hero, Gilgamesh, who was two-thirds divine but mortal (the math escapes me). However, we do not agree with the majority opinion that says if you are a hero, one of your parents was divine. The majority also makes this claim for Isaac:

> Yahweh visited Sarah as he had said;
> Yahweh did to Sarah as he had spoken.
> Sarah became pregnant; . . .
>
> (Gen 21:1-2a)

In our world, the majority believes that the mother is the only obvious parent. The father does not want to claim the below average or deformed child; perhaps the mother was impregnated by some evil god. This being the case, he cannot claim the hero or the renown, who was surely fathered by a god. I suppose the father could claim the average child. This view does not make any sense to us.

Our minority opinion would suggest that education, character, time and circumstance have much to do with shaping a hero's life. People can learn and think. We do not have to give human achievement to the gods. And what of the handicapped among us? Why should one say that one parent was an evil god? Magon has told us that there is a Sumerian story supporting such a view, but the same story makes a place in society for such people to live and perform a service. One interesting example concerns the one who is born blind. The Sumerian god Enki said that this one should excel in music. It is interesting that scribes have thought about such problems, but in our opinion, we are the ones, not Enki, who should make a place for the handicapped among us, and we should admit that we do not know why such things happen.

Chapter Three

Jonathan and His Poem on Job

I had just finished my third entry when Jonathan came home. The children were outside playing. He was smiling, and I was glad. In fact he kissed me again and again.

"I don't know why you are so happy," I said, "but I like it."

"Khety has agreed to teach."

"That's wonderful news."

He nodded. "I am certain things are going to get better around here now. I tried to see David today, but he was gone. I will go over and talk to him about building the new houses in the morning. And," he said, still holding me in his arms, "I finally finished my poem on Job."

"I need another kiss; I can't believe it! After all these years you are finally finished."

"Yes! During the last few weeks, I have worked on it every day; today I put down the last word."

"But now we have a problem. Of course, I want a copy for *The Minority Report*, but we will have to find a way to present it to more people."

"Maybe we could have a party, and you could read it, but that would not reach many people. As we have said before, it needs to crush the old story of Job."

Jonathan was silent; he kissed me once more and began to pace around the room. Then he turned and said, "For now we won't tell anyone that I'm finished. We will wait for the next big occasion, and perhaps it will be just right for such a reading. Something will come up, and we will be ready."

"I am willing to wait for the public 'occasion,' but I cannot wait to see the poem. How long will it take to make me a copy? I will want to read it and keep it safe for *The Minority Report*. This is exciting."

"I want also to show it to Naam. I think it will help him. He still suffers from the loss of his grandfather."

Jonathan went outside to play with the children, and I cleaned up some of my mess. I would work more tomorrow, but now it was time to think about our evening meal. We have always had our best times at the table. I still had food from last night when Khety was here, and I decided to call the children and Jonathan. They had to get ready.

As we were eating, I said to Jonathan, "Today I was able to start my writing again. I finished three entries. I want you to look at them in their finished form."

"That's great," answered Jonathan. "I have an idea. Naam and I will both look at your work, and you can read to the girls."

"That will be a pleasure."

We did not stay too long at the table, and everyone helped me clean up and put things away.

Jonathan and Naam read my entries. Also he told Naam that he had finished the Job poem. Naam said, "This is good; you have finished a major work, and mother has finally returned to work on an important project. When can I see your poem?"

"As soon as I make a copy for your mother's book. But your mother and I have decided that we will not tell anyone that the poem is completed. We want to wait for just the right occasion to announce and read it. As you know the poem confronts and denounces the old story of Job."

Naam said, "Won't the people, who live according to the old story be angry?"

"They will be angry. We will have to be prepared for that

anger, and that is another reason why you need to read the poem."

After I had read to the girls, we all went to bed. Before we went to sleep, Jonathan said that my three entries were well done. Then he said, "I'm still sorry that we used the story about Mrs. Lot in our epic."

"Don't worry about it. It provided the context for one of our best discussions during those great evenings. But I would like to know if you remember that line in the love song that you wrote for our wedding about your garden?"

"Yes. I do. Listen:

> I have come to my garden,
> O my sister and my bride.
> I've gathered my myrrh and spice;
> I ate my honeycomb and honey;
> I drank my wine and my milk;
> We were together as one."

"You did remember. I think you should come to your garden for your honey and spice."

And he did.

In the morning Jonathan left the house early to talk with David. I thought I could do another three entries before he returned for lunch. Again these were ones that Jonathan and I had discussed many times. In fact, Jonathan discovered the long poem on wisdom, which I have used in "The Fear of the Lord."

Four

No Surrogates

I remember the evening when father, Jonathan, and I planned our wedding. We were sitting around our table, and Jonathan with a serious look on his face told father that he would need a marriage contract. He wanted the marriage contract to name the surrogate who would have our babies if I were barren. He added that Jacob had such a contract from Laban. Leah's surrogate was Zilpah and Rachel's surrogate was Bilhah. He said that this was all according to our traditions. Also he told us that other countries had the same legal traditions, for example, the city-state of Nuzu.

In response, I said: "You had better be joking, because I'm not living in the past. As members of the minority, we will be living in the future. I come without dowry, and I'll have the babies, if there are babies. I'm starting new traditions."

We laughed and had a good time. By the end of the evening we had decided that there would be no marriage contract. Instead Jonathan would write a love song for me. We were having fun, but there is an important issue here. Most families in Jerusalem would not joke about such things. We are aware that the more important minority opinion in this case has to do with our view of tradition. Tradition is helpful, because from it we gain a sense of our identity. But if one part of our identity has to do with openness to change then tradition must not be allowed to stifle our freedom.

Five

The Fear of the Lord

Among the majority of the scribes, the fear of God, the Lord, or Yahweh is the beginning of wisdom or can be equated with wisdom. The ancient Job is described as "one who feared Elohim and avoided evil." This majority view is not difficult to hold. After all when David took Bathsheba and had her husband, Uriah, killed, the prophet Nathan said that their child should die. Also in the story of Judah, Yahweh killed Judah's first two sons. If Yahweh is like that, he is a God to fear. Likewise the God in the ancient story of

Job is to be feared. On this last point Jonathan has recently found a poem by one who supports the ancient story of Job. Jonathan has created a poem denying any truth in the story of the old Job, and now this new poet has written one to uphold the old Job. It summarizes the old story and its basic teaching. The point of view is not good, but the poetry is actually rather nice. Here is the poem that Jonathan calls, "Where Can Wisdom Be Found?"

> Yes, there is a smelter for silver,
> And a place where they refine gold.
> Iron is taken from ore,
> And stone produces copper.
>
> [Man] made an end to darkness,
> And to every end he searches
> [For] dark and gloomy rock.
> Foreign people broke shafts,
> [Shafts] forgotten by pathways,
> They hung; [far] from men they swayed.
> Earth, food comes from her,
> And under her, it was changed by fire.
> Her stones are [the] source of sapphire,
> And particles of gold are in them.
> [The] path no raptor has known,
> And [the] falcon's eye has not seen it.
> [The] proud beasts have not used it;
> [The] lion has not come upon it.
>
> [Man] put his hand into the flint;
> He overturned mountains from [the] root.
> In the rocks he hewed out channels,
> And his eye saw every precious thing.
> [The] sources of the rivers he stopped,
> And hidden things he brought to light.

And wisdom, where can she be found?
And where is [the] place of understanding?
Man does not know her dwelling,
And she cannot be found in the land of the living.
[The] Deep said, "She is not with me,"
And [the] Sea said, "Not with me."
Fine gold cannot be given for her,
And silver cannot be weighed out [as] her price.
She cannot be purchased with the gold of Ophir,
With precious onyx or sapphire.
Gold and glass cannot equal her,
Nor vessels of fine gold be her exchange.
Coral or crystal will not be mentioned;
[The] endurance of wisdom surpasses rubies.
The topaz of Ethiopia cannot equal her;
She cannot be purchased with pure gold.

And wisdom, from where does she come?
And where is [the] place of understanding?
She is concealed from [the] eyes of all living;
From the birds of the heavens she is hidden.
Abbadon and Death said,
"With our ears we have heard a rumor of her."
Elohim has understood her way,
And he has known her place.
For he looks to the ends of the earth;
He sees everything under the heavens:
Giving weight to the wind
He measured the waters with a measure.
When he made a channel for the rain
And a path for the thundershower,
Then he saw her, and he evaluated her;
He established her, and he tested her.
He said to Adam,

"See, the fear of [the] Lord, that is wisdom,
And to turn from evil is understanding."

(Job 28:1-28)

This poem makes wisdom so remote and unobtainable that a mere human does not have a chance of finding it. Certainly, human skill has nothing to do with wisdom, and of course it cannot be purchased. It is only God who knows wisdom, and the human who fears god is also "wise" or at least smart and religious.

My father, Jonathan and I have always had a different opinion concerning the nature of God. We don't know much about him. Perhaps he ordered this not-so-perfect world and made life possible for us, but there is no need to fear such a God and to do so hardly would seem to be the beginning of wisdom. For us wisdom is born of understanding based on observation. Note one of our favorite accounts of the birth of a proverb:

I passed by the field of a lazy man,
And by the vineyard of a senseless man.
Here, thorns climbed up all over them.
Its surface was covered with weeds,
And its stone wall was broken down.
I observed; I took it to heart.
I saw; I studied [this] lesson:
A few naps, a few drowsy times,
A few times of folding the hands to rest,
And your poverty will come marching on,
Even as a [charging] warrior your dire straits.

(Prov 24:30-34)

Here the sage has learned something about "poverty" or "dire straits." The lazy farmer will have nothing. But the important thing to note is the method of the sage. The sage observes and studies. We suggest that the conclusion is exaggerated, because the sages also talk about the need to enjoy one's work and to rest (this is true for all of us, the humans and the other animals as well). In fact we have another proverb that says:.

> The fool is one who folds his hands
> And the one who devours his flesh.
> Better is one handful of rest
> Than two handfuls of labor and [the] pursuit of
> wind.
>
> (Eccl 4:5-6)

Once again our view is that wisdom is the result of observation and study. It does not come from the fear of the Lord.

I could not finish three. As I was preparing lunch I heard the children, home just a little early today. Naam and Elissa were happy and vocal, but Ruth had tears in her eyes. I asked her why she was sad.

"I can't read, and it's too hard."

I sat her on my lap and said, "Ruth this is your first year. Naam and Elissa had difficult times when they started to read. You will do fine. Can you help me get some of this food on the table? Your father will be here soon, and we want to be ready."

Ruth liked to help me, and she dried her eyes on my skirt and seemed happy again. We were ready when Jonathan arrived. I did not ask him about his conversation with David, but I could tell that he must have been pleased with it; he was in a good mood. There would be plenty of time to talk about that after lunch. I did announce that I had finished two more entries, and he said, "Children, your mother is a hard worker. We will have to let her rest after lunch."

"I don't need to rest, but I do need some food and some happy smiles from my family."

The children all put on silly grins and helped clean up and put the food away. Naam said that he would help the girls with their reading, and Jonathan said, "I want to tell you exactly what David said to me, so I will speak for him, word for word."

"'Jonathan, I want to make a statement before you say or ask anything. You are my father Jesse's brother, and that is important to me. I am getting close to fifty years old and that makes you close to forty. I have never thought of you as my uncle; you were always my younger brother. Our lives have diverged, and we are different in many ways. I have made some mistakes, and I will probably make some more, but I do hope that we can repair whatever is broken between us. I want to know what you are thinking even if I do not agree with you. In my view, my army commander, the great Joab, had too much power. You relieved him of his balls for his attempted rape of Keziah and the murder of her father. I don't blame you for that, but it is time for you and me to restore our relationship.'"

Then I said, "I am glad to hear you say such things, because we have at least one thing in common: we both want to have a great academy. We have appreciated your willingness for us to search for an Egyptian scholar, and we had a good interview with Khety. He has agreed to join us in the academy, and this will help us achieve one of our goals. We must be able to study all the classical literature from our world. We all thank you for allowing this advance."

"David said, 'I am glad that you have found a good teacher, and I hope that you can somehow include Sheva in some of your new projects. You have to get beyond the walls of the past.'"

"We will try to do that," I said. "But all of this brings up a request. We need to build two new houses: one for Khety and one for Magon and Naomi who have been living at some distance from the school. There is room for two houses, and we hope you can see this as a possibility."

"David said, 'I will send some builders tomorrow. I want you and Sheva to meet with them. You tell them what you want, and we will get started at once.'"

I said, "I will speak with Sheva about this, and we will meet the builders. Now I have one more request. In the near future, I would like to show you my poem on Job. My poem is meant to demolish our old story of Job. Some people will not like it, but I hope that it will start an important discussion concerning the way in which human beings deal with the problem of suffering. Are you willing to read it?"

"David said, 'By all means, I want to see it, but I may not like it. Personally I try not to think about such things.'"

"I told him I would let him see it as soon as I could make a copy and thanked him."

"That was some conversation," I said. "You got what you wanted, but I noticed that he did not mention Joab's murder of Ahban."

"You are right, and he did not really speak to our problems with Sheva. But he did say that we should solve the problems. However I suppose that he said about all he could say, and he left it to us to work it all out."

"But Jonathan, I don't understand why you asked him to read your poem."

"I wished that I had discussed that request with you, but it just entered my mind on the spot, and for a reason. He wanted to restore our relationship, but that did not mean that we would always agree. I felt like he could not ask me to forget my poem even if he did not like it. I asked him to read it, because I will want to publish it someday. He may not like it, but he will let me publish it. But now I am repeating myself."

"Yes, you are, but I get the point. One of the first things he said was that he was interested in your thinking even if he did not agree. So we can hold him to that statement.

That is helpful, and I agree that it was a perfect time to mention the poem."

"I'm glad that you agree."

"However, on second thought, I doubt if we can ever hold David to any statement. If he wants to change his thinking, he will, but you are his uncle. That helps just a little.

Chapter Four

New Houses

The next morning Jonathan said to me, "After breakfast I will see Sheva and tell him about my meeting with David and inform him that the builders will be here this morning. Will you watch for them and let us know when they arrive?"

"I will do that, but I want to do something else as well. When Naomi brings her children for school, I want to ask her to stay here for the meeting with the builders. Also Magon should be included. It may be awkward for Naomi to meet with her father, but conversation has to start sometime. This is an opportunity, and besides Magon and Naomi should have some say about their future house."

"Keziah, you are always thinking; that is a great idea. It just might work."

With that Jonathan left, and I decided to clean house and keep a watch for Naomi and the builders. It is strange how sometimes things can happen so fast. Just the other night Naomi expressed her belief that somehow conversation would be restored in her family, and today there would be a first attempt. As it turned out I did not see Naomi come in the gate, but after bringing her children to school she came to see me. "I'm glad you stopped by," I said. "I need to talk with you."

"That's good, because I was afraid that I would interrupt your work."

"I don't want you to ever think that way. If I'm here you are more than welcome. I have some good news for you. Jonathan got David to agree to build two new houses. Naomi, you will have a house here."

"That is the best news that I have had in a long time. This will be exciting."

With that she hugged me, and we both danced around the table. Then I said, "The builders will be here any moment to talk with Jonathan and your father about the new houses. This may not be easy, but Jonathan and I want you and Magon to be in on this planning session. We don't want this to dampen your happiness of this moment, but you said the other evening that things had to get better."

"I said that and I meant it, but I did not expect such a thing so soon. I will do it though. I will go to Magon's office and get him. I will need him to lean on."

"That's a good idea, but don't be too long. The builders are due here now."

"We'll be back soon, and by the way, thanks. I'm nervous, but I'm still happy."

It was not long before the builders arrived. Jonathan and Sheva were talking in front of the main school building, and I took the builders over there. "Sheva," I said, "I hope that we can wait just a moment to start this session, because Magon and Naomi are joining us. We need their ideas since they will be living in one of the houses."

Sheva was flustered, "Jonathan, perhaps you can handle this. I have some other things that I should do."

Jonathan said, "Sheva we need your ideas."

And I added, "I know that sometimes I talk too much, but Sheva, we need you to be here. Naomi and you need to be able to talk. She has the courage, and I'm sure that you have it too."

Sheva did not have a chance to respond or leave. Magon and Naomi came just in time.

The school building was located at the back of the

courtyard. Sheva and Sarah's house was to the right of the school building, and Elishama and Deborah's house, to the left. Our house was just to the right when you entered the front gate. Jonathan suggested that the two new houses could be built across from ours.

Sheva said, "That is the only place for them."

"I agree," said Magon. "Also I have been wondering if we need two houses. Khety could live in Zadok's old room in the Old School."

Sheva shook his head. "No. We should save that room for the next person that we will want to hire. If David is willing to build two houses now, we should take them. We may not have another chance like this."

Magon said, "You are probably correct."

"I agree with father," Naomi said. "I would really like to have the first house from the gate, and then we would be just across from Jonathan and Keziah."

The group broke up after completing the plans. I invited Magon and Naomi to our house for some lunch. As we prepared the food, I said to Naomi, "You did a wonderful thing in your first comment to Sheva. You said, 'father.' That was a word that Sheva needed to hear. There was a tear on Naomi's cheek, and I gave her a big hug.

After lunch Sarah came over, and Naomi ran to her and Sarah held her. "You helped your father this morning; you put a smile on his face. Just give him a little time."

"I will, mother."

After everyone left, I said to Jonathan, "That was a great morning. I know that things will be better. What is going on here will bring healing."

"I hope so, but it is not an easy situation. We need the school and that means we must get along with David and Sheva, but our freedom is essential for our work."

"So the tension remains."

"And it may just empower us to get a few things done. I am still thinking about the right occasion for reading the Job poem."

"But for now begin that copy for me. Naam can help to make one for David."

Jonathan left for his office, and I decided to try for one more entry. "The Word of God" was still a little vague in my mind, even though my father, Gad, had talked about it many times, as had Jonathan and Ahban.

Six

The Word of God

In our stories and ancient traditions God speaks to many of our ancestors, such as Abraham and of course Moses. But I remember from many conversations with my father, Jonathan, and Ahban comments like: why is it that God always speaks to the ancients but never to us? Ahban gave a short poem to father, and it made the same point.

> To the ancients, came God's word;
> In the present, there's no word.
> Yes. He spoke to Samuel,
> But then only a few words,
> And to King Saul, not a word.

Ahban and father talked about how easily we ascribe greatness to the past while making the present rather dull. We forget that the present is our opportunity to make a real difference. After reading Ahban's verse Jonathan said, "We must give the past its due, but we must also rethink everything in the present if our thought is going to make a difference. Most of us are not bold enough or certain enough to stand by our best thinking."

Father said, "It empowers a prophet to claim that his 'best thinking' is a word from God, but after David dismissed me, I decided to never make such a claim. I like to solve problems, and if the solutions are helpful, that is enough.

We will always have people who claim that God spoke to them. I cannot say that their claim is false, but my best thinking says to me, 'Don't believe it.'"

In light of several years of such conversation and thinking, we have decided that "the word of God" should remain in the past. It certainly is not a part of our experience. Many of our fellow human beings know all about God, and they know exactly what he wants them to do. But we do not know such things, and we have a suspicion that their God does not exist. Nevertheless, we think it is important to love and to care for others. We need to do those things that a loving father would want us to do if he spoke to us. I would like to use one of Ahban's stories to make this point.

When he was young, he journeyed to Egypt and was gone for about two years. His father had built for his family a wonderful house, and he had well kept vines and olive trees. But after many years his health was bad. Just before Ahban left on his trip his father said, "If I am not alive when you return, I want you to know that you have my blessing."

Ahban said, "Though I did not know it, my father died a few weeks after I left for Egypt. During my stay in Egypt, I encountered many problems, but I knew what to do. Why? Because I had my father's blessing, and I knew how he cared for us, for his fields, and for others. He was no longer alive, but I did not need a new word."

Humans have always wished for a clear word; many have claimed it. For us it is more important and interesting to attempt the creation of a better future. True, our world is not perfect and suffering is all around us, but it is our home. According to our story of the first human, we are here to guard it and care for it. That is the word we hold dear.

I was not really satisfied with "The Word of God," but I was sure Jonathan and Naam would go over it for me.

Chapter Five

A Decision to Read

A week went by. Yesterday Jonathan finally finished the copy of his poem, and this morning I read it twice. Some of it I had seen before, or Jonathan had read for us on several occasions. But to have it all together was thrilling. It was not what I would call a "happy" poem. But it did destroy the fantasy of the ancient poem of Job: "Just pray, worship and do well, my friend, and all will be well with you, your family, and everything that you have; you will prosper." Until this fantasy is destroyed it is difficult to build a life and to build it together. Suffering is a part of our world; we can escape the fantasy but not the suffering. Reality and truth provide a better foundation for re-building a life together than this fantasy.

This poem should have been read years ago; it needs to be read before one needs it. I wondered if we could create the right time to read it, rather than wait for the right time to come along.

Jonathan came home a little before lunch. He sat down at the table and said, "I just finished teaching my class on the history of the ancient Job story. The students are interested in the subject, and it will be a good class."

"That may help us. I know I agreed that we should wait for just the right moment for a public reading, but after reading it this morning I'm about to change my mind. Let's invite your class and some of our friends here for an evening reading as a first step. We would begin to create a conversation with a small group. From them you would gain support, and this would help you when you did your public reading. What do you think?"

"You may be right. It would be nice to have some support before undertaking the public reading. Of course when we create this conversation, the word will get out to some of our enemies, so we can't wait too long."

"We'll probably have to wait until David has had a chance to read it. I'm hoping that he will go along with you on this even if he is not convinced."

"He may go along. After all, he did say that he wanted to restore our relationship."

"So, we should get a copy of the poem to David, and this afternoon we can start inviting people for the first reading. Can we do it three days from now?"

"Yes. Keziah, you do help me get things done."

"I thank you for your kind words," I kissed him. "I want to warn you that tonight after the children are asleep we will start another conversation that will prepare us for joy in our bed."

"I do not consider that to be a warning but rather an exciting invitation."

We ate our lunch together, before the children came home, "I love the children but thanks for coming home a bit early. This has been a good time. Do you have another class today?"

"No. I can start the copy for David, and Naam can help me."

After Jonathan went back to his office I wrote number seven.

Seven

Humans and Beasts

We have already discussed the equality of men and women as human beings. We also believe that some of those same traditions emphasize the relationship between the humans and the beasts; they are all classified under one term: *nephesh hayyah* ("living being"). This does not mean that we cannot distinguish between the various types of animals. The human is different in many ways from the horse, but they are both valuable as separate parts of creation; they are both called *living beings*. Our views on this subject are derived, once again, from our second creation story in the *Royal Epic*. Note the following:

> Yahweh-Elohim formed the human [from] the
>> clay of the ground;
> He blew into his nostrils the breath of life;
> The human became a *living being*.
>> (Genesis 2:7)
> Yahweh-Elohim formed from the ground all the
>> wild animals
> And all the birds of the heavens.
> He brought [them] to the human to see what he
>> called them,
> And whatever the human called each of the *living beings*,
> That was its name.
>> (Genesis 2:19)

In this section of our epic it is clear that the human can see the differences among the creatures. It is also clear that the human cannot find one exactly like him for a mate. Therefore there has to be a special formation of the woman from the same substance as the man. Nevertheless, the humans (male and female) function within the framework of creation and with all living beings. This is important for us to remember, and this opinion has found a place in some of our traditions. The commandments that Moses gave include a commandment for the Sabbath. In that law the domestic animals are also given rest just as the humans. The Sabbath is for all the *living beings*; it is for *all flesh*, to use a term from the flood story. After the flood Elohim says that the rainbow is a sign of his covenant. Then he says:

> I will remember my covenant that is between me
> And between you and between every *living being*
>   among *all flesh*,
> And never again shall the waters become a flood
>   to destroy *all flesh*.
> When the bow is in the clouds, I will see it,
> Remembering the eternal covenant between Elohim
> And between every *living being* among *all flesh* that
>   is upon the earth.
>
> (Genesis 9:15-16)

I like this entry, but not many people pay any attention to such things. They don't really consider the livestock as a part of our community; they would rather listen to one of our psalms, which makes the majority opinion:

> What is man that you remember him,
> And [the] son of man that you visit him?
> You have made him a little less than [the] gods,
> And [with] glory and honor you crown him.
> You make him ruler over the works of your hands;
> You put all things under his feet:
> Small and large cattle, all of them, and even [the]
>   wild beast,
> [The] birds of [the] heavens, and the fish of the sea,
> That travels [the] paths of [the] seas.
>
> (Psalm 8:5-9)

Chapter Six

An Evening with Jonathan's Poem

Three days came and were gone. This seems to happen when you really need more time to prepare. We did get ready for the reading; we had the food on several tables, but our problem was one of space. Eight students from Jonathan's class were coming, and among our friends Magon and Naomi, Elishama and Deborah, Danel, Noah, and Elimelech were also coming. It will be difficult to get seventeen people in our house, but that many crowded in for our discussions during the dedication of David's palace. I can't believe it: twelve years ago. We will work it out. I was glad that Deborah was willing for Naam to take the children to her house. She said that Naam and Rachel, the same age as Naam, could keep them entertained. Magon and Naomi were trying something new. They were going to leave their children with her parents.

We did manage to find room for everyone. Some of the students sat on the floor, comfortably leaning against some cushions. Jonathan read the entire poem, but in the following report, I have only given the parts that sparked most of the discussion. For the brave, the entire text is attached to this book in *The Minority Report*.

"About thirteen years ago," Jonathan began, "I talked with some of this group about the ancient story of Job. Lately I have been discussing this in my class. So most of you are aware that I do not like the old story of Job (Job 1,2,27-31,38-

42). That story is false. It claims that if you are religious and worship your God you will prosper and have a long and happy life, and if you are not pious you will suffer and be taken away. Many say that such a fantasy helps one in a difficult world. It may help until one discovers that it is false, but the real tragedy is the way this idea of retribution and reward has been used to control people.

"It has taken me a long time to write a poem that I hope will crush the power of the old story. I know that it has dominated the thought of many people for many years and is known throughout our world from Babylon to Egypt. But I have waited long enough, and perhaps some of you can help me with a public reading later.

"My poem is a response to the ancient story, and therefore I use almost the same prologue, but I turn the characters upside down. Job is not pious as in the old story. His wife is praised for suggesting that her husband 'curse God and die,' and the three friends do not go along with Job's wife but take up the arguments of the ancient Job's religious orthodoxy; they use them against this rebel Job.

"I don't go into great detail about Job's losses, but let me quote what his wife says and Job's response:

> 'Curse God, and we will hold a funeral for our
>   children.'
> Job said to her:
> 'You speak as one of the wise women might talk.
> Should we, indeed, accept all of the evil with no
>   explanation?
> In any case we must bury the children. We will
>   bury them,
> Call forth their names, and tell their stories.'

During the next seven days burial rituals for the children were recited, and the three 'righteous friends' were confused and shocked at Job's anger."

The youngest of Jonathan's students, Eli, only seventeen, raised his hand and said, "In the old prologue we are told that God is testing Job with all of this suffering. In your prologue is any reason given for Job's suffering?"

"No. Who knows why there is suffering? The three 'friends' think they know, but I hope that my Job shows that they are wrong in every way."

Eli persists, "But you give no clue as to his suffering?"

"That's correct. The poem is in the form of a debate. First Job speaks and then one of the 'friends.' Then Job answers, and another 'friend' speaks. They alternate until Job has spoken nine times, Eliphaz three times, Bildad three times, but Zophar only speaks two times. The epilogue is a conversation between Job and his wife."

Magon says, "Why not begin with Job's first speech."

> Afterward Job opened his mouth; he cursed his day.
> Job answered; he said:
> Perish the day on which I was born;
> The night that said, "A hero is conceived."
> That day, let it be pitch-black.
> May Eloah from above not find it,
>
> . . .
>
> Do not count it among the days of the year;
> Within the number of months, it shall not enter.
>
> . . .
>
> Why did I not die from [the] womb,
> Or expire [when] I came out from [the] belly?
> Why did knees receive me,
> Or why breasts that I could nurse?
> For by now, I would have lain down; I would be
>   quiet;

I would have been asleep; then I would be at rest,
With kings and counselors of the netherworld,
The ones who built for themselves ruins,
Or with princes who had gold,
The ones who filled their houses [with] silver.
Or [why] was I not like a buried stillborn infant,
Like babies who never saw light?

· · ·

Why does he give light to [the] overworked
And life to those bitter to the core of being;
The ones who wait for Mot, but he is not [there];
They dig for him more than for treasure;
The ones who would rejoice [with] the gods of a grave;
They would gladly discover a tomb,
For a hero whose way is hidden,
Whom Eloah has protected?

· · ·

(Job 3)

Magon said, "Job's first speech is powerful. Someone has to be really hurting to dig for Mot, the God of Death, more than one would dig for treasure and is glad to find a tomb. I am anxious to hear how Eliphaz answers."

The students were also anxious.

"Well he begins with no compassion:

If one attempts a word with you, could you handle it?

· · ·

Is not your fear your confidence,
And the integrity of your ways your hope?

Remember now, who of the innocent has ever
    perished,
Or where have the righteous been destroyed?
As I have seen, those who plow evil
And who sow trouble, they will reap the same.
From the breath of Eloah they perish,
And from the wind of his nostrils they are
    destroyed.

. . .

A word came to me as a thief [in the night];

. . .

'Can a man be made righteous by Eloah?
Or can a hero be made pure by his Maker?
If he cannot trust his servants
And charges his angels with error,
How much the less those who dwell in houses of clay,
Whose foundation is in the dust,
Who are crushed before a moth.
From morning to evening they are crushed;
Without accomplishment they perish forever.
Is not their tent cord pulled up with them?
They die and not with wisdom.'

                                        (Job 4)

. . . .

Yes! Evil does not come up from dirt,
And trouble does not sprout from the ground.
Yes! Humanity is born for trouble,
And the sons of Resheph go flying high.

But, I myself, I would seek El,
And before Elohim, I would place my case,
Who does great deeds and none can be fathomed,
Wonders beyond number;
Who gives rain upon the face of the earth,
And sends water upon the face of the land?

. . .

Indeed, fortunate is the man whom Eloah corrects;
Do not reject the discipline of Shaddai.
Yes, he injures, and he treats;
He wounds, and his hands heal.
From six troubles he shall rescue you,
And in seven, evil shall not touch you.
In famine, he saves you from death,
In war, from the wielders of the sword.
From [the] scourge of [the] tongue, you shall be
    hidden,
And you shall have no fear of destruction that
    comes.
At destruction and at famine you shall laugh,
And from the beasts of the earth, you shall not fear.
For with the stones of the field is your covenant,
And the wild beasts shall be at peace with you.
You shall know that your tent is safe;
You shall visit your fold and miss nothing.
You shall know that your descendants are many;
Your progeny are like the grass of the earth.
You shall come in full vigor to [the] grave,
As a shock of grain is brought up in its time.
Here it is! We have investigated it; it is so!
Listen and you shall know it for yourself.

(Job 5)

Eliphaz begins his long response with no compassion, and he ends with no understanding. He says, 'Seek El, and you shall know that your tent is safe.' Where has Eliphaz been for the last seven days? The children have just been buried! Conclusion: Job did not seek El. Eliphaz makes me angry."

Then I said, "My dear husband, you put those words into the mouth of Eliphaz; why are you angry? He is the orthodox fundamentalist who opposes our every move. You have given him the right words if he makes you angry."

"You are obviously right, Keziah, but it's too bad that people like Eliphaz, in the face of real suffering, have to recite the entire orthodox list of falsehoods and thus force me to do the same. The one who suffers does not fear God and has sown trouble and reaped the same. Then he asked that awful question, 'who of the innocent has ever perished?' This is so wrong!"

Naomi said, "I liked the line: 'Evil does not come from the dirt,' and 'Humanity is born for trouble.' That makes things clear; we are at fault."

"So all we have to do is seek God, feel fortunate under the blows of God's rod of correction, and our progeny will be many. 'Obey and you will know it for yourself.'" This was Elishama's response.

Then I said, "Before Jonathan reads Job's second speech, I want all of you to get something to eat and some wine."

After that, Jonathan said, "If I'm going to read this poem I must resist commenting on each speech. I'll try, and here is Job's second speech:

> O that my anger could be weighed
> And together with my misery be put on the balances,
> Right now, it would be heavier than the sand of
>   the sea.

. . .

For the sick [there should be] loyalty from his friend,
Though he forsakes the fear of Shaddai.
My friends have been treacherous like a torrent,
Like a wadi of torrents they pass away.

. . .

Have I said, "Give to me,
From your wealth, pay a bribe for me,
Rescue me from [the] hand of an enemy,
From [the] hand of evil men, redeem me"?
Teach me, and I will be silent;
Where am I wrong? Bring understanding to me.
How trenchant are [the] words of the upright!
How does reproof from you reprove?
You think to reprove [with] words,

. . .

Relent! Let there be no injustice!
Relent! My justification is in this.
Is there injustice on my tongue?
Can my palate not distinguish words?

(Job 6)

. . .

Whenever I lie down, I always think,
'When can I get up?'
But an evening always drags on,
And I am sated with tossing until dawn.
My flesh is now covered with maggots and lumps
    of dirt;
My skin has cracked; it is dripping [pus].
My days are swifter than a weaver's shuttle;
They are finished without hope.

. . .

I despised [my life]; I will not live forever.
Let me be, for my days are a breath.
What are human beings that you make them so great,
Or that you pay attention to them?
You have visited them every morning;
Every moment you test them.
How long will you not turn your gaze from me?
Will you not let me alone till I swallow my spit?
Have I sinned?
What am I doing to you, O watcher of humanity?
Why have you made me your target?

. . .

(Job 7)

In this speech Job is angry with his so-called 'friends,'
and he comes up with a series of questions for their God.
We will go right to Bildad's first speech:

How long will you utter these [things]?
The words of your mouth are a mighty wind.
Does El pervert justice?
Does Shaddai pervert [the] right?
If your children have sinned against him,
He has sent them into the power of their
    transgression.
If you will search for El,
And from Shaddai seek mercy,
If you are pure and upright,
Now he will rouse himself for you;
He will restore your righteous dwelling.
Your beginning will seem a small thing;
Your end will be very prosperous.

. . .

So, El does not reject a perfect person,
Nor take the hand of evildoers.
He will yet fill your mouth with laughter,
And your lips with shouts of joy.
Your enemies will be dressed in shame,
And [the] tent of the wicked will be no more.

                                                    (Job 8)

Bildad does not add much. He repeats Eliphaz' words concerning the need for Job to 'search for El,' and if Job becomes 'pure' all will be well as in the ancient story of Job. He does imply that Job's children were sinners as well as Job. His big lie is the following: 'the tent of the wicked will be no more.'

"I guess it is impossible to do away with comments between speeches. In Job's first two speeches he complained; he desired death; and he asked questions. Now he will get down to business in a long speech. He knows that it is pure folly to file a lawsuit against the God of his 'friends,' because as creator of this world he is so powerful. No one can answer such a God, and besides God has already condemned him and all the innocent. The earth is controlled by the wicked. But why? Once again Job looks to the grave:

Indeed I know that [the following] is so:
What human can be acquitted before El?
He could not answer him once in a thousand.

. . .

Him, though I am innocent, I could not answer;
I would be pleading for mercy from my judge.
If I summoned, [if] he answered me,
I do not believe that he would hear my voice.

. . .

He mocks [the] despair of the innocent.
Earth has been placed in [the] hand of [the] wicked;
The faces of her judges he covers.
If not, then who is he?

. . .

For he is not a man, like me, whom I could answer,
'Let us come together in the trial.'

. . .

(Job 9)

My being is disgusted with my life;
I will give free rein to my complaint;
I will speak from the bitterness of my being.
I will say to Eloah, 'Do not condemn me;
Let me know for what you are charging me.
Does it seem good to you that you oppress,
That you despise the labor of your hands,
And on the counsel of [the] wicked you have beamed?

. . .

Why did you bring me from the womb?
I would have expired;
Not an eye would have seen me.
That which I was not, I would have been;
From womb to tomb, I would have been carried.
Are not my days few? Desist!
Stand away from me, and let me smile a little
Before I go (and I will never return)
To the netherworld of darkness, to the shadow of Mot,

A netherworld of darkness like gloom,
The shadow of Mot and chaos;
[The netherworld] was brightened with gloom.'
(Job 10)

That was a long speech."

"It was long, but Job made some good points," said Elimelech. Your last few lines were wonderful; you must have spent some time on them. The last line, 'The netherworld was brightened with gloom,' is a great line."

Magon said, "The wording and style is certainly creative. I liked two lines earlier in that last section. Jonathan let me see your text. Ah, yes, here it is: 'That which I was not, I would have been; / From womb to tomb, I would have been carried.' Language like that is bound to win."

Jonathan said, "I hope so, but Zophar who speaks next does not agree with you. His speech is quite short. He repeats the words of the other two: 'spread out your palms to him' or seek El, but his first words are:

Should a multitude of words not be answered?
Or should an articulate man be acquitted?
Should your idle talk silence men?

. . .

Zophar just sees Job as a stupid man. He says:

An empty headed man will get understanding,
When the wild ass of the steppe is born
    domesticated.

. . .

(Job 11)

Poor Zophar. He is the one with the empty head.

"Next we have another long speech by Job; there is no doubt that I give him more space than the others. The 'friends' have an equal opportunity, but they don't take advantage of it. So, here we go with a few sarcastic lines:

> Indeed, you are [educated] people,
> And with you wisdom will die.
> But I have a mind even as you;
> I am not less than you.

. . .

> But indeed ask please the domestic animals,
> And they will teach you;
> And the birds of the heavens, they will tell you.
> Or speak to the earth, it will teach you.
> And the fish of the sea will recount to you.
> Who does not know among all of these,
> That the hand of Eloah has done this?

. . .

(Job 12)

. . .

> Indeed I want to speak to Shaddai;
> I will be pleased to argue with El.

. . .

> Be silent before me, and I will speak.
> Let come upon me whatever.
> I will take my flesh in my teeth,

And my being I will place in my palm.
So, he will kill me; I have no hope.
Yet, I will argue my case to his face.

. . .

O El, do only two things for me,
Then from your face I will not hide.
Remove your palm from me,
And let your dread not fall upon me.
Summon me and I will answer,
Or let me speak, and you reply to me.
How many are my iniquities and sins?
Make known to me my transgression and my sin.
Why do you hide your face,
And count me as your enemy?

. . .

(Job 13)

A human, born of woman,
Is of few days and sated with strife.
Like a flower that came forth; he withered;
Like a shadow, he fled, and he does not endure.
Indeed, on such a one you opened your eye;
And me, you bring into judgment with you.

. . .

Yes, there is hope for the tree;
If it is cut down, it will grow again,
And its young shoots will not cease.
Or, if its root grows old in the earth,
And in the dirt its stump dies,
At the scent of water, it will sprout,

And make branches like a plant.
When a hero dies, he has collapsed;
A human has expired, and where is he?

. . .

And you have destroyed man's hope.
You overpower him forever; he is gone.

. . .

(Job 14)

I told you that this speech would be a long one. Notice
that Job teased his 'friends' about their wisdom, and he
suggested that they could learn something from the other
animals. He stresses that God defeats all, but nevertheless
Job is willing to debate with him. Of course he knows
that this God will kill him. For trees there is hope but not
for humans.

A human dies, and 'where is he?' He is dead!"

I said, "It is time for a break. I know that Jonathan
needs a cup of wine. Also, this is taking a long time. Do
you want to continue tonight or come back tomorrow
evening?"

Everyone wanted to continue. Deborah came to me and
said that she was going home to watch the children, so that
Rachel and Naam could come for the last part of the reading.
We all ate some more raisin cakes and filled our cups. About
then Deborah returned and said that Sarah and Sheva had
brought Magon and Naomi's children over to join with the
other children and their fun.

Jonathan said, "We have read one cycle of speeches in
this debate, and now we will listen to the second speech of
Eliphaz."

Magon said, "Before we hear from Eliphaz, I have two comments. Job is willing to face God, but it seems that God is not willing. Job asks, 'Why do you hide your face?' It appears that El condemns *in absentia*. Also from what we have heard so far, the three 'friends' seem to speak in a descending order of ability. Bildad and then Zophar are heard as weakening echoes of Eliphaz' thundering orthodoxy. Is that what you intend?"

"Exactly, but I could be criticized for not making Job's critics stronger. However Job's critics do have old and fading arguments.

"So we will listen to Eliphaz once again:

> Does a wise one answer windy knowledge,
> And does he fill his belly with an east wind?
> Should he argue with speech that is not profitable,
> And words in which there is no value?
> Indeed you destroy religion,
> And you do away with meditation before El.
> For your iniquity instructs your mouth,
> And you choose a crafty tongue.
> Your mouth condemns you, not I,
> And your lips testify against you.

. . .

> I will tell you, listen to me,
> And what I have seen, I will declare,
> What sages make known,
> And their fathers did not conceal,
> To whom alone the land was given,
> And no alien passed among them.
> [The] wicked writhes in pain all his days,
> And few years have been stored up for the ruthless.
> Dreadful sounds are in his ears;

When all is well, the enemy falls upon him.
He does not believe in returning from darkness,
And he is destined for the sword.

· · ·

(Job 15)

Eliphaz does not add much in this speech. He openly attacks Job for his lack of religion, and then goes on to repeat the orthodox position at length: the wicked will suffer. This is not the case, and repeating it does not make it true.

"Job speaks again:

I have heard many things like these;
Painful comforters are you all.
Is there a limit to windy words?
Or what afflicts you that you answer?

· · ·

My enemy narrows his eyes at me.
They have opened wide their mouths against me;
They have slapped my cheeks with scorn;
Together they mass themselves against me.
El hands me over to [the] vicious,
And into the hands of the wicked he throws me.

· · ·

(Job 16)

My spirit is broken;
My days are finished;
[The] tombs are for me.
Surely the mounds are before me,
And in their slimy pits, my eye fixes its gaze.

. . .

My days have passed,
My plans have been broken,
My mind's possessions.

. . .

To the pit I have called forth, 'You are my father,'
To the maggot, 'My mother and my sister,'
Then where, where is my hope?
My hope, who can see it?
It will descend into the power of Sheol;
We shall rest in the slime together.

(Job 17)

This is a sad speech."

Naomi said, "You have pointed out earlier the meaning of the 'where' questions. When Job asks, 'Where is my hope?' it is clear; there is no hope. There is only slime."

"True," responded Jonathan. "This is perhaps the low point in the poem for Job. After this Job seems to find some new strength, but first we have to listen to Bildad who once again repeats Eliphaz' point that the wicked will be punished:

Indeed, [the] light of the wicked is extinguished,
And the flame of his fire does not shine.
[The] light in his tent became dark,
And his lamp above him is extinguished.

. . .

He devours his skin with two hands,
The first-born of Mot with both his hands.
He is torn form his tent, his security,
And he is marched to the King of Terrors.

In his tent is set fire;
On his abode is scattered brimstone.

. . .

He has no offspring and no posterity among his
    people,
And there is no survivor in his old haunts.
On his [last] day, westerners were appalled,
And Easterners were seized with horror.
Surely these were the dwellings of [the] wicked,
And this is [the] place of one who did not know El.

(Job 18)

On this section I want to ask Magon a question. Years ago
you translated for us a letter from the king of Tyre to the
King of Ugarit. It had to do with a ship from Ugarit that was
about to sink. The King of Tyre rescued the ship and its
crew from the hands of the 'Master of Death.' As I was writing
this speech for Bildad, I was thinking that 'the first-born of
Mot' and the 'King of Terrors,' which we sometimes use
were titles that were close to the 'Master of Death.' What do
you think?"

"I think these titles are related, but as I remember, we
did not think about any additional titles at that time."

"Right, so this shows us that it takes a long time for us to
finish our work."

"If we ever do. The mention of these titles reminds me
that the orthodox position of a just God, who is always absent,
lends itself to a 'Master of Death' or 'King of Terrors' to
hand out the punishment."

Jonathan continued, "Our rebel Job is ready to speak
again, and he will make one of his most important points in
this speech:

How long will you torment me
And crush me with words?

· · ·

Though, truly, you are overbearing against me,
And you argue my disgrace against me.
Know then that Eloah has perverted me,
And he has thrown his net over me.
So, I cry, 'Violence,' and I am not answered;
I cry for help, and there is no justice.

· · ·

All the men of my association have abhorred me,
And those whom I have loved have turned against me.
My bones have stuck through my skin and my flesh;
I, myself, have escaped by the skin of my teeth.

· · ·

O that my words would be written!
That they would be engraved on the stela;
With an iron stylus and lead,
They would be carved in rock as a witness.
But as for me, I know that my avenger lives;
And a guarantor by [my] grave will stand.

· · ·

(Job 19)

The most important words in this speech are 'I cry for help, and there is no justice.' There are no rewards, and there is no justice. Those who think otherwise are living in a fantasy world. One has to move beyond fantasy in order to deal with the harsh facts of this world and to fashion a life with a few moments of joy."

One of the students asked, "Does that mean there is no justice anywhere?"

"The answer is yes; there is no justice from our leaders, from other humans, from the God of the pious, or from our world, and we should not expect it. I have to be honest; this is a minority opinion, but it is, I think, correct. Experience bears it out. Keziah is producing a book on minority opinions, and my Job poem will be one of the longest parts of that work.

"I would also like to call your attention to another line, 'All the men of my association have abhorred me.' Some of you went with us to Bethlehem when we buried Gad, Keziah's father. You will remember that the men of the Marzeah, or the house of mourning, were helpful during those sad days. I belong to that association, but what if those men abhorred me? That would be tragic. In Job's case there will not be much help at the end. However he will have at least one friend who will stand by his grave and give him a proper burial.

"Zophar follows with his second (and final) speech, and once again it is a repeat:

· · ·

Have you not known this from old,
Since a human was placed on earth,
That [the] triumph of [the] wicked is brief,
And [the] joy of [the] impious is for a moment?

· · ·

He will perish forever like his own dung;
They who saw him will say, 'Where is he?'
Like a dream he will fly away, and they will not
   find him,
And he will flee like a vision of [the] night.

· · ·

There is nothing left for his meal,
Therefore his good times will not endure.

. . .

This is [the] lot of a wicked human from Elohim,
And [the] inheritance appointed him from El.
(Job 20)

The only new thing here is the admission that the wicked
may seem to have joy for a short time, but 'good times will
not endure,' says Zophar. It is obvious that Job does not go
along with this. Rather he asks:

. . .

Why do the wicked live on?
They have grown old;
They have even become wealthy.
Their seed has been established in their presence
    with them
And their offspring before their eyes.
Their houses are safe from fear,
And the rod of Eloah is not upon them.
His bull has bred and never fails;
His cow calves and never aborts.
They send out their young ones as a flock,
And their children dance about.
They take up the timbrel and harp,
And they rejoice at [the] sound of [the] flute.
They finish their days with good times,
And in a moment they go down to Sheol.

. . .

Have you not asked those who travel [the] road[s],
And do you not acknowledge their evidence,
That on the day of disaster [the] wicked is spared,
From the day of fury they are led forth?

. . .

(Job 21)

Once again we have a strong speech by Job. The wicked do not live short lives; they do well; they even have a quick death when the time comes. Then he stresses that 'on the day of disaster [the] wicked is spared!' Again, there is no justice."

I said, "Jonathan let me read a couple of speeches. Your voice is tired, and you need some wine."

"That would be great. You will begin with Eliphaz' last speech. He first enumerates Job's sins and then tries to bring him back to God."

I began:

. . .

Is not your wickedness great,
And your iniquities have no end?

. . .

Serve him and be complete;
In this, good will come to you.
Take instruction from his mouth,
And put his words in you mind.
If you return to Shaddai you will be restored;
You shall put iniquity far from your tent.
So, set on the mud [your] gold,
And on the rocks of the stream [your] Ophir.
Shaddai will be your gold
And a mountain of silver for you.

When you delight in Shaddai,
And lift up your face to Eloah,
You shall pray to him, and he will hear you,
And you shall fulfill your vows.
And you will decide something, and it will stand,
And on your path, light has shone.

. . .

(Job 22)

Goodness. Old Eliphaz makes a strong plea, but I note from the beginning of Job's next speech that he is not interested in serving the God of Eliphaz:

Even today my complaint is bitter,
[His] hand is heavy on account of my sighing.
O that I knew where to find him,
That I might come to his dwelling.
I would set [my] case before him,
And I would fill my mouth with arguments.
I would [like] to know [the] words he would
    answer me,
And I would understand what he would say to me.
Through an attorney would he prosecute me?
Surely not! He would charge me.
There [the] upright could reason with him;
I could bring forth my case to an enduring life.
Lo, I go east, and he is not there,
And west, and I cannot discern him.
North, in his work place, and I do not behold
    [him].
He hides in the south, and I do not see [him].

. . .

(Job 23)

. . .

> From [the] city [the] dying groan,
> And a person with wounds cries out.
> Yet Eloah does not pay attention to prayer.

. . .

> If it is not so, who will prove me a liar,
> And make as nothing my words?
>
> (Job 24)

Jonathan, do you have anything to point out about these words of Job?"

"Yes. Here Job is searching for the God of his friends, but that God is not to be found. When Job says, 'I could bring forth my case to an enduring life,' this is sarcastic. Job cannot find God, and this is like asking, 'Where is he?' Answer: 'dead.' At least that is what I was trying to convey."

Then I said, "Let me read a short response by Bildad:

> Dominion and dread are with him;
> He is the one who makes well being in his heights.
> Is there a number to his troops,
> And upon whom does his light not rise?
> How can a man be righteous before El,
> And how can one born of woman be pure?
> Even [the] moon does not shine,
> And [the] stars have not been pure in his eyes.
> How much less a man, a worm.
> And the son of Adam, a maggot.
>
> (Job 25)

I guess that this means that since everyone is born of a woman no one is pure. So how can Job talk about being innocent? I'm beginning to dislike Mr. Bildad and his views.

In fact he makes me angry. Now, Jonathan, you should read the last speech of Job."

"I would be glad to read Job's last word to his 'friends':

. . .

How have you helped [the] powerless?
Have you aided a weak arm?

. . .

By his power he stilled the Sea;
By his cunning he smashed Rahab.
By his wind the heavens were cleared;
[By] his hand he pierced the fleeing Serpent.
Lo, these are just traces of his rule;
What a whisper of a word we hear from him;
Who can understand the thunder of his might?

(Job 26)

In this poem Job cannot find the God of his 'friends.' He implies that he is dead. However, he does want to end his speech with some kind of a call to care. We may not know much about God, but this world is an interesting, ordered, and amazing place, and it and its 'powerless' need our care. We can respond to this calling. Since poor Zophar had nothing more to say here is my epilogue:

"Job expected Zophar to respond, but he did not say a word. Job had made his case; he was tired; he went back to the tomb where they had buried their children. His wife was there, and he sat down beside her. 'So what do we do now?' Job asked his wife. 'We have buried our children; we have lost everything. What do we do now?'

"She answered; she said: 'I have been thinking about what we should do, but first what happened in your long talk with your pious 'friends'?'

"He said: 'The whole thing was a heated debate. They thought that our loss was a sign of our sin. I said no! I told them that I would like to go to court with their God, even though I knew I would be defeated. Why? Because their God does not care about the cries of those who suffer. There is no justice in his court or any place, and in fact their God does not exist. Where is he? He is not to be found. They finally just quit; they could not answer. This does not mean that I could ever convince them. Their ears are filled with righteous wax, and they are probably praying for us. In my last words I did suggest that the one who conquered chaos did give us an ordered world, but "What a whisper of a word we hear from him."'

"She said: 'What you have just said helps me, just a bit. Earlier you asked, "What do we do now?" Well, we can moan; we can cry out; we can wish for death. But we can also remember our children, call forth their names at this tomb, and try to build new lives out of these ruins. I think we must avoid the night terrors when the God of the pious creeps into our dreams and marvel at the wonders of this world though it is also full of suffering. I am certain of one thing: it will take more than "a whisper of a word;" there has to be between us a shout and a hopeful song of love and support.'"

Eli's friend, Nahum said, "The fantasy in the 'friends' position is difficult to believe, but your Job does not have an attractive alternative; your Job does not have a happy ending."

"That's right. But the ending is realistic. No more fantasy. There is no time to worry about justice, but there is time to help each other, with no expectations or rewards. There is no escape; we live in this world and not another, and a bit part will do in this world of wonder."

"I am sorry that this reading was so long," Jonathan said. "You have been faithful friends. Since it is late, you should feel free to leave at any time, but you can also get another cup of wine, and we can talk. If you agree that this poem is important then I will want you to help me when we make it public."

Some of the people left at this point, but others stayed to ask questions and to talk about a public reading. Elimelech said, "I think it is a good poem, and it should be read soon."

Jonathan said, "After David reads it, we'll set a meeting of the entire school. I would like for all of you to spread yourselves out among the audience to get a feel for the mood. It will also help to have your questions coming from all around the room."

"What do you want to achieve with the public reading," asked Elishama.

"I want to create a debate that will result in getting my poem published even if it is published alongside the old story of Job. I hope that David will help us to do that, even though he may not like my poem."

"Even if he did like it," said Eli, "he probably would have to publish it 'alongside the old story of Job.' His position would remain more confusing that way."

"You are probably correct."

After everyone had gone, Naam said, "Your reading went well. I enjoyed it, and I hope that your students help you win your points. I talked with Rachel, and we both thought that most young people would rather stand with the rebel Job than with the old orthodox teachers."

I said, "You are probably right, but as your father has reminded me, the old teachers will have many priests and royal prophets on their side. Still as you know, we believe in pushing minority opinions. Now, I must go get the girls. Jonathan, you and Naam can start to create some order while I'm gone."

Chapter Seven

The Public Reading

We only had to wait about three weeks for the big day. As soon as Jonathan heard that David had read the poem, he asked Sheva to schedule an assembly for the entire school. "We will need the big hall in our class building for this event."

"Do you think it is wise to have a public reading of your poem? I have heard that your position will be opposed by some of our teachers and students. Also I was informed that David wants to send some of his prophets and priests to hear it."

"Well, I have never thought that everyone would like what I have to say, but I have worked on it for a long time and want to share it. It should start a conversation that will move throughout our country and beyond our borders. Perhaps it will shape our future. I knew that David would send people from his staff, and that does not bother me. The poem does contain my views, but they are not mine alone. As one looks back in the literature of our world, it is clear that there have been other voices concerned with some of the same issues. This will be important for our school even if we never fully agree on these matters. In the end we must clarify what we think about pain and suffering in our world even if we remain divided in our answers."

"Jonathan, you are persuasive."

I began thinking of ways that I could help. Jonathan was already prepared, and I thought the best thing for all of us would be to relax for three weeks. I decided not to push too hard on my writing. I spent extra time with the children and had some fun with our friends.

Jonathan noticed that some the teachers avoided him. They probably knew most of his views and were the ones getting ready to oppose him.

Then suddenly it was time. I took the children to the hall, and we sat with Magon and Naomi. Then the children found seats in a big windowsill. We referred to this space as "the big hall," but it wasn't very big. I supposed it could hold a hundred people. The hall was soon filled. Before we arrived, I had asked Naam to count how many came and how many left before the end. I knew that Jonathan would need about the time that most people spend during a long lunch break to read his poem, if he didn't make comments. After the reading I supposed there would be some questions. I noticed that Jonathan had just taken his place and was ready to read. Someone had built a small platform for him to stand on. They also had a rather high table for his scroll.

During the reading the audience was quiet; they wanted to hear. When Jonathan finished, four or five men jumped to their feet, and they all tried to talk at once. Sheva stepped up beside Jonathan and called for silence. He said, "You can direct your questions to me, one person at a time. First, I will take questions from the five who are standing; I will start from the front to the back of the hall. Magon, you are first."

"I know that you have spent about twenty years dealing with this subject. I know that it has been an important topic in our world's literature, but why is it so important to you?"

"Every human being in our world lives under the tyranny of death, pain, loss, and all forms of suffering. Even infants will soon learn to deal with such experiences. My purpose is to start a conversation that will give some the courage to stand tall in the face of such tyranny. We need friendship, support, and love to find moments of joy and to realize a few accomplishments within the swift years of our lives.

The next speaker was one of our older teachers. He said, "I have been teaching at this school for many years, long before it became The Jerusalem Academy. On this subject I have always gone along with the scribes of many other schools. Therefore I subscribe to the arguments of Eliphaz in your poem. We need to fear God and praise him. Your rebel Job is not in a position to help himself or anybody."

After this statement most of the crowd voiced their approval. The next two speakers said almost the same thing. Then Jonathan said, "All three of you are following an ancient tradition. Also, this is exactly what some Babylonian texts teach. I disagree with such texts, and this illustrates why we need this conversation."

The next speaker, a priest, was angry; he said, "You and your rebel Job will bring utter chaos to our people. You have Job arguing his case with three pious men; you created those three, and you put weak arguments in their mouths. Your Job has no real answer to your 'important subject.' What I want to know is this: since you like the form of the debate, do you have the courage to argue Job's case before three real persons of faith, obedience, and integrity? These three will be righteous men and followers of the God whose funeral you have announced."

Jonathan said, "If you can find three righteous men, I have the courage, and I will ask Sheva to schedule it."

From the other side of the room Elishama stood and addressed Sheva. He said, "As a helpful introduction to this debate, I would like to request that Jonathan, and also others if they want, give us some facts about the ancient story of Job from our traditions and from the Babylonian traditions. This will help us to understand the debate."

Jonathan said, "I can do that; I have been collecting such material for my class."

That concluded the program, but it was easy to see that

many were angry. In fact, I heard some remarks that were unkind and even threatening. One man said to a small group, "Jonathan should be thrown out of this school, but King David would not allow such a thing to happen to his 'uncle,' even if he agreed with us."

Naam told me that ninety had shown up for the reading, and he said. "I did not see one person leave before the end. They were interested."

"Thanks for that report," I said.

Jonathan joined us as we walked to our house with Magon and Naomi. "Well, I got what I wanted, a debate," he said. "I asked Sheva to hold it soon."

When we got to our house, we discovered something that we did not want. A message was painted above the front door; it said in big letters, "DOES THE REBEL JOB HAVE A GOD? WHERE IS HE?"

Jonathan asked Naam to get some water and some brushes. He said to the rest of us, "I hope that I have not put any of you in danger. The only good thing about this is that it appears that whoever wrote this actually understood my message."

Magon said, "We will help you wash it off."

I said, "Naomi and I will fix some refreshments, and when you are finished we can talk about the debate."

Jonathan, Magon, and Naam scrubbed the stones above the door. Sheva came by. "I'm sorry to see what has happened here," he said. "Jonathan, do you really want to go ahead with this?"

"Yes. I am ready. It needs to be discussed. Even if all participants retain their present positions, they will know that when pushed in any conversation their remarks will have to be qualified with 'I know that others do not agree with me.' Over time I hope that such qualifications will make it easier."

"I will set it up soon," said Sheva. "We are certainly moving into a new and different future. I wish that Khety was here to participate in this conversation."

"He'll be here soon," said Magon, "and this conversation will be ongoing."

Sheva left, and soon the men were finished. When they came into the house Jonathan said to me, "The stones above the door look better than before. I suppose you will want us to wash the entire house."

"That won't be necessary, so sit down and relax. I will even serve you."

"I thank you for such service. I feel good about the reading. I suppose that David will want to talk about it, and I want to do that soon. It will be important for us to know what he thinks and what his staff thinks. Of course we already know what one of his priests thinks."

Magon said, "That was an interesting remark when you said to the priest, 'If you can find three righteous men, I have the courage.' I'll bet you that to meet that quota, he will only look for two."

"I had the same thought," said Naomi.

"I wonder if his name is Eliphaz?" I said.

"We are joking," Jonathan said, "but we are on to something. We should find out his real name and check out his background. Tomorrow I'll talk with Danel and Noah; they will be able to check him out. I noticed that Abiathar and Nathan were not at the reading. I think they are still David's main priest and chief prophet, but I don't know that for sure. It wouldn't surprise me if they sent their underlings."

"I hate to break up this conversation," Naomi said, "but we should take a quick look at our new house and pick up the children. So, we will see you soon, and Jonathan perhaps you should put up a message board out in front of the house. It would cut down on washing down walls."

Chapter Eight

Khety's Return

During the next few days Jonathan and Magon spent a lot of time together working on the ancient Babylonian traditions that dealt with the problem of suffering, parallel in many ways to our ancient story of Job, not even close to the new views in Jonathan's poem. One of the Babylonian texts Magon had received from his friends in Tyre. He thought it was a copy of a text used in the scribal school at Ugarit.

Jonathan talked with David, who had enjoyed the poem, because he had always thought that his prophets and priests were too certain about a lot of things. But he also said that he would have to support his prophets and priests in their belief that the ancient story of Job was better for the general public, because obedience to God is better than chaos. Jonathan told David that the issue was not between obedience and chaos, but between fantasy and truth and the ability to deal with suffering. David didn't agree but supported the idea of the debate. Obviously they did not settle their differences, but Jonathan was pleased that David had liked his poem.

On the day before the debate, Noah reported to Jonathan and Magon concerning the priest who would lead the opposition. Noah said, "His name is Elyahba'. I thought that his name said it all: 'El hides.' After all, your rebel Job accused El of hiding, so this priest has the right name. He works for Abiathar and is someone who wants to make it to the top. His righteousness and 'humility' is the most conspicuous thing about him, and he has offended most of his family and friends. I don't know if this will help you or not. If I hear anything concerning the others who will be with him, I will let you know."

That evening Jonathan and I talked about the debate. I suggested that if David enjoyed the poem it would not hurt one bit to throw in some humor from time to time directed toward the priests. Jonathan agreed. Then he said, "I want to forget about the debate for tonight. I would like for the five of us to eat some of your cakes, drink a bit of wine, and tell some stories."

"That sounds good to me."

We called the children, but before we could get started with a story there was a knock on the door. There was Khety! "You are back from Egypt," Jonathan said. "We did not expect you so soon. This is great. Tomorrow we are having a public debate. I am defending my poem on Job against some orthodox 'friends' who don't like it. But tonight we are relaxing and were just about to tell some stories and eat a few cakes. Won't you join us?"

"I will be happy to. Sheva gave me a room in the school building, and I was just out for some evening air. The refreshments will be good, and I will even earn my keep. I will tell a story for this event."

The children clapped and shouted. Ruth said, "We want you to tell your story, because Naam and Daddy always tell the same old stories."

Khety settled down among the children, "Well the story I have is an old story—somehow they are the best—but it is an old Egyptian story, and I doubt if you have heard it. It is called *The Story of the Shipwrecked Sailor*, and it is probably about eight hundred years old. I do not have a written text with me, but I know it by heart. I won't leave out anything that is essential, and I won't add much. I learned this story from a text copied by a skilled scribe, by the name of Imeny, from an earlier text.

"A prince went on a mission by ship that was not successful, and after he returned he was afraid and worried about what the king would say. The ship's chief mate tried to advise the prince and also cheer him up by telling him about one of his sea-going adventures. But the sailor's tale did not really help the Prince, and when we are finished, I will ask you why the tale did not help. Also you should know that the Egyptian expression 'the great green' (*w₃d-wr*) means 'the sea.' With that here is the story.

"The chief mate said, 'Take heart my Prince. Behold, we have reached the palace. The mallet was seized; the mooring-post struck; the prow-rope placed on land. Give praise, and thank God. Each man embraced his fellow; your crew has returned in good condition; there is no loss among our troops. We have left Wawat; we have passed by Senmut. Behold we have returned in peace, and we have reached our land. Listen to me O Prince. I make few demands, but wash yourself and put water on your fingers. Then when you are addressed you must answer. Speak thoughtfully to the king; you must answer without hesitating. *A man's mouth saves him.* His speech brings forgiveness for him, but do what you want. Speaking to you is wearisome.

'But, let me tell you a similar thing that happened to me. I was going to the mines of the king, and I went to the great green in a ship of a hundred and twenty cubits long and forty cubits wide. One hundred and twenty of Egypt's choice sailors were in it. They watched the sky; they watched the land; their hearts were braver than lions. They could predict a storm before it came and a raging wind before it happened. While we were on the great green, a storm came before we reached land. [The storm] brought a wind with it; it repeatedly made a wave, which was eight cubits high.

Behold a [piece] of wood struck me, and then the ship died (*dpt mwt*). From those in it, no one remained. I was cast on an island by a wave of the great green. I spent three days alone; my heart was my companion. I lay in the midst of the covering of the trees and kept to the shade.

'Then I stretched forth my two feet in order to find out what I might eat. I found figs and grapes there, many fine leeks, ripe and unripe sycamore figs there, and cultivated cucumbers. Fish were there and birds; there was nothing that was not in this place. I satisfied myself, and I placed [the rest] on the ground, because my arms were so full. I made a fire drill; I started a fire; I gave a burnt offering to the gods.

'Just then I heard a thunderous voice, and I thought, "It is a wave of the great green." Trees broke, and the ground trembled. I uncovered my face, and I found it was a serpent; he was coming. He was thirty cubits [long]; his beard was more than two cubits [long]. His body was overlaid with gold, his eyebrows with the best lapis lazuli. He coiled himself forward. Then he opened his mouth to me while I was on my belly before him. He said to me, "Who brought you? Who brought you, poor fellow, who brought you? If you delay in telling me who brought you to this island, I will introduce you to your [new] self, [since] you will be as ashes, having become as one not seen."

'"You speak to me, [but] I do not understand it. I am before you, [but] I am ignorant."

'So he placed me in his mouth. He brought me to his lair. He sat me down without hurting me. I was whole and nothing was torn from me. Then he opened his mouth to me while I was on my belly before him. He asked me, "Who brought you? Who brought you, poor fellow, who brought you to this island of the great green which is surrounded by water?"

'Finally I answered him; my hands were raised before him. I said to him, "I went down to the mines as a messenger

of the king in a ship of a hundred and twenty cubits long
and forty cubits in wide. One hundred and twenty of
Egypt's choice sailors were in it. They watched the sky;
they watched the land; their hearts were braver than
lions. They could predict a storm before it came and a
raging wind before it happened. Each of them, his heart
was braver; his arm was stronger than his fellows. There
was none who was ignorant. While we were in the great
green a storm came before we reached land. [The storm]
brought a wind with it; it repeatedly made a wave, which
was eight cubits high. Behold a [piece] of wood struck
me, and the ship died (*dpt mwt*). From those in it, no one
remained except me. Behold I am at your side. I was
brought to this island by a wave of the great green."

'Then he said to me, "Do not fear! Do not fear, poor
fellow. Do not let your face blanch; you reached me. God
has caused you to live; he brought you to this fantasy island.
There is nothing that is not in this place; it is full moreover
of all good things. Behold you will spend month upon month
until you have completed four months in the midst of this
island. Then a ship will come from the palace with sailors in
it that you know. You shall go with them to the palace; you
shall eventually die in your city.

'"How joyful is he who tells what he has experienced
after the pain has gone away. Let me tell you a similar thing
that happened on this island. I was here with my brothers
and with children in their midst. All together, [we were]
seventy-five serpents, my children with my brothers (I will
not mention to you a little daughter whom I had obtained
by prayer). Then a star fell, and they went up in the flames
from it. Now it happened that I was not with them; they
were burned. I was not among them. Then I felt dead
because of them. I found them, one [pile] of corpses.

'"If you are strong and completely subdue your heart,
you shall embrace your children; you shall kiss your wife;
and you shall see your home. It is more beautiful than

anything. You shall reach the palace; you shall be there
among your brothers.”

'Now I was extended out upon my belly; I touched the
ground before him. Let me speak to you, “I shall tell of your
nature to the king. I will acquaint him with your greatness. I
shall send you two kinds of oil, herbs, incense, and the
incense of the temple, which makes content all the gods in
it. I shall tell what happened to me from what I have seen of
your nature. One will praise god for you in the city before
the magistrates of all the land. I shall slaughter oxen for you
as burnt offerings; I shall sacrifice geese for you. I shall send
to you ships laden with all the riches of Egypt as is done for
a god who loves people in a far land not known to mankind.”

'He just laughed at me for what I had said, which seemed
foolish in his mind. He said to me, “You do not have much
myrrh or all kinds of incense; I am the ruler of Punt, and
myrrh belongs to me. That oil which you spoke of bringing,
it is the main thing of this island. It will happen when you
have left this place, you will never see this island again; it will
have become water.”

'Later the ship came as he had foretold beforehand. I went
and placed myself up in a tall tree; I recognized those that
were in it. When I went to report it, and I found him, and he
knew it. He said to me, “In health, in health, poor fellow, to
your home and you will see your children. Cause my name to
be fair in your city. Behold, that is my due from you.”

'Then I put myself on my belly; my hands were raised
before him. Then he gave me a load of myrrh, oil, herbs,
incense, spice, perfume, eye paint, giraffe tails, wood,
incense, tusks of ivory, greyhounds, monkeys, baboons, and
all kinds of riches. I loaded them on the ship. Then I placed
myself on my belly to thank him, and he said to me, “Behold
you will reach the palace in two months. Behold you will
embrace your children. You will be young and vigorous at
the palace, and you will be buried.”

'I went down to the shore in the vicinity of this ship.

After calling to the crew, which was on the ship, I gave praise on the shore to the lord of this island. Those in the [ship] did the same. We sailed north to the palace of the king. We reached the palace in two months, just like all he had said. So I went in before the king. I presented the gifts I brought from the island. He praised god for me before the magistrates of all the land, and I was made a chief mate and endowed with two hundred persons. "Look at me! After I was endowed with land, after I have seen what I had experienced, now you listen to my mouth. Behold it is good for people to listen."

'Thus the Prince said to me, "Don't use such skill my friend. Who would give water to a goose at dawn that will be slaughtered that morning?"'

Ruth said, "I would give water to the goose."

"I'm sure the goose would appreciate your gift," I said.

Then Khety asked his question. "Why did the story fail to help the Prince?"

Naam said, "The chief mate was a great success, and he was treated accordingly. This did not help the Prince, who did not bring home a ship loaded with gifts."

"That is exactly why the Prince was not helped," said Khety. "But I think the chief mate was thinking along different lines when he offered his story."

Elissa said, "In the beginning of the story, the chief mate said, 'A man's mouth saves him.' The chief mate's real success came because he was forced to speak to the serpent. So, the Prince should listen, and he should speak before the king."

"You're right," said Khety. "When we listen to stories, the author's point of view and intention, in this case the chief mate's, needs to be stressed. So is this a good story or a story that failed?"

Naam said, "It is a good story, because it was entertaining. That is important. It is a sad story in that the Prince could see nothing but the ship loaded with gifts."

I said, "I suppose that one could say that the chief mate could have made his point with greater clarity. However, many times clarity appears as preaching and is rejected as such. You have to hope that people will be entertained and perhaps learn something along the way as Jonathan has said with reference to the Joseph story in our epic. But people are going to see what they want to see in a story, and success is never guaranteed."

Jonathan said, "I want to thank you for that great story. It is clear that we have all enjoyed it."

I said, "Khety, you need some more wine after that story."

I poured some wine and excused myself. I had to see that the children got ready for bed. After that Jonathan and I talked a little more with Khety. Jonathan said, "I was interested in the fact that the chief mate says, 'Then I put myself on my belly; my hands were raised up before him.' When we describe a person seeking the favor of a superior, we say, 'spread out your palms to him' (Job 11:13). I suppose that the two expressions are about the same."

"Yes, and this can be seen in our art."

"Also I was interested in another point. In your story, the chief mate reports that 'the ship died.' This is exactly the way a sinking ship is described in a letter from the King of Tyre to the King of Ugarit, which Magon translated for us a few years ago. We just talked about Magon's translation of this text the other night when I was reading my Job poem to a few friends. It is interesting that in Egyptian, Babylonian, and I suppose in Ugaritic the phrase, 'the ship died,' is used in this way."

"It is interesting," said Khety. "The expressions of the sailors penetrated all of our languages. This is doubly interesting, because in Egyptian we use the same root for our word 'to die,' (*mwt*) as you have in Hebrew, and it is of course seen in your Mot, the god of death."

"You just gave me the answer to my next question. Thanks. It is good to have you here."

I said, "I have a comment on the story. In this story the serpent is kind and generous. This tale is so completely different from one of our creation stories where we give God the credit for placing an eternal enmity between the humans and the serpent, and most humans do fear serpents. But your story attempts to counter that fear. Do you think that your story tries to give another view?

"It is a story for children, and I do think that it challenges the accepted fears of all humans. At least it opens up other options."

"That is so interesting. Please come by again; we had a good time."

"I'll do that. You have a lovely family. I will see you at the debate."

Chapter Nine

The Debate

The next morning I did not see Jonathan. He had gone to his office to prepare for the debate, which would start just after lunch. When he came home for lunch he said that he had been reading his poem again and preparing some remarks about the ancient story of Job that he would make just before the debate. After lunch the girls went over to Deborah's place to play, and Naam, Jonathan, and I went to the debate. There were more people for this event than for the public reading. As soon as Sheva saw Jonathan, he called the meeting to order. He asked Jonathan to come forward along with Elyahba' and his two friends. Sheva explained that Jonathan would open the meeting with a background statement on the ancient story of Job. Then the debate would start, and Elyahba' would make the first speech. Jonathan would respond to each of the three challengers in order. Jonathan began the background speech.

"My poem, which we will be debating today, argues against the ancient story of Job. But what is the ancient story of Job, and how ancient is it? There is some material from Egypt that relates more to my poem than to the ancient story of Job, so I will go to the Sumerian and Babylonian material to answer these questions. In the near future I will want to discuss some of the Egyptian material with our new teacher from Egypt, who is with us today. Khety please stand so that all will be able to recognize you.

"We do not know much about the Sumerian story, but it is like the ancient story of Job in that someone suffers, and he prays. As a result of his prayers, his suffering is turned to joy. The first Babylonian story of this type is *Ludlul bêl nêmeqi,* which means, 'I will praise the Lord of Wisdom.' Magon brought this text to my attention some years ago, and we have discussed it on several occasions. It is like our ancient story of Job. It goes into great detail concerning a faithful man who endures great suffering. He is finally brought back from the edge of the pit, from death itself. Recently, Magon has come up with another text of this type. This new text is also Babylonian, and is much shorter than *Ludlul bêl nêmeqi.* The interesting thing about this text is that a scribe probably brought it to Tyre from Ugarit just after the fall of Ugarit, about two hundred years ago. It seems to be a short form of *Ludlul bêl nêmeqi* or perhaps both of them came from a common source.

"I have asked two of my students to hold up two charts. Those of you who are close to the front will be able to see, and I will read them for the rest of you. Note the following parallels in the structure of the two texts:

Ludlul bêl nêmeqi	The text from Ugarit
1. The diviners and priests are confused and cannot explain his condition. (Lines I: 51,52; II: 108-110)	1. The diviners and priests are confused and obscure concerning his pain. (Lines 2-7)
2. They cannot fix a time limit on his illness. (Lines II: 111)	2. They have not fixed the term of his illness. (Line 8)
3. The sufferer was prepared for burial before death. (Lines II: 114,115)	3. The sufferer was prepared for burial before death. (Lines 9-12)
4. Marduk was worshipped. (Lines III: 1-60)	4. Marduk was praised with a hymn. (Lines 25-37)

5. The sufferer was rescued.	5. The sufferer was rescued.
(Lines IV: 5,35)	(Lines 38-41)
(See W. G. Lambert, *Babylonian*	(See Jean Nougayrol in *Ugaritica V,* pp
Wisdom Literature, pp 33, 45, 46, 59)	265-273, text 162)

"These two texts do not really deal with the question of why a faithful person must suffer, and they do not come close to the subject matter in my poem, but they agree that the worship of Marduk can heal. This is like our ancient story of Job. A good man suffers, and he finally bows before the creator and everything is restored. This old story is everywhere, and most people live by it.

"I have spent twenty years writing my poem with a central message: the ancient story of Job is false. It is false in the Babylonian tradition and in the Hebrew tradition. The Babylonians have another text that is of some help for me; it begins to question the ancient stories and to ask the 'why question.' It is an acrostic poem of twenty-seven verses, and each verse has eleven lines, which begin with the same syllable. We do not have the first line and hence the title, but we can call it 'A Dialogue Between An Orphan, Who Suffers, And His Friend.' It is in the form of a debate and this has been used in my poem. The standard Babylonian views of suffering as seen in the ancient stories are questioned but not solved. I had to pursue and expand their arguments in my poem.

"Now I want to make a suggestion. It may be easier for our debate to call the ancient story of Job: *Job I,* and my poem: *Job II.*

"In *Job II* there is something new; it is the knowledge that *Job I* contains a fantasy. What is this fantasy? It is the belief that you will have a life without suffering if you seek God and fear him. Only by knowing that this is a fantasy, can we build again after experiencing loss and suffering; with this knowledge, one is free to build on old ruins knowing that there is no one to blame not even a god. We live in a world where there is no justice. True, our misguided decisions and the greed of the powerful can make things worse, but the fact remains: there is no justice. I welcome the words of my challengers, and I want all of us to have an enjoyable afternoon."

Sheva said, "After the formal debate we will be open for questions. Now we will hear from Elyahba'. He is a priest, who works with Abiathar."

Elyahba' stood and introduced his two friends: Ahimelech son of Abiathar and Ira the Jairite. I thought, "Goodness, they are all priests. Where are the prophets? Such priests always think they know exactly what God wants us to do, but prophets might have some good ideas as to what is needed in a given situation unless they are royal prophets who only say what the king wants to hear."

Then Elyahba' began his speech:

"I want to thank King David who allowed us to see his copy of *Job II*, as Jonathan wants us to call it. It is clear in *Job II* that Job got more time in the debate than the three who opposed him. I hope that today we get equal time. I found myself angry with those three friends, because they could not find the words to answer Jonathan's rebel Job. Words had fled from them. But then I realized that Jonathan had set them up; he took the words away from them. As a result, his Job won that debate. Now the situation is different. The three of us stand before you, and Jonathan cannot steal our words.

"'I will make known my knowledge, even I, / For I am full of words (Job 32:17b-18a). The wind in my belly pushed me. / Therefore my belly is like unopened wine, / Like new wine skins it will break. / I will speak, and it will break wind from me (Job 32:18b-20a). . . . My words are from an upright heart, / And my lips have spoken pure knowledge; . . . See, I am like El's vessel (Job 33:6a).'"

I thought to myself, "It sounds like he is an old fart. He brags but leaves himself open to ridicule."

Elyahba' continued, "Indeed your *Job II* has said, 'I am pure without transgression; / I am clean without guilt (Job 33:9).' And he accuses God of injustice and of heaping upon him unbearable suffering, but God has chastened him upon his bed. God has rescued him from the Pit. So *Job II* needs to repent; he needs to sing:

> 'I sinned, and I perverted the right,
> And he did not pay me back.
> He saved my being from passing into the Pit,
> And my life sees the light.'

(Job 33:27b-28)

Therefore I say to *Job II* (and to Jonathan, who is to be identified with *Job II*):

> 'Heed, Job; listen to me.
> Be silent, and I will speak.
> If there are words, answer me;
> Speak, for I have desired your righteousness.
> If you have nothing, listen to me;
> Keep silent! I will teach you wisdom.'"

(Job 33:31-33)

Elyahba' sat down and Jonathan stood up and said, "Since this is a debate, I cannot take your last imperative seriously; I will not 'keep silent.' You have said that you were so full of knowledgeable words that they will spill forth as if from a new wine skin. But it seems that you are confused. New wine breaks old skins, only wear or poor construction breaks the new ones, and your words are not new; *Job II* heard these same words from his so-called friends. Your skin may be old, but if you break wind it will not be because you have any new ideas. It may be because the old ones have fermented too long; they have turned sour!

"You began and ended your speech with an admonition to listen to you and your wisdom, because you were God's vessel. You have claimed to be the great teacher, but a great teacher should be truthful. *Job II* does not claim to be 'pure without transgression,' and he does not claim to be righteous. He does claim to be innocent, and many times he asks God to tell him what he has done wrong (Job 7:20; 13:23). He does say that he has kept God's ways (Job 23:11), but these are the ways of the God who does not respond in any way and who cannot be found. This is the God who 'hides his face!' Elyahba', you should know all about this since your name means, 'El or God hides.' I should add that *Job II* does not believe that prayer is useful, because Eloah does not hear the cries of the innocent (Job 24:12), and yet Job does say 'my prayer is pure (Job 16:17).' At this point Job is saying that his desire is real or pure; he is ready for the tomb (Job17:1-2).

"You are correct in saying that *Job II* accuses God for his troubles, but what other answer is possible? You have said that Job is 'chastened by pain upon his bed.' Therefore your God must use pain in this way. You have a strange religion, and you claim that your God will deliver one from the Pit? This I doubt. After telling us that God uses suffering as a discipline, your confused mind asks us to sing, 'I sinned, and I perverted right, / And he did not pay me back.' This makes no sense."

At this point, I was worried as to how this debate would end. The audience became unruly, and Sheva had to call for order.

When the people became quiet, Ahimelech began his speech. He said, "*Job II* has said, 'I am righteous, and El has taken away my justice (Job 34:5).' In fact he goes on to say that 'A man gains nothing from his favor with Elohim (Job 34:9).' God controls all flesh, and he could end all flesh. God cares for us, and he deals harshly with the wicked. Jonathan does not agree with this, but he is wrong. Also Jonathan says that God does not hear the cries of the innocent, but again he is wrong. It is the wicked, who do not bring before God the cries of the afflicted (Job 34:28-29), so if he is silent who can condemn?

Job II is a rebel as he multiplies words against El."

Jonathan responded, "Elyahba' claimed that you would have strong arguments against me. As I see it, I gave Eliphaz, Bildad, and Zophar stronger arguments against *Job II* than you are making against me; I even gave them more time than you are taking. Ahimelech, you have repeated some things that I have just shown to be false. *Job II* has not said, 'I am righteous.' But he does say there is no justice (Job 19:7b). I wrote the poem, and I know what *Job II* has said. You waste everyone's time by inserting things into the poem and then disagreeing with those items. If you want to say that Job is wrong when he says there is no justice then you have a valid argument. Again you are wrong when you accuse *Job II* of saying, 'A man gains nothing from his favor with Elohim.' Even though *Job II* might say such a thing, *Job II* at one point says just the opposite; the wicked say, 'What is Shaddai that we should serve him (Job 21:15)?' You claim that God deals harshly with the wicked, but this is just not the case. Just look around this city; they live on in grand style (Job 21:7). You threaten evildoers with the statement that God could take back his spirit and breath, so that 'All flesh would expire together (Job 34:15).' But you also say that El would not cause evil. This sounds like a new flood? Does your God go back on the promise he made after the flood, 'Never again will I destroy all life as I did (Gen 8:21).' Your response to Job's claim that Eloah does not hear the cries of the innocent seems strange to me. You blame the unfaithful for not bringing the cries of the poor to God. Therefore, God's silence cannot be condemned. This is a word spoken for a God who is deaf. But your final accusation is true; Job is a rebel."

Next it was Ira's turn. He said, "Jonathan you have said that Job does not claim to be righteous, but it still seems to me that he considers himself to be better than El. Also he is so bold. There are plenty of people who are oppressed and suffer, but 'nobody has said, "Where is Eloah my Maker?" (Job 35:10).' When Job says this he is proclaiming the death of Eloah, and at the very least he claims that God cannot be found (Job 23). If Job can not see him, then he should wait for him (Job 35:14)."

Jonathan said, "Ira, you are like Zophar in my poem; you don't say much. But at least you did bring up an important matter. It is true that *Job II* considers your God, be it Shaddai, El, Eloah, or whatever, to be dead or perhaps he never existed. At best he is hidden and cannot be found. *Job II* is still bothered by your awful God in his dreams of the night, but he knows that the creator who brings us order and life must somehow be more gentle and kind. Or perhaps completely different than we have ever imagined."

Elyahba' jumped to his feet, and he immediately began bragging about his great knowledge and defending the power and compassion of El. He said, "El will not let the wicked live, 'and justice he gives to the oppressed (Job 36:6). The people, 'If they listen and serve him, / They will end their days in the good, / And their years with the pleasures [of life] (Job 36:11).'

"In our old story of Job or *Job I*, I really like it when God speaks from the storm, and his thunder does speak concerning him (Job 36:33). 'He thunders with his majestic voice (Job 37:5),' and he asks Job questions that Job cannot answer concerning the creation and the workings of our world. I would like to ask *Job II* some of the same questions. 'Give ear to this, O Job; / Stand and consider the wonders of El. / Do you know how Eloah commands them, / How he flashes lightning [from] his clouds? (Job 37:14-15)'

"Our God flashes his lightning; he commands and guides it 'Whether for discipline, or for his earth, / Or for kindness, he makes it find [its mark] (Job 37:13).' God controls the natural forces in order to help the earth or to punish human beings."

I thought, "That is awful. This God can help or discipline with his lightning. How cruel. From then on Elyahba' questioned Job, or perhaps Jonathan, all about the creation and the natural wonders. He took God's role as seen in *Job I*. But his ending was really stupid. He praised Eloah for strength and justice, saying that he will not oppress. 'Therefore mankind should fear him (Job 37:24a).' Why should we fear him if he does not oppress? His last line was 'God does not pay attention to any who are wise of mind.' Obviously the priests do not like the teachers in this school, or perhaps Elyahba' is explaining why he is God's special friend!"

Jonathan said, "In this last speech we have heard more exaggerated claims to 'perfect knowledge,' and a repeat of how Elyahba' defends El. What is interesting to me is that Elyahba' defends the creator's role in *Job I*. He likes the questions that God puts to *Job I* from the storm. So he takes God's role and asks such questions of *Job II*. In *Job I* the creator crushes Job with his presence and questions, and Job finally repents for demanding an audience with God. But I would like to remind Elyahba' that *Job II* will not be crushed by such questions, because God is not present, and 'Who can understand the thunder of his might? (Job 26:14),' to quote the last line of my poem.

"Elyahba', you have given us an incongruous picture of a cruel God who can strike us with lightning but does not oppress. He rewards service but demands fear. Everything you say speaks loud and clear concerning your desire to control the people. You want their support of altar and state. You claim 'perfect knowledge' but turn against those who use their minds in a school like this. Your influence needs to be tempered by this academy and by the prophets. I thought that you might bring a prophet with you. Where are the prophets? The royal prophets are of little use, but isn't there at least one who stands beyond altar, state, and academy to help us balance our powers?

"Does the fear of God bring safety? Does fear preserve our children and reduce our suffering? To answer yes to these questions is to live in a land of fantasy. Since there is no justice in state or world, we do the best we can to build a new community on the ruins of the old, but the old orthodox fundamentalism of altar, state, and academy is not helpful; it does not meet our needs. So what do we need in order to build our community? Beyond our food and clothing and other physical needs, we need to recognize that change is the only thing that we can count on; we need freedom to think; we need love and support as we build for a new future. We do not claim 'perfect knowledge,' but we look forward to increasing our understanding."

Sheva stood to ask for questions, but there was such a roar from the crowd that he could not be heard. The priests and some older teachers were shouting mostly at Jonathan. They wanted to burn his scroll, and some wanted Jonathan thrown out of the academy. Just as things were getting out of hand once more, Benaiah, David's commander of the mercenaries (the Cherethites and Pelethites), stepped through the back door. He stood beside Sheva, and the crowd became silent. Sheva thanked Benaiah for restoring order, and then said, "I enjoyed the debate, but I did not enjoy the unruly response. Therefore the participants and I will meet in a few days to decide the future course of this conversation."

Sheva came over to where Jonathan and I were standing. He said, "I hope that you can join Sarah and me at the house for some refreshments. I have already invited Magon, Naomi, and Khety. We need to get acquainted with Khety."

Jonathan said, "We will be there as soon as we check with Deborah about the children."

Sheva said, "You won't have to check with Deborah; Deborah and the children are already at the house. Come on."

When we arrived, we saw that Sheva was right. Ruth ran over to me, and she had a raisin cake in each hand. Here we were back in Sheva and Sarah's home. It really did seem like old times. Magon and Naomi seemed at ease, and we were all happy that a re-birth of our community was taking place. The debate brought out a lot of anger on the part of many, but we were glad that our school was able to stand together against some of the outside pressures.

Jonathan asked Khety if the shouting priests should discourage us. Khety said, "No. Such a reaction should be expected. But, it is important for you to publish your thoughts on these important issues even in the face of anger. Publish when you can; you publish for the future. In Egypt most of the scribes are grateful that we have the essay on kingship addressed to Merikare and the story of *The Eloquent Peasant*. Both of these works were written about one thousand years ago, and they both show the importance of fine speech and stress the equality of a peasant with a lord or an official; both had the right to defend their interests with bold and effective speech. This was a great moment for our people, but later we were only interested in expanding our empire. Orderly conduct and devotion to our state became more important than the rights of individuals, and people were advised to be silent. This is a tragic story. But, these documents were published when it was still possible; they remind us of some great truths, which should be resurrected in our time. However, I doubt if this will happen in Egypt. It seems that the time is never right to do the right thing."

Jonathan said, "Has your disappointment in such things caused you to leave Egypt?"

"That is part of the reason. Also, to come to a new state, which is building a strong school, could present one with creative possibilities. You have written about a new understanding of Job, and now is the time to make it known. There is opposition to your understanding, but the state and the school is still in its creative period. You will be able to publish it, but that does not guarantee its acceptance."

At that point, Khety noticed that everyone was listening to his words. He said that he did not intend to make a speech, and he wanted to taste some of Sarah's cakes. While he was eating I asked him for a few more details about the story of *The Eloquent Peasant*. He gave me the basic facts of the story, which were interesting. I thanked him, and I said, "I need to know more about your literature."

Then I noticed that the children needed some help with their refreshments. We all had a good time, and I said to Sarah, "I want to thank you for all your work and for the way you always look after the children when the rest of us talk on and on."

"You don't have to thank me. I want these children to enjoy the party. After all, I helped to bring all these children into this world, and I love them."

As we were leaving, Magon asked Khety if he would like to see the copies of the tablets that were sent to Egypt about three hundred and fifty years ago. Magon said, "I mentioned these Babylonian letters from 'Abdi-Heba, king of Jerusalem, to your Pharaoh in Amarna on that first evening we were together."

Khety said, "I would like to see them. I'll come to your office tomorrow after lunch."

We gathered up our children, thanked Sheva and Sarah, and walked home. When we got home there was nothing written on the house, but there was a note that had been slipped under the door. Naam noticed it as he opened the door. He handed it to his father.

We went inside, and we all sat down at the table. Jonathan looked at the note. It was a small scrape of parchment. Jonathan said, "There are only five words in this message. I will read it for you. 'Burn it or we will.' It is not signed, but we should do exactly as they say."

Elissa said, "Don't burn your poem Daddy!"

"I won't burn the poem; I'll burn this message. We'll use it to start the fire in the morning."

I said, "Jonathan, this could be serious."

"I'm sure it is, but we can't let them stop us. As Khety said, it is never the right time for such things."

Naam said, "I wonder who left the message? Some of those people were really angry after the debate, but they got quiet fast when they saw Benaiah. Did David send Benaiah in case the crowd got too rowdy?"

"That is a good question," Jonathan answered. "I heard Sheva say to Magon that David probably sent Benaiah, because David had read the poem. Magon said that David was willing to keep things calm, but his actions did not really tell us what he thought about the poem. At that point Sheva said, 'I will find out what he thought.' I am glad that Sheva will talk to David about this. I'm sure that he will do it before he meets with the priests and me."

I had been holding Ruth. She was not worried; she was asleep. I said, "Ruth has the right idea. We should all get some sleep, and we should not worry too much. We will find out more about all of this in the next few days."

Before we went to sleep, I said to Jonathan, "I would like to write an entry for *The Minority Report* on the subject that Khety brought up: the need for free speech and the importance of eloquent speech. If I keep adding new ideas, I won't have space for some of the others subjects that we have discussed. What do you think about an entry on speech?"

"It is an important subject; you should do it. Do you remember that one of the things that qualified Joseph as an Egyptian ruler was his 'perfect speech'?"

"That's right. I could start with Joseph. I don't want to say any more about this, or I won't be able to sleep. But I do want to say that you made some fine speeches today, and I imagine that your speeches reminded Khety of the importance of the right to speak."

For that I received a nice kiss.

Chapter Ten

Sheva Meets with Jonathan and The Priests

Sheva, Jonathan, and I sat on one side of the table, and Elyahba', Ahimelech, and Ira on the other side. I came along to take some notes. The priests did not want me to be there, but Jonathan prevailed.

Sheva opened the meeting with a report. He said, "Yesterday I talked with David. He told me that after he had heard the reports of the public reading, he knew there would be problems at the debate. That is the reason he sent Benaiah. He has rightly blamed the priests for their unruly actions, but he also has excused them. He calls their actions 'an overly zealous response.' David has read Jonathan's poem, and he said, 'It is a wonderful work, but it does not offer much hope. In order for us to have a calm unity for our united Israel, the old story of Job should be published, because it gives hope for those who are obedient. Also the old story represents the way most people think about the problem of suffering. However, we should allow Jonathan's poem to be published as well, along with the arguments that the priests advanced during the debate.' Later in the conversation he said that these publications would be accomplished under the supervision of Nathan, his prophet, and Hushai, his counselor and 'friend.'"

Elyahba' said, "King David is a wise man, and we see this as a wise plan. The three of us plan to combine our

arguments against Jonathan's poem, and give them the title
of 'The Speeches of Elihu.' This will be our way of honoring
David's brother, Elihu, for he agrees with us on every point."

Jonathan said, "I do not like this solution to our problems,
because it is not a solution.

During the debate, I asked, 'Where are the prophets?'
This was a serious question. After Gad was thrown out of
David's administration, we have only heard from Nathan.
Other prophets must be afraid to speak. I speak freely, but I
am related to David. Publication under the supervision of
Nathan and Hushai is not to be understood as free speech,
and thus it is not a solution. A real solution would be the
publication of three separate books:

The Ancient Story of Job, The Poet's Job, and *The Speeches of
Elihu.* I know what royal and priestly editing did to our text
of *The Royal Epic,* and David's solution will result in the same
thing. But what David proposes is better than the message
we received the evening of the debate at our home. It said,
'Burn it or we will.' Elyahba', do you know who wrote that
message?"

"No! I know nothing about it, but many said such things
after the debate. I agree with their desire to put an end to
it, but we do not need to burn it. 'The Speeches of Elihu'
will neutralize your poem for all time."

Jonathan continued, "I doubt that. But allow me to add
to my comments on David's views. David said that the old
story of Job gives hope to the obedient, but what he does
not say is that such obedience is to a cruel God and that to
be religious and wise is to fear that God. This is a way to
control people and to catch them up in the fantasy of
rewarding such fear. This is wrong."

Sheva said, "It is obvious that you folks disagree. David's
decision on this seems to please the priests, but Jonathan,
you are not happy. I do not really know how to proceed. In
fact, I am not sure that we can do anything to change David's
thinking on this."

Elyahba' said, "We are happy with David's solution, and we will leave now. I will not tell Jonathan how mistaken he is in the presence of his wife."

"Don't let me stop you," I said.

But the priests left, and Jonathan said to Sheva, "I want to thank you for talking with David and for calling this meeting. The best thing to do at this point is to do nothing. Perhaps it will take Nathan and Hushai a long time to do their work, but that may just be wishful thinking. I will publish my poem. At least I will make some more copies for friends, and it will appear in Keziah's book."

Sheva said, "I would like to have a copy, because I too have had problems with the old story. David even told me that Bathsheba did not like the old story, because Nathan had said that her first baby died because of sin; a view that fits the old story. David cannot admit that this problem is real, because the old view is more helpful to him as king. By the way, you should keep me informed if you receive any more threats or notes."

"I will get you a copy of the poem, and we will keep you informed."

I said, "I'm glad that you told us about Bathsheba's views. It makes me feel better; we are not completely alone."

As we walked home, I said, "Those priests did not say much. You were right about doing nothing just now. We will have to wait and see what happens."

Jonathan said, "While we are waiting, we must be careful. The "righteous" could do more than send notes, and they will act in the name of their God. God seems to have given the orthodox an additional shot of zeal."

Chapter Eleven

Khety's Class Plus Another Entry

Before the children left for school, I said to Naam, "The girls will go to Deborah's after school, but I want to take you and Rachel to Khety's first Egyptian class. We will see if he has room for us. It will be interesting, and I need to know more about Egyptian literature for some of my entries."

Naam was excited and anxious to tell Rachel, and he ran out the door. I worked hard all morning in order to be ready for the class. Jonathan was enlisting some of his students to help him make copies of the Job poem.

When we arrived at Khety's class we noted that there were eight students. I said to Khety, "Will you have too many if Naam, Rachel, and I sit in?"

"That will be fine. There will be one or two more with us for our next lesson. We will have a good time."

Then Khety said, "As far as I know we Egyptians are the only ones who have divided the day into twenty-four hours. We have twelve hours for the day and twelve for the night. In Egypt I would not say, 'we will meet after lunch,' but I would say, 'we will meet at the seventh hour (*wnwt*). The Egyptian way is easier and it is more accurate, even though in the summer each hour during the day is a bit longer than it is in the winter. But enough of that.

"Egyptian is a difficult language, but you will find that it is a lot of fun. The fun will carry you through the rough spots. We have words that copy the sound of that to which they refer. For example, *miw*, pronounced *meyu*, is our word for 'cat.' You will have to listen to a cat to get the correct pronunciation. This is like your word for bottle, *baqbuq*, which imitates the gurgling sound when a bottle is emptied. Also Egyptian will be interesting for you, because you will find Egyptian words that are the same in Hebrew. This is the case for the Egyptian word for 'death' (*mwt*) or Egyptian 'to' (*r*). This last example will be confusing for you at this point in your studies, because the Hebrew word is '*l*.' But you will soon learn that in Egyptian we use the 'r' sign (a picture of a mouth and sometimes a picture of a lion) for 'r' and for 'l.'"

As Khety talked, he also wrote on a sheet of papyrus. His drawings of the "mouth' and the "lion" were excellent. He did it with such quick and talented strokes of his pen. Naam and Rachel sat with attention and amazement.

Khety continued, "Now I must decide what we should read first. I want to read with you *The Eloquent Peasant, The Story of Sinuhe, The Journey of Wen-Amon,* and *The Story of the Shipwrecked Sailor.* I will start with *The Story of the Shipwrecked Sailor.* I told this story a few nights ago to Jonathan and Keziah's children, and they enjoyed it. Also it will be an easy place to start our work.

"During each class you will copy a few lines for the next class. You should re-copy these lines several times until you can draw each sign accurately and with ease. Bring your best copy to class, and we will learn to read what you have copied. It will be slow at first, but again you will have fun. Egyptian is difficult, but it tries to help you. After each word there is a determinative. A determinative is a picture that determines the meaning of the word to which it is attached. For example, if I write the word for 'sun' (*r*') I would draw a picture of the sun (a small circle with a smaller circle in the center) and place it immediately after this word."

Khety had two lines on a large sheet of papyrus for us to copy. It took us some time, and he walked around and helped us with our work. We used black ink and a reed pen. After we finished our work we thanked Khety, and went home. On our way, I suggested that we would have to get some help from a cat if we could find one. Naam and Rachel agreed, but they were excited and ran on ahead. They wanted to start copying their lines.

I decided to do at least one entry for *The Minority Report.*

Eight

Free and Eloquent Speech

Khety inspired this minority opinion. After the public debate about Jonathan's Job poem, we were at Sheva and Sarah's party. Khety urged Jonathan to publish his poem even with all of the opposition. He was speaking to Jonathan, but soon everyone was listening to what he said about free and eloquent speech. He spent most of his time talking about *The Eloquent Peasant.* This story was written about one thousand years ago, and it shows the importance of fine speech and points out the equality of a peasant with a lord or an official; both had the right to defend their interests with bold and effective speech. Khety added that this was a great moment for the people of Egypt, but later, Egypt was only interested in expanding its empire. Orderly conduct and devotion to the state became more important than the rights of individuals, and people were advised to be silent. Then he said, "This is a tragic story."

In *The Eloquent Peasant,* a poor man was robbed of the labor of his hands and imprisoned illegally. Since his wife and children were also in dire straits, he pleaded with the chief steward for the return of his goods. He needed to market them and return to his family. After prolonging his prison stay in order to hear his great speeches, the peasant's goods were returned to him. Even the poor could speak up for their rights by means of true and perfect speech. It is important to have eloquent speech, but it is even more important to have the freedom to express your thoughts in such speech. It appears that the majority of the ruling class and their officers, priests, and royal prophets are always ready to take away this freedom, which is so vital.

This is a different sort of minority opinion than we have discussed earlier. In other words, most minority opinions never become important in our lifetime, but here is an important majority opinion that soon became a minority opinion. At one time in Egypt, good speech and the freedom to use it equaled a great moment in its history. But soon the rulers took it away. Free speech became a minority position that only a few among the oppressed people dared to practice.

In our Royal Epic, it is said that Joseph had perfect speech:

> His brothers saw that their father loved him more
> than any of his brothers. They hated him, and
> they could not overcome his perfect speech.
> > (Gen 37:4)

Joseph needed such speech when he was in prison. He used it again when he became a ruler in Egypt. I wonder if the Joseph story was told as if the days of the eloquent peasant were still intact during Joseph's time? Or was Joseph rewarded not for his speech but for his skill in dealing with dreams?

It is interesting that David has allowed Jonathan to speak, but he did not like it when, Gad, my father, spoke his mind. David dismissed father from his position as a prophet in the administration. The freedom of speech must be guarded at all times. We do not want to lose it and be forced to say what Khety had to say, "This is a tragic story."

Naam and Rachel ran in just as I finished my entry. They wanted to show me their copies of the text for our Egyptian class. I said, "This looks nice. I should stop writing and make my copies."

Naam said, "I had a difficult time with this, but Rachel is a real artist. Her copies were good on her first try."

Rachel said, "So, we have different talents. I have always been able to draw what I see, but as you know I cannot run fast; I can't catch you."

I said, "I must make my copies. Naam let me borrow your pen and ink."

Rachel and Naam watched as I made my first copy. Naam said, "I can see that Rachel has a better hand for this than you or me."

"Yes, you are right, but I am going to keep trying."

Naam said, "I can't wait until we can read with ease. I would like to know more about the Egyptian belief in immortality. I have heard that we do not believe as the Egyptians. For us, humans are mortal, and yet we call forth the names of our ancestors at the tomb. Why do we do this, if we believe that humans are mortal?"

"You are asking some good questions. I will devote my next entry to clarifying our views on the subject of mortality. I am glad that you asked about it, but it is complicated. I will need to talk with your father about this one."

Chapter Twelve

More Opposition

That evening as we were gathered about the dinner table, Jonathan told us that he had more problems. Some students in his class on the ancient Job story were pressured to drop the class by other teachers. Three of these students had even attended the private reading of the poem here at the house. Jonathan said, "Our teachers who have pressured students in this way are acting like government officials rather than teachers. They are afraid of freedom, and they do not trust our students; they deny our students the right to know about a variety of opinions. I will have to speak to some of them. Also, someone broke into my office last night and took a copy that we were making of the Job poem. I have been bringing the original home each evening. The work they took was about half finished. I will have to see Sheva about this."

I said, "This is awful. It is difficult to understand such teachers, and they obviously have no idea what they are teaching by their actions. Perhaps they are teaching students to steal?"

Jonathan replied, "I am going to spend a few nights in my office. I just might catch someone."

Naam said, "I would like to go with you."

"I'll do the office duty by myself. I want you to be here at the house in case there is any trouble here."

I said, "It is tragic. In your work you have tried to lift the burden of fantasy from the backs of suffering people, and yet they prefer the burden."

Later in the evening after the children were asleep, I talked with Jonathan about Naam's interest in the question of mortality. And we came up with the following:

Entry Nine

On Being Mortal

Most of the great literature in our part of the world teaches that human beings are mortal. Death is real. This is certainly the case for the Babylonians. Gilgamesh searches for eternal life but he does not find it. Also Adapa gives up any chance for eternal life. At Ugarit, Aqhat, son of Danel, rejects an offer of eternal life from the goddess Anat. In our own Royal Epic, our first humans elected to be mortal in order to have all knowledge, and our flood hero or Noah remains mortal unlike the Babylonian flood hero, Utnapishtim and his wife. So in our literature this seems to be the majority opinion: humans are mortal.

As I have said in my prologue, this is not the case in Egypt. In Egyptian texts it is clear that death is not real. Death is a door to a better life in the land of the "West." There you will have good food and a wonderful life. However in the Harpers' Songs we find a minority opinion; in these songs there is grave doubt and uncertainty concerning immortality. These Harpers are skeptical and suggest that that you should have a good time now. "Make holiday" is the word. We are also interested in *this* minority opinion coming from a land that celebrates immortality. Also it is interesting that some of these skeptical songs were carved on the tombs.

When Naam asked me why we called forth the names of

our dead at the tombs if we believed that humans were mortal, I did not have a ready answer. In our stories we do talk about Sheol, the Pit, the Netherworld, and other such places where our dead reside. Does such talk also point to a kind of immortality even though it is dark and slimy? It is certainly different from the Egyptian "Land of the West." It is possible that many people think that when we call forth the names of the dead we are thinking in literal terms. But is this the case? In our funeral rituals when we "call forth" the names of our dead, our main purpose is to tell their stories. We do ask for blessings, but is it the dead who bless or is it God who blesses those who remember? Our actions have nothing in common with necromancy and the work of the witches. The witches, for a fee, bring up the spirits of the dead or the dead, and with their magic they ask about the future. The fact that king Saul had forbidden such activity is proof that there are people who visit the witches. In fact there is the persistent rumor that Saul visited the witch of En-dor shortly before his death.

Jonathan suggests that those who visit the witches and practice other forms of magic do not believe that human beings are mortal; they are close to the majority in Egypt. We stress that human beings are mortal and do not understand our tomb rituals to argue against mortality. We find that we agree with the minority opinion of the Harpers in Egypt. Mortals who accept death have a deep desire to enjoy life.

I close with this poem:

Life: A Precious Moment

Death is a destructive reality.
We mourn the loss of a beautiful mind,
Of wisdom and friendship of every kind.
Even for happy souls there is a cloud,
A dark reminder of our brevity.

Our world will not miss us; perhaps our kin?
But we'll miss out on the future of all.
The human and Eve wanted all knowledge;
They gave up immortality to know,
And what they gave us was freedom to know.

Their gift makes our moment interesting.
But can we enjoy a precious moment?
It cannot be detained or extended;
It can be savored but note: not for long.
It is "swifter than a weaver's shuttle."

A popular fantasy says, "Fear God!
Fear God and live," but death is all around.
The rebel Job said, "There is no justice."
We must face this to enjoy our moment
And with love share our small accomplishments.

Our youth is our prologue that seems so long,
But soon enough our story takes its shape.
Joy, work, love, and suffering find their place.
Then we need to set our house in order.
Our epilogue moves on, our final song.

Chapter Thirteen

The Tension Continues

Jonathan had an uneventful night in his office, but on his way home in the morning he met Sheva who was full of bad news. "What are you doing?" Sheva said. "You are up early this morning."

"I stayed in my office all night, because the night before someone took a half-finished copy of my Job poem. I was going to tell you about it today. There are other problems as well. Some of our teachers have pressured students to drop my *Job I* class, but this should not be a big surprise."

"Sad situation, and I have some more bad news. David is going ahead with his plans to publish *Job I, Job II,* and *The Speeches of Elihu* all in the same volume with 'royal' editing, and Elyahba' was here yesterday speaking to a group of students about your position."

"Elyahba' must be behind most of our troubles. At least he is holding up the priestly tradition as it appears to me. Thanks for your information. I should get home and see how things are going there."

Sheva gave Jonathan a smile of encouragement as they parted.

As Jonathan got near to the house he saw the charred remains of the copy of his Job poem in the courtyard. He hurried on to the house and called us. We came out and saw what was left of the scroll. We went back in the house and sat around the table. Jonathan told us about Sheva's news.

"I would say that things are getting worse," I said. "Let's put some of our important scrolls in jars in the cellar."

"I will do that today," said Jonathan. "Also I am going to get some more help. I want to make more copies. Elimelech will help and perhaps Noah and Danel."

Just then Magon came to the door, and I said, "Come in and eat with us."

We soon informed him of what was going on, and Magon suggested, "Let's send your Job poem to my sister, Elissa. She will be interested in it, and it should be safe in Tyre."

"Good idea," I said. "I have not written Elissa in a long time. I must do that, and I will also send her a copy of my book as soon as I finish it."

"Will you finish it soon?"

"That depends on how many 'minority opinions' we include. The most important one is *Job II*. Jonathan and I have a long list of other opinions, but we do not have to use them all to make our point that there are a few people who are excited about creating an interesting future with new thoughts. So far I have written up nine 'minority opinions' in addition to *Job II*."

"There is always the option of doing a second volume," said Magon.

I raised my brows, "Good idea. I like that."

Jonathan nodded, "That is an option. The main thing is to wait until we see how David's publication of *Job I, Job II*, and *The Speeches of Elihu* turns out. I have a feeling we may want to review the 'royal editing.'"

We smiled, and I fetched us more fig cakes.

"Are you satisfied with the progress on your house?" I asked Magon.

"Yes, in fact it looks like they will be finished in about two weeks. Let's step over there now and take a look."

We had been too busy to notice, but Magon was right. The builders were really making progress.

Naam said, "Look mother! Look at those poor children standing at the gate."

There were about ten of them from toddlers to Naam's age. The younger ones had been crying; white streaks from tears ran down their dusty faces. As I approached them I saw their mothers begging in the street. The two women saw me and approached the gate.

"Please could you help us," one said. "We have no food for our children. The priests will not help us. They told us to glean in the fields of Absalom and Joab, but when we tried to do that we were chased off."

I nodded, "Since Absalom was killed during the rebellion, I suppose Joab has taken over his land, and he would never help anyone. You wait right here, and we will bring you something."

Then I took my three to the house, and we gathered up some bread and cheese. When we took the food to the children there were lots of smiles, and I thought of *Job II* and his question to his "friends" at the beginning of his last speech: "How have you helped the powerless?" The mothers and the children thanked us again and again. I told the two women that we would try to do something about their right to glean. I said, "Your right to glean what the reapers leave is one of our best laws. You come back tomorrow to see if we have been able to do anything about this." And another minority opinion began to form in my mind.

Jonathan and Magon had been talking to the builders about a problem. They did not realize that we had given the children some food. I walked over and got their attention and said, "We just gave those poor people some food. Apparently they were run off of Absalom and Joab's estates where they were gleaning. Did Joab take over Absalom's land? If he did, I wonder who takes care of Absalom's sister, Tamar."

Jonathan said, "I can see what you're thinking, but you may create trouble if you pursue it."

"But these people have the right to glean, and I want to help them. If Tamar is in charge of her brother's land, she could be approached on the matter. If Joab has taken charge of Absalom's land, this does nothing for Tamar's interests. In that case we should speak with David."

Magon said, "Jonathan, you will need whatever favors David owes you for other things. Let me speak to him about this. I can thank him for the new house and ask him to help these starving children and perhaps Tamar."

"I did not mean to involve you, Magon, but if you are willing, I think it would work. Jonathan says that sooner or later I give everyone a task."

"That's right, but you are a good boss. Magon, if you want to see David about this, I agree with Keziah; it will probably work."

"I will see him in the morning and be back tomorrow afternoon."

Chapter Fourteen

A Conversation with Tamar

$\mathbf{M}$agon did see David the next morning, and at noon he gave us his report. "I was the first person to see David. I thanked him for the great progress on the houses and for bringing Khety to the academy. I told him to let me know if and when he wanted to build a temple and said that I would personally ask King Hiram to help. Then I said, 'I know that there is some opposition to Jonathan's poem, but the rebel Job does ask his critics at the beginning of his last speech, "How have you helped the powerless?" Yesterday Keziah gave some food to ten starving children, whose mothers had been gleaning and were chased off the estates of Absalom and Joab. In your legal traditions such people have the right to glean, and so I ask, does Joab control what you granted to Absalom before his death? Or did that grant pass on to Tamar? If so, Joab should not control it, and he should not deny the right to glean on that land or on *his* land. He's caused you a lot of trouble in the past, and it appears he is still intent on causing trouble for everyone.'"

Jonathan looked up intently, "You were very direct."

Magon nodded grimly, "He acted like he didn't want to hear about it, but did say he would look into the matter. He said, 'I am more concerned about Tamar than anyone else. If Joab is hurting her in any way, I will find out about it, and I will solve the problem. Also if Joab has denied the rights of the poor to glean, I will force him to give them some of his harvest.'"

We looked at each other. "Do you think David will do something?" I asked.

"I hope so."

"I'm afraid I'm not so hopeful," said Jonathan.

I nodded.

After Magon and Jonathan went back to work, I put another jar in our cellar, which we had dubbed "the crypt," and I thought about Tamar. Naomi and I would have to give David some days to act, but we would follow up.

"We will have a nice walk even if we don't get to see Tamar," Naomi said.

It was a bright mid-summer day just eight days after Magon had spoken to David. "So Keziah, what do we know about Tamar?"

"We know she was used and abused by Absalom and raped by Amnon, who 'loved' her, but we know almost nothing else. Let me tell you the story Jonathan heard when he visited Elhanan in Bethlehem."

"Please do," said Naomi linking her arm through mine.

"Absalom wanted to get rid of Amnon, David's firstborn and next in line for the throne, because Absalom wanted to be the next king. It was known that Amnon 'loved' or at least he desired Tamar, who was his half-sister, since they had different mothers. Amnon was either sick or pretended to be sick, and he asked David to send Tamarr to his house to prepare some food for him. Absalom thought that this was a perfect opportunity. He told Tamar to wear her royal robe, which all of David's daughters kept for special occasions. He guessed Amnon would be overcome with lust, and Absalom instructed her to be extra nice. She followed those instructions. Amnon was overcome by Tamar's kindness and beauty and raped her. All went according to Absalom's plan.

Tamar lamented that day; she put dust on her head and rent her royal robe. She continued to live in Absalom's house but was in constant mourning. Absalom didn't seem to care about her. He only waited for an opportunity to kill Amnon supposedly for the rape of his sister. At a sheep shearing, after Amnon was full of wine, Absalom had his companions slaughter him. We know Joab urged Absalom to execute his brother. Joab, the beast, wanted to get rid of everyone who might someday get in his way."

Naomi shuddered. "That is a tragic story," she said. "Do you think Tamar will tell us any more?"

"I hope so. My main concern is how she is getting along. I want to know if Joab has taken over the estate she probably received after Absalom's rebellion and death. I suspect that Joab has, because I don't think Tamar would send the gleaners away from her fields. Or perhaps my hatred of Joab is clouding my mind."

Naomi squeezed my arm, and we fell silent. It was good to be away from the city where the only sounds were those of some delightful birds.

We walked north of Jerusalem for half of the morning before reaching Absalom's estate. Just a little farther lay Joab's estate. We were in luck. Tamar was working in her garden when we arrived. We introduced ourselves, and she asked us to sit on a bench under an olive tree at the edge of the garden. Then she said, "Excuse me for one moment, and I will get us something to drink."

"She must be about our age," Naomi said, "and she is beautiful with her shining thick hair and her skin is so flawless."

When she returned, she offered us some fresh figs and cool water. "I seldom have any visitors. However two days ago, father came by, and now you are here."

"It was good that David came to see you," I said.

"Yes. I appreciated it. He wanted to make sure I was well. He also wanted to tell me that he had warned Joab to stay on his own property."

"Has he been bothering you?" I ventured.

Tamar shrugged, "Not really, but David was firm that after Absalom's death this estate was mine. It seems that Joab's servants had chased off some gleaners, women and children, from my land a few days ago. Also David sent two young men to help me with some work that needs to be done around here."

"I'm glad. We were fearful Joab might be causing some trouble," I said, "because those gleaners came to Jerusalem, and we fed them."

"Joab has taken some of my crops, but he has not threatened me in any way. Still I wish he lived somewhere else. My problem with him is that he helped Absalom with the plan to kill Amnon. I take it that you are both acquainted with the events of those days. Everyone seems to be."

"Yes. We know the story," I said. "Since we first heard about these things, we have always been concerned about how you were treated."

"I was mistreated by both my brother and Amnon. Amnon was my half-brother. He was good looking and had always been kind, and I did not think he would harm me. I was wrong. Before Amnon raped me, I pled with him to ask David for me as a wife, but he would not listen. Afterwards, he realized I was Absalom's bait, and he hated me. If he had listened to my pleading and if we had married, Absalom and Joab would have found some other way to eliminate him and probably me. Absalom's three children and his wife all died of a fever when they were in Geshur. As you probably know, Absalom was exiled to Geshur for three years after he killed Amnon. I wish that the children were with me now. He named his daughter Tamar. My main problem is that I am alone."

"I can understand some of your feelings," I said, "because Joab tried to rape me, and he did kill my father."

"The past has left scars upon you both," said Naomi, taking our hands.

Tamar nodded, and I smiled at my friend.

"Would you allow us to send the gleaners back to your fields?" I asked Tamar.

"Of course. Send them back. Joab will not bother them again with David's men working here."

We visited with Tamar for some time, and she took us around to see her beautiful garden. It was clear that she spent a lot of time here.

"My son, Naam, would love to help you in the garden. I have an idea. You should come to our home some evening for dinner, and you can meet our families. We live at The Jerusalem Academy."

"Oh, I have not gone anywhere for so long. It would be difficult for me to visit you, but if you want to bring your children here, I would love to meet them."

Naomi and I agreed, and Tamar said that in three days, with the help of David's men, things would look better, and she would be ready for us. We told her that we would be there and thanked and embraced her. As we were leaving, Tamar said, "Wait just a moment."

She ran to her cucumber patch and picked a few for us. We thanked her again.

"She is lovely," said Naomi on our way home.

We were so pleased that we had come. Our interest in the rights of the gleaners had given us a new friend.

Chapter Fifteen

Egyptian: An Interesting Class

Naam, Rachel and I were getting ready for our Egyptian class with Khety. I made a few more copies of the text just before we left for class. We had to wait a few moments for Khety. When he arrived, he apologized for being late. He told us that he had just returned from Magon's office where he had taken a second look at the copies of the clay tablets that were sent to Amarna about three hundred fifty years ago. He said it was a thrill just to touch them.

"Well, we need to get to work. Or is it work?" Khety asked.

"It is hard labor," I said.

"But the results of your labor will be beautiful," he said. "First, let me see your copies of the text for today. The assignment was just the last few lines of the prologue."

"This is beautiful work, Rachel," he said. "The head of your owl is flat, and that is important. Good work."

Rachel said, "Thank you. I made many copies, and every time I was pleased. The images got better each time. It was fun."

We began to read. Khety helped us to identify each character and gave us its phonetic value or, in some cases, its meaning. We read these lines:

> "Wash yourself and put water on your fingers.
> Then when you are addressed, you must answer.

> Speak thoughtfully to the king; you must answer
> without hesitating. *A man's mouth saves him.* His
> speech brings forgiveness for him, but do what
> you want. Speaking to you is wearisome."

When we were working on the phrase, "Speak to the king with your mind" or "Speak thoughtfully to the king," Khety spent some time with us on the word "mind." He said, "Notice that we are dealing with a picture of the human heart. We pronounce it *ib,* and we translated it into Hebrew as *lev.* The Egyptian and the Hebrew words for heart are used to refer to the 'inner being,' to the 'mind' or 'intellect.' We have to depend on the context to get the exact meaning or sometimes the meaning is clear from the way two words are combined. We have the word *kefa'* that means 'bottom' when followed or determined by an image of the hindquarters of a leopard. Now if I add the word *ib,* 'mind/ heart,' the expression means 'to be trustworthy.' This context suggest the meaning 'heart' for *ib,* because we trust from 'the bottom of the heart.' I have been reading your Royal Epic, and I have noticed that in the Joseph story this Egyptian word for heart is used. In fact there is an Egyptian sentence. When Pharaoh puts Joseph in charge of the land of Egypt, he gives Joseph his signet ring and dresses him in fine Egyptian linen; he puts him in a chariot and runners go ahead of him shouting to the people, *ib.r.k* (Genesis 41:43). If we translate each word we have in Hebrew *lev le ka* ('heart/ mind to you'). Here the meaning of *ib* equals 'mind,' or in other words, it means, 'pay attention.'"

He also spent some time on the phrase, "A man's mouth saves him." He said, "In Egyptian schools the teachers and the stories stress the importance of fine speech. It is also the main theme in the story of *The Eloquent Peasant,* and it is important in the story of Joseph. Remember where it says that Joseph's brothers hated him, 'and they could not overcome his perfect speech.' (Genesis 37:4b) This meant that Joseph was qualified to be a great leader in Egypt. In our story the chief mate is encouraging the Prince to make a good speech, and all will go well."

Khety gave us our lines for the next class. We were now through with the prologue and were going to start on the main story.

After class Naam and Rachel went to the house, but Khety said that he wanted to explain a few things to me. "You will have to explain to Rachel and Naam that the Egyptian language is extremely graphic, and I should ask you to forgive me if what I am going to say offends you. In Hebrew you prefer to soften your speech. You sometimes use the word *yad,* 'hand,' when you mean 'penis,' but in Egyptian we draw a picture of an erect penis with the scrotum and testicles. It is used as a determinative in words referring to a male, and it has liquid issuing from it in the word 'to urinate.' Well, you use your own judgment as to what you need to say, but I felt the need to say something about this."

"I think we can handle this, and you have not offended me. I thank you for the warning, but it will not be a major problem. Perhaps you should also warn the other male students to read such words with understanding, so that they won't laugh and make fun."

"You are right," he smiled. "I will do that."

On my way home, I thought about what a concerned teacher Khety was. It was obvious that he had not had female students in the past. I may have blushed a bit when he began talking about the penis, but he was right to do it. I hope that I was not too blunt, but both male and female students need to deal with other's writings and art with an open and a respectful approach. Rachel and I are a minority in the class, and I hope that we will not dampen the style of the class but rather help to create a new attitude that is beyond the majority or the minority views. It might be a new way of being human.

Chapter Sixteen

Friends

It was too hot to hike in the early afternoon, so Naomi and I asked Deborah to come with us, and we brought all the children; the children were glad to take the day off from their studies. Three mothers and eight children walked together; we made quite a procession. The children ran around us chasing each other. When we arrived at Tamar's home, they had traveled twice the distance.

With the help of David's men, Tamar had fixed up the place: grass was cut; weeds were pulled; and the terraces and rock walls were re-built. Tamar greeted us happily and invited us for refreshments under the old olive tree. The children were not bashful about accepting the cool water and the raisin cakes. We introduced Deborah to Tamar, and Deborah said, "These children are usually at school in the mornings, so today is a treat for them. But they should learn something. Could you show them your garden? They need to know more about the source of their food."

"I'll be happy to, and they can help me pick a few things for our lunch. I'll need some beans, onions, and cucumbers."

Tamar took the children to the garden, and we followed at a distance. She seemed to enjoy talking with them, and they were their curious selves. She had to show them how to stand on the path just below a terrace in order to pick the produce.

She said, "If we got up on the terrace by the plants we might do some damage."

"But I can't reach," said Ruth with a sorrowful cry.

"Don't worry," said Naam as he picked up a stone. "You can stand on this large stone."

They soon had enough for our lunch, and they handed us the baskets. Then Tamar took them to see the vines. "When it is time to pick the grapes, you will have to come back and help me."

"I'll be here," said Naam. "I would love to pick grapes, and I also enjoy the view of the mountains from here."

"We are near Gibeah where Saul had his headquarters," Tamar responded. "I like it as well. As you know, we are not far from Jerusalem, but here we do not have the noise of the city when people are walking and talking in the evening. But sometimes it's lonely, and I enjoy your company. Can you help me prepare our lunch?"

"I am a good cook," said Rachel.

The children helped Tamar by washing what they had gathered, and Tamar and Rachel began slicing the cucumbers, onions and beans. Tamar mixed them together and put them over our bowls of yogurt. Everyone enjoyed the tasty and fresh food. Ahinoam, Dinah, and Ruth were the youngest, but I think they ate as much as the older children. Dinah said to Ruth, "This food is better than we have at home."

"Did the gleaners ever come back?" asked Naomi, over lunch.

"Yes they did," Tamar responded with a smile, "but I have to tell you that Joab walked by that day, and he looked angry, even though the gleaners were on my land."

"He could still cause some trouble, but he is probably afraid," I said.

"I hope so," said Tamar. "But I want to tell you about my brother's return from Geshur, because you have told me that some of you are studying Egyptian. Joab persuaded David to allow Absalom to return to Jerusalem, I think because Joab wanted to keep track of what Absalom was thinking and doing. On his way home from Geshur, which is several days north of here, Absalom stopped at Beth-Shan for a few days. That's near Mt. Gilboa where the Philistines killed Saul and his sons. Then they impaled their bodies on the walls of Beth-Shan. Absalom stopped there, because he had been told that there was a place in the city where you could see the foundation of an ancient Egyptian temple."

"How did they know that it was Egyptian?" asked Naam.

"Absalom told me that you could see the top part of two large stones in this temple, and they had pictures carved on them and Egyptian writing. He was able to get papyrus, a pen, and some ink from a scribe, who helped him copy the top part of these two stones. He brought the copies home, and I have them in the house."

"This is important," I said, and Naam and Rachel were excited but silent. "Our teacher's name is Khety. He would be interested in these copies. Would you allow us to bring him here on another day?"

"Oh yes. I would like to know what those stones have to say."

All of us nodded; we all wanted to know. Naomi said to Tamar, "Magon is from Tyre. He has told me that in every port along the sea there is a great deal of evidence that the Egyptians were there. I suppose that Khety could find many monuments to read."

"Khety would not have the time to do that, but if I can learn enough Egyptian from him, I would like to discover and read Egyptian inscriptions," said Naam.

"You will learn enough to read them," teased Rachel, "but your writing is somewhat lacking."

"Before these witnesses, I swear that Rachel is correct. My writing is not so good. Rachel is an artist, and that helps in writing Egyptian. Of course it does not seem to help her reading."

Naam had to dodge a small clod, which Rachel threw at him, and he fell off the rock on which he was sitting. Deborah said, "And I thought our children were growing up."

We all laughed as Naam picked himself off the ground. Deborah continued, "Tamar, do you find any signs of the past inhabitants of your land?"

"Yes I do. In fact just the other day when we were redoing some of the terraces, we found some pottery, sling-stones, and one bronze spearhead."

She went to the porch, and brought a basket filled with such things. We all looked at them, and I said, "When I touch these items, I have a strange feeling. I don't mean to say that the past is communicating with me, but it is important to touch what others have touched and created. Somehow it reminds us that others have had their moments in the past and that our moment is just that—a moment."

As we were preparing to leave, I said, "We will bring Khety in a few days."

She smiled, "I'll be pleased."

We were almost to Jerusalem when we met Joab on his way home. He was tired, dirty, and bitter. He said nothing as we passed, but then turned and hissed, "There they go, three meddling bitches."

We did not look back.

At our evening meal, Jonathan asked us about our trip. All talking at once, the children told him all about their delightful time. Finally Naam was able to tell him about Tamar's invitation to Khety to read from Absalom's copies of the tops of the Egyptian monuments at Beth-Shan. Jonathan was interested in this project, and he volunteered to speak with Khety the next day.

Later in the evening when we were alone, I told Jonathan about Joab. "He is still a hateful man."

"That he is. He does not do much anymore. Most of his officers deal with army affairs, but he is always angry. But I will speak with David again about his threatening behavior. He is a sad case."

"He is. I still have a mixture of fear and rage whenever I see him."

He held me close. "David should take back the royal grant from Joab, and give it to someone more deserving."

Chapter Seventeen

Khety Reads Tamar's Texts

When Jonathan talked with David the next day, David told him he had already taken back Joab's land grant. It had made Joab raving mad; he was out of his mind. David thought Joab was living in the wilderness of Judah, and that Zeruiah, his mother, provided him with food and water. He had given Joab's grant to Sheva, who would step down as the head of the academy in a few years.

"This is good news," Jonathan said. "Tamar will not have to worry about Joab, and Keziah can also begin to forget. I thank you."

When Jonathan told me about this, I was relieved. I was happy for Tamar's friendship, but when I had seen Joab, bad memories rushed into my mind like a great flood in a dry wadi. This was great news. "Does Sheva know about his grant?" I asked.

"I think so, but this only happened yesterday."

Later Naomi told us that Sheva was happy about the grant. I thought that Tamar would be pleased as well.

It was two days later when Jonathan, Khety, and I visited with Tamar. When I introduced Jonathan and Khety, she seemed to be a little nervous. But, that soon passed. She was excited about the fact that she would have new neighbors. "I have already met Sheva and Sarah, and they seem nice. They said that they would find one of the older students to stay in the house until they felt ready to move. I want to thank you all for taking an interest in those gleaners, because that investigation caused David to reconsider the entire situation."

"This helps you, and it also makes me feel better," I said. "I'm glad to know that Joab is living in the wilderness."

Tamar served us some cakes and cool water, and then she brought out Absalom's copies of the Beth-Shan stelae. She laid them out on a small table, and it was easy to see that Khety was extremely interested. He said, "This first one is a good copy. Let's see. It is a little less than two cubits wide here at the top, so I'm guessing that the full height of this stela was about five cubits. The first thing that we have is the traditional winged sun disc extending across the slightly curves top of the stela. Then we have some writing and note the two figures facing each other. According to the inscription the figure on the left is Pharaoh Seti and he is offering a libation to our god Re-Har-akhti with his hawk's head and the sun or Re' above his head. We don't have much of the inscription, but this monument must have been set up about three hundred years ago.

"Now this second copy is much like the first one except here just under the winged sun disc is the god Amon-Re on the left and Seti's son, Rameses, on the right. I can't tell you how important this is to me," he said, looking up at Tamar. His handsome face glowed. "I know from inscriptions in Egypt that Seti and Rameses were in control of Beth-Shan, but to have this evidence from Beth-Shan is a verification of what we know. I would like to go to Beth-Shan and see these stelae. We might be able to clear away some dirt and rubble in order to see more of the inscriptions."

"We should try to do that," Jonathan said. "I don't think there should be any objection on the part of David or on the part of the people of Beth-Shan."

"But when could the two of you find time to go to Beth-Shan?" I asked.

"I don't know," replied Jonathan. "It would take us about three days or six days for going and returning by donkey."

"Yes, and you would want to stay there for three or four days."

"I don't know how we will do it, but it must be done," said Khety. "Tamar you have placed us in your debt; showing us these copies amounts to a great gift. I thank you."

Tamar smiled and said, "Not a word. I'm glad that this will help you, because all of you have certainly helped me."

We had some more refreshments, and a lot more conversation, but the men kept going back to the Beth-Shan story. Jonathan said, "The Egyptians were certainly in control of Beth-Shan in those days. Absalom thought that these monuments were located in a temple. Before the rule of Akh-en-Aton, the Egyptians were certainly here, but during his reign the Egyptian presence was less. The Canaanite kings wrote to him in Amarna as we have discussed, but he did not give them much help. But these invasions of Seti and Rameses show a new push for the Egyptian Empire. Also it is interesting that there were a few Hebrew people in Egypt during the time of Rameses; Hebrew people who later escaped."

"Yes, and some of your ancestors were taken by Seti to Egypt as prisoners of war," Khety added. "We have pictures of this at Karnak. Also during the reign of Marniptah Hatpamua, after Rameses, I know that he sent letters to the king of Ugarit in which he promised to help in the renovation of the temple of Ba'al. In fact he also said that he would send a monument like these in Beth-Shan to the city of Ugarit to be placed in the temple of Ba'al. It had an image of Marniptah standing before an image of Ba'al. At Beth-Shan, Seti and Rameses were standing before Egyptian gods, but since the Egyptians had identified Ba'al with their god Seth, Marniptah is in fact standing before Seth and Ba'al of Ugarit. Letters like this were written in Babylonian. We will have to send Magon to Egypt to see some of these things."

"Goodness," I said. "It appears that all of you want to travel."

"Where is this Ugarit?" asked Tamar. "I have never heard of it."

"You will have to ask Naomi's husband, Magon, for details," Jonathan answered, "but it was an important port north of Tyre. It was destroyed about two hundred years ago, but some of the scribes escaped, and they moved down the coast to Sidon and Tyre."

"It would seem that Marniptah's gift to their temple was only a few years before that city was destroyed," said Tamar. "The gift did not help them."

"I suppose not," said Khety, "but the Sea People from Caphtor (Crete) and other places in the far west were powerful. They conquered the Hittites, Alashiya (Cyprus), Ugarit and the coast of this country. The Philistines came from Caphtor and were one of the tribes in this big move to the east. Also Amenophis, Seti, and Rameses used some of the Sea People as mercenaries at an earlier time. Still later the Sea People helped to destroy the entire coastal area, and David had to put the Philistines in their place, but even David has some mercenaries from the west, his Cherethites and Pelethites. We need to know more about all of this. We do know that after Marniptah a later Rameses stopped them from taking Egypt."

"This is fascinating," said Tamar, shaking her head. "I'm afraid that my world is much too small."

"But it is obvious that your mind is open, and you are curious," responded Khety, smiling appreciatively. "That's what keeps life interesting."

We had talked so long Tamar insisted on giving us some lunch before we left. Khety wanted to see her garden, and they took their time. On the way home, Khety was talkative "Tamar is so generous, so beautiful."

We laughed.

"Well she is," he said blushing. "Don't you agree?"

Chapter Eighteen

The Trip to Beth-shan

After about two weeks, Jonathan and Khety began to plan for their trip to Beth-Shan. David let them use mules from the royal stables, so they could make it to Beth-Shan in two days. By donkey it would have taken three days. David was anxious to know if the citizens of Beth-Shan were still loyal to him.

Khety was not sure he could ride a mule. "Don't worry. You may not ride now, but by the time we reach Beth-Shan, you'll be an excellent rider."

"Yes, and that is the problem! My *butt* will be sore and as red as an Egyptian warrior in our paintings. Did they all ride mules?"

"I doubt it," Jonathan said with a smile. "They were tough. We would say *'admoni* or 'ruddy,' but you knew that."

"I did, but I'm not ruddy."

On the morning of their departure, we were all up before sunrise. I had prepared food for the trip, and I fixed a good breakfast for the travelers. Khety came over to help Jonathan pack the last few items, and they checked their lists. When we finally sat down, the girls were full of questions, but Naam was silent. He wanted to go to Beth-Shan. I felt sorry for him, and I did not know what to suggest. Jonathan sensed the problem. "Khety, it is obvious that we need to revise part of our plan. We could use more help at

Beth-Shan. It is a little late to make changes, but I think we can. If Keziah will pack a little more food, Naam can find a place for it on the pack mule. I'm suggesting that Naam go with us as far as the stables, and if they have an extra mule, he should go with us to Beth-Shan."

"But that might be asking too much of Naam," Khety remarked.

Naam was on his feet running to Jonathan, "I'll go! I'll go! I'll help with all the work."

"Obviously I was wrong," Khety said.

Naam was beside himself. "If you go on this trip," I said, "you'll have to help me. I'll do your work here, and you'll have to keep a journal for me. I will need an account of everything. Also remember that this all depends on that extra mule, and if you do not go, your father will have to keep the journal."

"Thanks mother. I'll keep the journal."

"Jonathan, I'm going to miss you and Naam," I said. "Take good care of yourself and Naam."

Outside the girls ran over to the mules. Elissa said, "Their big brown eyes are beautiful, so soft yet rich in color."

Ruth was more impressed with the way they pursed and moved their lips.

Jonathan kissed the girls. I stayed in his arms a little longer. "We'll stop by to see Tamar," he said to me, "and then head on north to Shechem. I'm taking a letter from Elishama to his folks, and we will stay all night with them. The next day we will continue north until we start down toward the Jordan. We will go through Hamath, Rehob, and finally Beth-Shan. I do hope that we can get another mule."

Naam gave me a big hug, and Khety said, "I'll just pretend this mule is a camel."

Naam is a good writer. He noticed things the rest of us would have overlooked. I have copied it from his original:

Our first stop was at Tamar's place. We enjoyed her baked goods, and she gave us one of Absalom's maps for traveling to the north. As it turned out we did not need it, but I corrected it thinking it might be useful in the future.

We were not able to get to Shechem before dark, and then had trouble finding Elishama's father. Finally we gave up and looked up Elishama's friend, Joshua, one of the minstrels who sang at the tomb of Joseph in Shechem and at the dedication of David's palace. Joshua and father had a lively conversation as Joshua took us to Elishama's parents. Father delivered the letter from Elishama, but he decided that we should go back with Joshua to his house. Abraham, Elishama's father, was ill. Jonathan told Abraham that when they returned to Jerusalem, he would suggest to Elishama that he should make a trip to Shechem.

At Joshua's place we had a good meal. Joshua was interested in father and Khety's project, and we stayed up too late. Nevertheless we were up early and soon on our way to Beth-Shan. In the light of morning we were able to see that Shechem was situated between Mount Ebal and Mount Gerizim.

On the way, I noticed that Khety was sitting on an extra shirt. "Khety," I said, "you will get your shirt dirty sitting on it. I can put it in my pack for you."

"It is fine just where it is, my dear fellow. In fact, my butt is so sore that I may put another garment on top of the shirt."

Father said to me, "You have discovered something about scribes: Their occupation does not condition them for such travel."

"I don't understand. They sit all day, don't they?"

"Yes, but our benches don't bounce.

"Well, if they need to look at ancient texts in far away places, you had better get them conditioned."

"Jonathan, I think your son is trying to make our lives more difficult."

As long as we traveled in the high lands, the weather was

cool, but as we started down towards the Jordan, the air was much warmer. By noon it was hot, and we stopped for some lunch and shade. Two shepherds came by with their sheep, and father asked about the distance to Beth-Shan. The older boy said we would be there before dark. Father offered them some bread, and they ate it as if they were starved. The hot weather was hard on their sheep, they told us, and they had to climb to higher ground. Father said that seeing those boys reminded him of his days of tending flocks.

Khety was worried about the heat. "I hope that it does not make our task too difficult."

"We should go easy at first," father replied. "I think we can adjust to the heat."

We passed Hamath without stopping and went on to Rehob. The mules were thirsty as were we. In Rehob we asked directions again and arrived in Beth-Shan well before dark. We were amazed at the size of the mound. Beth-Shan had been rebuilt many times and building upon the ruins of older cities had created this tall mound. Not many people lived on the mound; most had found places to build and live below the city, hence the 'sub-urb.' Father asked some people in the market if there was a scribe who lived here. They told him yes and gave the directions to his house. When we found the scribe, we asked him if he was the one who had made copies of two Egyptian stelae for Absalom. "I am," he said.

"We are from The Jerusalem Academy," father said. "King David has sent us here to investigate these stelae. Can you show them to us?"

"I can, but it would be better if we wait until morning."

"That is fine," said father. "We do not need to do it this evening. We will find a place to camp and see you in the morning."

"You may stay here," said the scribe. "My name is Abdi-anati."

"You have an interesting name," father remarked. "In ancient Ugarit Anat was an important goddess, and I remember Magon, one of our teachers from Tyre, mentioning a scribe from Ugarit by the same name; he was a 'servant of Anat.' Magon was comparing this name to Shamgar ben-anat, one of our early leaders. Since Anat was a goddess of war, Magon thought that to be a 'son of Anat' was another way of saying that Shamgar ben-anat was a great warrior."

"This is strange," said the scribe. "I went to school for a short time in Tyre, and I remember a Magon from that time. Of course it is a rather common name. But there is a tradition about a Shamgar ben-anat who was from Beth-Shan, and at one time Anat had many followers here. By the way, Shamgar is a Hurrian name. Both the Hittites and the Hurrians have influenced us in many ways."

"I can see that we will have some interesting conversations with you, but before we say more, I want to introduce my fellow teacher, Khety, who comes from Egypt, and this young fellow is my son, Naam," father said with his hand on my shoulder.

"I'm glad that you can help us," Khety said. "Perhaps after we set up our camp and fix something to eat we can ask you to tell us more about Beth-Shan."

"I will be glad to do that but don't fix a meal. My wife and daughters will soon have the evening meal ready. You just set your camp over by that old olive tree, and then you can tie the mules on the other side of it. We will have a good time over our meal."

Abdi-anati's welcome made us happy, and it did not take long for us to set up camp. The dinner was served outside, in back of the house, and we had a perfect view of the *tel* from where we sat. The meal was a welcomed treat. The bread and cheese were different but good. The bread was much darker than our bread, and the cheese had a hot spice in it. I liked it. I also liked the stew; it had bits of lamb among lentils and onions. And the melon was so sweet! Abdi-anati's wife and two daughters were beautiful but so quiet; they did not enter into any of the conversation. I am not used to that.

"Do you have enough work to keep you busy?" father asked Abdi-anati.

"Yes. I'm the only scribe left in Beth-Shan. There is enough work for another scribe. I write so many letters and legal documents."

"Can you tell us something of the history of Beth-Shan?" asked Khety.

"We do not have many written traditions, but there are lots of oral traditions. The Egyptians ruled our city-state for at least three hundred years, and they used mercenaries from Caphtor (Crete) and Alashiya (Cyprus) to keep order. Our own traditions were never too important to our rulers. After the Egyptians left, the mercenaries kept control of things. It was natural for them to join with the Philistines, who were also from Caphtor. After the Philistines defeated Saul on Mount Gilboa, they were welcomed by our rulers who helped them deposit Saul's armor in our temple of Ashtaroth and hang the bodies of Saul and his sons on the wall of our city. As you probably know, some warriors from Jabesh-gilead came one night and retrieved the bodies and buried them in Jabesh. When David sent his men to retrieve the bones of Saul and his sons from Jabesh, things changed around here. David's men entered our city and destroyed some of the temples. Most of the mercenaries fled to the west; they now live with the Philistines. Our neighbor, King Toi of Hamath, seems to be loyal to David. We will also work with David, but we need a lot of help. David should help us rebuild and defend our city, and since our rulers have left, we have no one to lead. Everyone does what is right in their own eyes. The result is complete chaos. I hope that you can help us."

"We can," father assured him. "As soon as we return, I will speak to David about this matter; he will send some help."

"Since the Egyptians ruled here for many years," said Khety, "I was wondering what the people thought of

Egyptians. Perhaps it would be best not to tell anyone that I am from Egypt. What do you think?"

"It does not matter. It has been a long time since the Egyptians were here. They were far better than their mercenaries. The people will be interested in what you find out about the stelae in the Egyptian temples. I would not worry about it."

I took notes during this conversation, and Abdi-anati said, "I see that you not only have a fine son but a young scribe. He deserves another piece of melon for such work."

He called to one of his daughters, "Sharmila, please get another piece of melon for our young scribe."

She served me a large slice and asked to see my notes. I was more interested in showing her the notes than eating my melon. She was interested, and it was clear she wanted to talk with me. "Wasn't that exciting?"

"You called your daughter 'Sharmila,' father said. "What is the meaning of her name?"

"You may have heard it pronounced 'Tharmila' as it was at Ugarit, but 'th' shifted to 'sh' in most of our languages as it had been in Babylonian. But *sharmila* is a fine white stone used by artists in their work. We thought she was a work of art."

"That she is," said Khety, "and your education at Tyre is apparent in your remarks. Did you study Egyptian?"

"No. But I wish that I had. Here at Beth-shan there are so many inscriptions in Egyptian, but we also have some writing by the mercenaries that I think comes from Caphtor or Alashiya. They wrote in a linear script, and I sometimes wonder if their writing influenced our own use of a linear script."

"You could be right," said father, "and such a revolution was helped along when we changed our writing material from clay to parchment and papyrus.

"We want to thank you for your fine food, and such conversation is always a delight for three old scribes and a young one. But we should get some sleep. We will see you in the morning. *Laylah tov*."

"And a good night to you," our host replied. "We should start our work early; it gets hot before noon."

It was already quite warm as they walked up a steep road to the top of the *tel* or the man-made mountain. The present generation always built on the ruins of their ancestors, slowly increasing the elevation of their city. There was a lot of activity in parts of the city, but nothing much was happening in the old Egyptian temple quarter. We were able to look around without attracting too many onlookers.

Abdi-anati knew right where to take us to see the two stelae. This was the exciting part for Khety. Abdi-anati explained that the stelae were at one time standing, but many years ago they had fallen to a horizontal position. Though they were made from hard black rock, the fall had cracked them. Abdi-anati said, "Absalom and I did not try to move the stelae, so we just removed some earth that had partially covered them."

Khety identified the first one as the Seti stela. Since it was lying on its side he did not have to remove much dirt to expose twenty-two lines of the text. "You can begin to copy the text," he said to me. "Your father and I will go to the next stela and clean it up."

"I'm glad that I sat in your Egyptian class," I told him.

More soil covered the other stela, but as Khety suspected it was the Rameses stela. However the inscription was worn; it would not be easy to read.

Khety said to father, "I will try to copy this one, and Abdi-anati could show you around to look at the rest of this mound."

"Good idea. Also I will enjoy just looking at the valley. This height gives one a great view."

"I would like to show you the ancient northern cemetery," said Abdi-anati. "It is interesting as some of the mercenaries were buried there."

Khety had a difficult time trying to copy the Rameses stela. From time to time he would come to where I was working. I did quite well with my twenty-two lines. Khety brought me over to view the Rameses stela. "Some of this looks impossible," I said."

"We will have a difficult time, but we will read most of it. There are twenty-four lines on this one, and some of it repeats the formal idioms that we see in the text you are copying."

Abdi-anati and father returned about noon. "We had better go back to the house for some lunch," said Abdi-anati. "We should not come back until it cools down."

Khety and I gathered our writing materials, and soon we were all on our way down from the *tel.* After lunch father described what he had seen. "The mercenaries were buried in clay coffins. One was decorated with a face and arms that started on each side of the head. They framed the face, and the hands came together just under the chin. Also the mercenaries brought some of their jars from their homeland. One jar handle had some of their writing on it. This is an interesting place. I wish that we could stay here for a long time, but I know that we cannot do that. How much longer is it going to take the two of you to finish your work?"

"I have finished," I said, "but I want to check several things again when we go back."

"I will need to work this evening in order to finish," said Khety. "The Rameses stela is in bad shape. If we can spend some time this afternoon translating what Naam has copied, it will probably help me restore some parts of the Rameses stela. I say this, because the titularies of both Seti and Rameses follow a set pattern (Seti, lines 1-3, and Rameses, lines 1-2), and the endings of each text will be similar. However the bodies of the two texts are different. In the Rameses text there seems to be a lot more boasting about the greatness of Rameses from what I have seen so far. I did see one interesting line. It was line 15 that continued the praise of

Rameses, and it mentioned his care of the widow, the poor and the afflicted. He is called 'a brave shepherd in caring for mankind.'"

"If he did care for mankind, he was a wise ruler, said father. "Our own way of describing the ideal king is almost identical."

So while Khety looked at my work and the rest of them gathered around to watch. Khety said, "The first half of line 1 gives us the date: 'Year one, month three of the third season, day ten.' This means that Seti came here during his first year as ruler of Egypt. We were right; it was about three hundred years ago. Believe it or not, I think they brought this stela with them from Egypt. Next we have the titulary (lines 1b-3). It gives the five great names that each pharaoh bears: 1) the Horus name, 2) the Two Ladies of the South and of the North, 3) the Horus of Gold, 4) King of Upper and Lower Egypt, and 5) his personal name. Now if this is like other inscriptions the scribes will have to praise Seti. The praise of Seti goes on for about ten lines (4-14a). Now I can see where the action starts. In the middle of line fourteen we have *Re' pn*. This is the usual way to start the story. It means 'On this day.'"

"But I thought that the small circle, which we read *Re'*, meant the God Re' or the 'sun,'" I said.

"It does, but it also means 'day,'" Khety answered. "Let's read this part:

> On this day, one came to speak to his majesty as
>   follows:

> 'The vile enemy, who is in the town of Hamath, is
> capturing many people for himself and taking
> the town of Beth-Shan. Then he made a covenant
> with those of Pahel. He did not permit the Chief
> of Rehob to go from his place. Then his majesty
> sent the first army of Amun, "Mighty of Bows," to
> the town of Hamath, The first army of Re', "Many

of Valor," to the town of Beth-Shan, and the first
army of Seth, "Strong of Bows," to the town of
Yanoam. It happened in the period of one day;
they were overthrown by the might of [his]
majesty, the King of Upper and Lower Egypt, Men-
maat-Reʿ, Son of Reʿ, Seti Mer-ne-Ptah, (may he
be) given life.'

Naam, you produced a fine copy. I hope that you noticed
in the translation that one of the towns uses your name.
Yanoam could be a verbal form meaning that this town 'will
make good.' I will want to check a few things with you when
we look at the text again. I am not sure why this scribe used
an 'r' for the 'n' in Beth-Shan. We expect the 'r' for words
with an 'l' because the sounds are not distinguished, but
this is something that I cannot explain."

"What an interesting text," father said. "It deals with the
towns close to Beth-Shan; all of them are just south of the
Sea of Galilee and near the Jordan. My question has to do
with the 'vile enemy.' Who is he?"

"As I said, earlier, in lines 4-13, Seti and his
accomplishments are praised. In line 9 it says that he 'crushed
the Retenu' or the original inhabitants of this area. The vile
enemy is probably one of their leaders."

Father had a second question. "Did the men in the various
armies have the name of their units inscribed on their weapons?
For example, did those who belonged to 'the first army of
Amun' put on their weapons 'Mighty of Bows.'"

"They probably did," Khety answered.

Abdi-anati said, "Would you like to return to the *tel* now?
You have made this day exciting for me, and I would like to
have a copy of your translations."

"I will make the copies this evening after dinner," I said.

"But we might not be finished with the Rameses
inscription for some time," said Khety. "We may have to send
you a copy of that one."

It was still very hot. I asked father, "Why?"

"I'm not certain, but we are low. On our return, you will notice that as we climb back up to Shechem the air will seem thin and become cooler."

"Our pack animals have a more difficult time when they go west to the sea," added Abdi-anati. "When they return it is easier for them. Therefore I think we are even lower than the western sea. The cities on the coast are hot compared with Jerusalem, but they are cooler than Beth-shan. Also in this area our people are plagued with a fever that does not exist in other parts of the country."

"Not to mentions the mosquitoes," father said.

Khety and I looked over my work and made a few corrections. Then we both worked on the Rameses stela. Khety said, "We will do our best, and then when we work on the translation it may become clear what a damaged sign has to be."

Abdi-anati and father looked around some more. When they got back to watch us finish our work, I said to father, "It all seems so strange to me. I touch these stones, and I suddenly imagine how they were transported here from Egypt, or I imagine the men who wrote on them. It is really quite thrilling."

"I know, my son. My mind runs away down some of those same paths. We are lucky that we have these texts to keep our imaginations from straying onto wrong paths, but at the same time giving substance to our thinking within the limits of the texts."

After dinner I made a copy of Khety's translation of the Seti stela for Abdi-anati. As I worked, Sharmila brought me melon as she had the night before, and I can say again that I enjoyed talking with her. But I felt just a little guilty because of my loyalty to Rachel. Still I reasoned that perhaps Rachel was more like my sister than a girlfriend. In any case, talking with Sharmila was fine.

The next morning we packed our things and were soon on our way, but not before thanking Abdi-anati and asking him to visit us in Jerusalem some day. Sharmila gave me a special package she had prepared. I'm afraid we were blushing as the others looked on, but she managed to say, "You will enjoy this on your trip home."

I thanked her and promised to write.

This is the end of Naam's journal.

Our travelers made good time on their return trip even though their initial climb was slow. Naam noticed when they got up in the mountains it was cooler. It was then that Naam opened his gift from Sharmila. She had packed raisin cakes and strips of dried fruit. Naam shared his gift with his father and Khety.

"I want to thank you for sharing your gift," said Khety. "It is good to have a young man as a traveling companion, who can attract young women and their gifts."

"Khety, you are a wise man," said Naam.

They all rested at Tamar's estate, and Khety remained for dinner. Jonathan and Naam came on home, anxious to tell us all about their trip. Khety said as they were leaving, "You can take my mule with you. You will want to return him with the others, and I will enjoy walking back in the morning."

"Are you sure," Jonathan said. "I think your mule likes you."

"He is nice, but my body will enjoy the walk."

Chapter Nineteen

Egyptian Proverbs and the Aton Hymn

When Naam, Rachel, and I walked into Egyptian class a few days later, we were surprised to see Magon instead of Khety. He explained to the class that Khety had not returned yet from his trip to Beth-shan. He went there to copy some of Egyptian inscriptions. Rachel, Naam and I looked at each other knowingly. "Khety has prolonged his visit with Tamar," I whispered.

Magon began the class with a statement and a confession. "Today you will not learn much Egyptian, but I hope to show you how important Egyptian has been for my work. I cannot read Egyptian like Khety, but I have studied some texts when I was a student in Tyre. One that was valuable to me was *The Instruction of Amenemope*. In it the ideal human is seen as one who is silent and honest, and this text prepares such a person to make a contribution to his country in the diplomatic corps. The instructions and proverbs in the text are arranged in thirty chapters. Khety and I have decided to arrange one section of Hebrew instructions and proverbs according to this Egyptian pattern. Our scroll of thirty sections will be shorter than its Egyptian counterpart. The proverbs that we borrow from Amenemope are usually expressed with fewer words. We are not finished with our work as yet, but I can give you four examples from our thirty chapters (Proverbs 22:17-24:22). Here is the way we start:

Chapter One

(Proverbs 22:17-21)

Incline your ear and hear [the] words of [the]
    wise
And apply your heart to my teaching,
For it is good that you keep them in your gut;
Together they will be ready on your lips.
May your trust be in Yahweh.
I have taught you this day, yes you.
Have I not written for you thirty [sayings]
With counsel and knowledge,
To make known to you truth [or] words of truth,
In order to return true words to the one who sends
    you?

. . .

Chapter Three

(Proverbs 22:24-25)

Do not make friends with one who possesses anger
And do not go around with a hothead,
Lest you learn his ways;
You will find yourself trapped.

. . .

Chapter Seven

(Proverbs 23:1-3)

When you sit down to dine with a ruler,
Consider carefully who is before you,

And you should put a knife to your throat,
If you are one who possesses an appetite.
Do not desire his tasty foods;
He and [the] food are deceptive.

Chapter Eight

(Proverbs 23:4-5)

Do not toil for riches;
From your understanding, desist.
Have you set your eyes on it? And it is gone,
For it surely makes wings for itself;
Like an eagle it flies to the heavens.

"The first of these four examples has two parallels with Amenemope. We took almost word for word the first lines of Amenemope, Chapter One: 'Give your ears to hear the sayings. Give your heart to understand them.' A few lines later we mention the 'thirty sayings,' but in Amenemope the 'thirty chapters' are not mentioned until the beginning of chapter thirty. We thought it should appear in Chapter One.

"Our second example is from Chapter Three. Here we depend on Amenemope, Chapter Nine: 'Do not associate with the heated man.' The third example from Chapter Seven is paralleled in Amenemope, Chapter 23. Here the emphasis is on good manners at the table of the king. This is an important part of the character of the ideal man and his worth in the foreign service. The last example is parallel to Amenemope, Chapter Seven: 'Do not set your heart on riches.'"

Naam asked Magon, "How do you decide to take the saying from Amenemope? Sometimes we may already have a similar saying."

"If we have one, we would probably use it, but our guidebook for foreign service will usually follow the Egyptian model. They have had many years of experience in this field. Also we change some things in a saying to make it fit our situation. In our Chapter One we have added, 'May your trust be in Yahweh.' That is certainly not Egyptian."

"Do you have another Egyptian text that has been helpful for you in your work?" I asked.

"Yes. At the present time I am using an Egyptian hymn, *The Hymn to the Aton*. I am writing a hymn about creation, and this lovely Egyptian hymn helps me in several ways. Sometime it says things in such a wondrous manner that I borrow the expression, or in other places it puts me in the right mood. I can give you an example:

> [The] moon determined the seasons;
> [The] sun knew its settings.
> It grows dark;
> It was night.
> In [the night] all [the] beasts of [the] forest prowl.
> The young lions roar for their prey,
> Seeking their food from El.
> The sun rises; they gather together,
> And in their dens they stretch out.
> [The] humans go out to their work
> And to their tilling until evening.
> How manifold are your works, O El;
> With wisdom you have made all of them;
> The earth is full of your creatures.
>
> (Psalm 104: 19-24)

The first two lines and the last three lines of this part are really not good Hebrew but rather good Phoenician. Note the last word 'your creatures' (*qinyaneka*) is typical in Phoenician texts. Perhaps I should replace El with Yahweh. But more important is the fact that this short section is full of Egyptian ideas and phrases from *The Hymn to the Aton*; in both texts we have the sunset and a night of darkness. Then the lions come forth from their dens. Next there is the sunrise and the humans go to their work. The Egyptian text is more detailed at this point. Thus the humans rise up, and they wash and get ready before they all go to work. Next god is praised for all of creation, but here the Egyptians stress that god is one. All is created according to god's wish, and wisdom is a theme in both texts.

"This Egyptian hymn has made an impression on many Phoenician poets, and I acknowledge that it has influenced me as I write this psalm for you."

Several students requested that Magon come back to class after he finished his psalm.

On our way home Rachel said again and again "Magon is so wise."

"He's able to relate to us so easily," added Naam.

When we got to the house, Jonathan was there. I said with a smile, "You will be interested to know that Khety is still visiting with Tamar."

"This is interesting, and I suppose that you, my darling wife, have it all figured out."

"That I do, my dear husband, and it puts me in a romantic mood."

"Good. I need some romance. By the way I have just the line for Khety."

"I'm waiting."

"Tamar is a name that is used among the Hurrians. Tamar means a palm like a date palm, straight and tall. There is a line from a love song that goes like this: 'What a figure! It is like a palm ('tamar'), and your breasts [are like] clusters [of dates].' (Song of Songs 7:8) I could tell him about this."

I put my arms around him, "You had better just keep it between us."

Chapter Twenty

The Houses Are Finished

The new houses were finished. I said to Deborah, "Let's go over to Sarah's and plan a party to celebrate."

Sarah welcomed us, and said she had been thinking of how to celebrate the event. "We can do it in four days," she said. "They will be settled by then. Sheva says we should have a small party but a good one."

"Yes," I said.

"Since this is such a special occasion, we will order a lamb for the dinner," Sarah said.

"Deborah and I will get busy, because we do want to help."

When we got to Deborah's house, I said, "We need to keep in touch on these preparations. We can talk again tomorrow."

When I got home, no one was there, and I decided to write up another entry.

Entry ten

Storing up Punishment for Children

In Jonathan's Job poem, he argues against the three righteous 'friends,' who claim that God will punish the wicked. Jonathan's Job says that this is not the case, and he asks:

Why do the wicked live on?
They have grown old;
They have even become wealthy.
Their seed has been established in their presence
     with them
And their offspring before their eyes.
Their houses are safe from fear,
And the rod of Eloah is not upon them.
His bull has bred and never fails;
His cow calves and never aborts.
They send out their young ones as a flock,
And their children dance about.
They take up the timbrel and harp,
And they rejoice at [the] sound of [the] flute.
They finish their days with good times,
And in a moment they go down to Sheol.
They said to El, 'Depart from us;
The knowledge of your ways, we have not desired.
What is Shaddai that we should serve him,
And what do we profit when we encounter him?'

. . .

[You say,] 'Eloah stores up punishment for his
     children;'
He should pay him that he might know.
Let his eyes see his destruction,
And let him drink the wrath of Shaddai.
For what does he care about his house after him,
When the number of his months has been cut off?
                              (Job 21:7-21)

Here the wicked are portrayed as doing just fine. But the righteous answer in the last section of this quote, "Eloah stores up punishment for his children." Job's answer is that God should pay the sinner; he should "drink the wrath of

Shaddai!" Job knows that the wicked are not punished by God, and their answer is an evasion based on one of our old legal traditions. In this tradition God warns the people not to worship images. Then he says:

> You shall not bow down to them or serve them,
> For I, Yahweh your God, am a jealous God.
> One who visits [the] sins of the ancestors upon
>   [the] children,
> Upon the third and upon the fourth [generations]
> Of those who reject me,
> And one who keeps covenant love with thousands,
> Who love me and keep my commandments.
>
>   (Exodus 20:5-6)

This old legal tradition is the majority opinion and resides in the tradition of Moses, but that does not make it correct in the eyes of Job. He asked, "Why do the wicked live on," and prosper?" He was expecting the answer, "Eloah stores up punishment for his children," and he got it. Anything to delay the truth!

The minority opinion in this case would emphasize that the wicked live on, because they are powerful. Of course we all have to live with the consequences of some of our actions, but it does not follow that there is any justice. God cannot manage it; the God of the righteous "friends' is helpless and absent, and if he plans to punish the children for the sins of their parents, he is cruel. When we say that there is no justice, we are not just saying that things are unfair. Rather we are saying that our leaders and their God cannot provide justice. God cannot direct our world to reward or bring punishment. God is not all powerful.

In the evening as we were sitting around our table, I informed everyone about the celebration we were planning, and I said, "I want some help with the baking. Jonathan said, "I will help you, but tomorrow I promised Magon that I would help with the moving."

"That's fine. We will have to bake on the next day."

On the day of the party, Naomi came by. She said, "Mother told me that you and Deborah were helping her with a party for us."

"Its hard to keep a secret. I hope that you are settled enough to put up with our invasion."

"Yes! It will be wonderful, and I will not have to cook our dinner. Mother is coming over to try our new fire pit and oven. We have a wonderful house. It is like yours with four rooms and a nice roof for extra space, but the good thing is that as your smoke from cooking floats towards your house, and our smoke also crosses over to your house. We are smokeless!"

"Well that means we will always know what you are cooking; we'll come over when you are cooking lamb."

"You will be welcome. Father said that he had talked to Khety about the party, and Khety's house will also be open for 'inspection.' I have noticed that he has been moving a lot of things. I don't know where he gets it all. I want to see what he has done, but I understand that the dinner will be at our house."

"Naomi, you are a wonder. You know more about our plans than I do. That is interesting about Khety. I wonder if Khety is planning for the future when he might need more furnishings. I know that he has been seeing Tamar."

"Really!"

"Yes, and I'm usually right about such things. I predicted that you and Magon would get married."

"Oh observant one."

After the dinner party, the children played on both roofs putting on plays for each other. Sheva gave a short talk about how The Jerusalem Academy was growing and taking on a cosmopolitan stance with Magon of Tyre and Khety from Egypt.

"They are helping us to understand the literature of our world, and by this we are able to relate our traditions and ourselves to others. These two houses stand here together, but we are not going to call this the foreign quarter. Magon and Khety are no longer foreign; they belong here as colleagues and friends. Sarah and I are also proud to say in this gathering that Magon is the generous father of our grandchildren. Would either of you like to speak on this occasion?"

Both Magon and Khety stood up, and Magon spoke first.

"We are excited about living here in our new home. I have enjoyed working here with all of you, and Khety has already helped me in many ways. We thank Keziah, Deborah, and Sarah for their preparations."

Magon sat down and Khety said, "Magon has just said all that I wanted to say; I thank you as well. But I do have something to add. I am thankful for such a fine home, because in the near future, I will carry my bride across my threshold."

We looked at each other, and Naomi whispered to me, "Keziah, you are always right."

"I have surprised some of you," Khety continued. "Do you know why there is so much good wine here tonight? David sent it. I asked him if he would allow me to marry his daughter, Tamar. He said, 'Yes' and sent the wine. Now I know that you can put on parties, but I need to know if you do weddings?"

Several of us responded at once, "Yes! We do weddings."

"You should have brought her here tonight," I said.

"I thought about that, but Tamar is shy. She said, 'I will meet all of your friends at our wedding.'"

"I hope that she will not mind if some of us go out to see her before the wedding. We can help her get ready."

"She will like that. In fact she appreciates everything that you have done for her."

Jonathan came by and filled our cups with the "good wine." He pointed out that the jars were stamped, *lemelek*, "Belonging to the King." By the end of the evening, we had all had more than enough.

I said to Sheva and Sarah, "I have had too much wine, but I think I can wash these cups. Why don't you pick up the left over food. Khety could help you, because he should take some of it home."

Jonathan and Magon were sweeping the floor, and Naomi was putting her children to bed. Mine had already gone home. When we finished cleaning up, Jonathan said, "I have just opened one more bottle of wine. Let's have one more drink, as we look to our future."

Chapter Twenty-One

Jonathan's Poem is Published

The academy seemed to be getting over its acute anger concerning Jonathan's Job poem. I was not making a lot of progress on *The Minority Report*, but I wasn't in a big rush. Jonathan thought that my last entry, "Storing Up Punishment for Children," was important. All was well until Jonathan received a copy of *Job* as edited by Nathan and Hushai and published by David's order. Jonathan brought it home as soon as he received it; we cleared our table and rolled it out. It did not take long to see what they had done. Jonathan said, "This is awful! I knew that they would not make three books, *The Ancient Story of Job*, *The Poet's Job*, and *The Speeches of Elihu*, but I was hoping that they might put the three works in that order in this scroll. They have mixed it up, and it appears as one book."

"Look what they did," I said. "They have put in the prologue of *Job I*; they have left out your prologue for *Job II*, and then they give your poem."

"Yes, and after leaving out my epilogue, they include the section on the final words of *Job I*."

Jonathan stomped around the room. "Keziah, this is horrible. God's speeches from *Job I* should be next, but they have inserted *The Speeches of Elihu* at this point. I would have expected these speeches to follow my poem; they should follow the poem, which they attack. Finally they give the rest of *Job I:* God's speeches, Job's repentance, and the epilogue for *Job I.*"

"Your poem is completely buried in a tomb constructed from the rubble of *Job I* and *The Speeches of Elihu.*"

"They have buried it, and I feel like they have buried me." He was still for a moment. "On the future copies of my work, I am going to make a chart to show how to find my work in the *Job* of Nathan and Hushai." He sat again. "Let's see; I will write the chart on this piece of parchment:

> *Job I*— Prologue (Job 1-2)
> *Job II*— Poem (Job 3-26)
>   with no Prologue or Epilogue
> *Job I*— Last words (Job 27-31)
> *The Speeches of Elihu* (Job 32-37)
> *Job I*— God speaks (Job 38-42:60
>   and Job repents
> *Job I*— Epilogue (Job 42:7-17)

If you look at this map my poem is not buried very deep, but deep enough to ruin it. It lies decomposing in a shallow grave. The editors have made a mistake by inserting *The Speeches of Elihu* between the call to God in *Job I* and God's answer. The speeches should be after my poem, but perhaps they could not find my poem. Keziah, this is a disaster."

"Well, we will have to get busy and make more copies of your work. There is still some room in the crypt, and there must be more people that want a copy. We could also send several more copies to Elissa in Tyre. She could send them to other schools in places like Sidon. Jonathan you are not dead or buried."

He kissed me, and I said, "Dead men don't kiss."

"Right, and I would like to start writing an entry for your book, with your editing, on 'Royal Editing.' Remember we said we would do this after we saw what David published. It is interesting that he felt he had to publish my poem not only because we are related, but also because there are some important people who agree with me. However when he allowed the editors to bury the poem, it also made the story in *Job I* confusing. But readers will probably just skip the confusing part and finish the story of *Job I* with all of its fantasy."

"They will also have to skip *The Speeches of Elihu* or be confused for a second time. You should make more copies and write the entry. I will write a few more entries and stop. It is important for us to get *The Minority Report* out, because it will also contain your poem. As we have said before, we can always do a second volume."

Just then Magon and Sheva appeared at the door. I said, "Come in and have a look at the royal edition of *Job*."

"We have seen it," Sheva said. "We came over to see if you had a copy, and to tell you that your enemies in the school are celebrating this publication."

"That is not surprising," Jonathan answered. "Yes, we have a copy, and it is disappointing to see what they have done. Magon, have you seen it?"

"Yes, and you are correct in your evaluation. The question is what do we do now?"

"I don't know. Keziah and I were just talking about what to do. She said that I should make more copies of the poem. I agreed and suggested writing an entry on 'royal editing' for her book. But can't we do more? I have another idea. Let my enemies have their celebration, and after things have settled down, we will have a celebration. We will have a funeral for the rebel Job; we can bury him in my tomb in Bethlehem. Keziah, we buried your father there; the rebel Job can be laid to rest beside Gad."

"But what good will that do?" I asked.

"It may not do any good," Jonathan responded, "but we will make a big thing out of it. We can start here at the school, and then have a long procession to Bethlehem in a two-part ritual. For me it will mean that I am done with it even if I failed. Yes, the editors have buried my poem, and they were wrong. But we will give the rebel Job a proper burial, and his words will be read each year when we call forth his name. This may be silly, but it will get the attention of these fundamentalists."

"It may help," said Magon. "You could gain some followers."

Sheva added, "It is ironic, but it is one way to keep the issue alive."

I was skeptical but finally agreed that it might work, "Let's wait until after Khety's wedding. Perhaps we will think of some other things to do as well."

It still seemed to me like a desperate attempt, but Jonathan had worked on this for so many years, and his options were few. His plan might work for the near future, but it is difficult to establish a lasting tradition.

Just then the children came in, and Naam reported that the students were getting loud and out of hand. Sheva left for the school. Magon said, "Jonathan, you should stay here, but I will go along with Sheva. They will settle down when they see us."

Naam was angry. His face was red, and he said, "I would like to ask them some questions; personal questions like, 'Has your family suffered? Why?' They are just linking arms with their closed-minded teachers."

"Which means they will not allow any other arguments to enter the conversation," Jonathan said. "These ultra orthodox people are like that, and David thinks he needs obedient people. He must not be aware that we united our country with the Royal Epic. We do need some order, but the promise of a good life in return for the fear of God is a cruel promise."

Naam said, "Someday I'll be a scribe, and I will continue to represent the wisdom of the rebel Job."

"We must all try to do that," I said, "and perhaps more people will become aware that since there is no justice we must help each other. The gleaners whom we helped will continue their lives in an unjust world; we will have to help them again."

Just then I noticed that Magon was returning. I ran to the door and asked him, "How did it go?"

"The students were a bit nasty, but it was not entirely their fault. Elyahba' was there claiming that *Job II* was published, and that all of Jonathan's arguments had been negated including his claim that there was no God. Then, Sheva walked up to Elyahba', and told him to leave the school. He said, 'You are inciting our student with something other than the truth. Jonathan did not say that there was no God, but he did say that your God was cruel and dead. There is a difference, but it would be difficult for you to understand it.'"

"I'll have to thank Sheva for those words," Jonathan said. "So what did the students do after that?"

"They disbanded and went back to their studies. Elyahba' was cursing Sheva and the school as he left, but Sheva just smiled and mumbled something about ignorant priests."

The next morning, I told Jonathan I was going to see Tamar. "If we can get things planned for the wedding, I will inform David about the date on my way home. We need to get things moving. We have a burial to plan."

Chapter Twenty-Two

Khety and Tamar

Later that week, Jonathan was working on some extra copies of *Job II* in his office when Khety came by for a visit. "He said Tamar and he appreciated what you have done for them," Jonathan told me when he arrived home. "I asked him what you had done."

I smiled, "I helped Tamar pick out her gown, and on my way home, I asked David to have the women's party at his palace, and he said yes."

"So Khety told me, and he said it would be a week from today. You do work fast.

"And will we have the men's feast here?" I asked.

"Of course. After our feast, Khety will go across to his house and wait for his bride, and the rest of us will walk to the palace to join you and the other women and start the procession."

"He will have to wait as you waited," I said.

"Yes. I asked Khety if he would incorporate Egyptian traditions in the ceremony.

'That is an amazing thing,' he said. 'Our traditions are almost identical to your traditions. On second thought, it is not so strange considering that if marriage traditions intend to bring two people together, they might have a similar structure. In Egypt young people fall in love, and they sing love songs. Usually the bride leaves her father house and goes to the home of the groom. Because she has a dowry and other belongings, the procession is a vital part of the wedding.'"

"And Khety just described our weddings as well," I said. "Also, we were interested in the wedding of Isaac and Rebekah, remember? You were convinced that their story was told in the form of a wedding. In this case the procession was a real journey."

"Which reminds me," Jonathan said. "In Egypt's recent past, we can point to the same sort of story. I am speaking of the marriage of Rameses to the Hittite princess, the eldest daughter of Hattusilis. Her procession was from the Land of Hatti to Egypt. Rameses dispatched an official escort to meet his bride and to help bring her and her things to his court. When the princess was brought before him, he marveled at her beauty and loved her very much."

"The two stories are similar," I said. "Goodness, we need to spend more time discussing such things. But the main thing is that Khety did not feel strange dealing with our traditions."

"No. Not at all. We did talk about a few other things. They will live here at the academy, so they need to find someone to stay at Tamar's estate during the week.

I suggested that they could get an older student, as Sheva is doing, but also someone like Noah or Danel might like to help out."

On the morning of the wedding, I got up early to prepare the house for the men's feast. Jonathan said to me, "Come back to bed for a little while."

"But we have a lot to do, and I don't want what you have in mind if it is only for a 'little while.'"

"Naam and I can get the house ready."

"I knew that I could count on you, but there are other things that must be prepared. Pace yourself today and save your strength for tonight."

Just then he jumped up and grabbed me and said, "I just needed a kiss."

I guess he did, because he must have kissed me ten times. "I also needed your kisses. But wait! Will Khety and Tamar kiss in the Egyptian way, nose to nose or will they press lips to lips?"

"I don't know, but you can watch the kiss when he lifts her veil."

"I intend to. And I want you to remember what happens at the men's party; I need the details for my journal."

David sent wine and food in the early afternoon for the men's feast. But I soon said farewell to my men. The girls and I left for the palace to help Tamar get ready. When we got there she had decided against wearing the things that we had picked out a few days ago and for good reason. The girls were looking at her royal robe, her *ketonet passiym*. "After I was raped by Amnon, I tore up my royal robe and went into mourning. Today David sent a new robe. And Khety had an Egyptian gown of fine linen sent to Tyre, and it arrived here yesterday. It will be appropriate for the party, and I will wear the robe over it for the procession."

The girls were looking at the robe. It was lavender embroidered with purple yarn. "David is being generous in every way for your wedding. Since his unmarried daughters wear such robes, you will not be wearing it after today, but it was still important to him that you wear it today."

"I will keep it and always remember today," she said smiling.

"I'm sure you will," I embraced her. "What can we do to help you before the other women come?"

"The palace servants are getting the food and wine ready, but you could help me pack my dowry and gifts that will be carried in the procession."

"You just tell us what goes, and we will do it. You should try to rest."

"I would rather talk to you as we both work. I am so thankful to you for what you have done for me. Before you came to visit me, I assumed my life was finished. Now I see that it is just beginning."

"And we are all looking forward to being a part of your beginning. We have all had some difficult times, but mostly we are joyful. I just thought of something. We will have to tease Jonathan about being a great uncle; he is your great uncle!"

"I've never thought about him as such, but if he is father's uncle then he must be my great uncle. All I know is that I'm happy, and I hope that my past will always be past."

"Tamar," I said as I put my arm around her. "Don't worry about your past. You have a great future, and as we say at our house, 'live it now.'"

"Thanks Keziah, but I just don't want to ever make things difficult in any way for Khety."

"You will not do that. He is intellectually and physically so able. He is also full of energy and joy, and believe me his joy has increased since he met you."

"I hope so."

Just then Naomi and Deborah arrived with their girls, and others were right behind them. Tamar suggested that we go into the next room where there was lots of food and wine. The girls liked that idea. Tamar asked Sarah, as her new neighbor, to preside, and Sarah was pleased to do so.

According to the report that I received from Jonathan with some help from Naam, here is how things went back at our house. Jonathan talked with Khety until the others arrived. "I'm glad that we took our trip to Beth-Shan when we did. It would have been impossible after your wedding. When Keziah and I were first married, we were upset when I had to travel from Hebron to Jerusalem."

"You are right, and I meant to tell you that I finally have the Rameses stela translated. That trip was important, and we should take more trips in the future."

"We should take a trip with our wives and before you have babies."

"And we will have babies. As you know from reading our love songs, Egyptians are people who fall in love and openly express their feelings. Right now I can only think of Tamar. Someday we will have to read *The Prince and his Three Fates*. The king's daughter loved the prince so much; her love saved him. There are a lot of people who do not know how to love, and if they learn, they are often too embarrassed to admit it."

"How right you are."

After the guests arrived, Sheva announced it was time to do some serious drinking. "The wine is good, and the food can wait. Get your cup, and we will give Khety a few moments to speak to us. Khety, tell us what's on your mind."

"Well I don't think I should tell you everything that is on my mind."

"We know what's on your mind," yelled Noah, "and we approve."

"Thanks, but that is in my heart. My mind says thanks to all of you for bringing me to Jerusalem, for being my friends, providing me with a house, and for introducing me to Tamar. Another Egyptian traveled to this area and was even given a wife, but he was never quite satisfied. He finally returned to Egypt for his last years and for burial. Of course I am thinking of *The Story of Sinuhe*. I am not a prophet, and I do not know the future, but I believe that I will be here to the end of my days. I have many things to do, and Tamar and I want to raise our children here in your presence."

Sheva said, "We are glad that you are here, and it sounds as if you are staying."

"This school has needed a voice from Egypt," said Magon. "We must thank Khety for providing us with many voices from his country. We hope you have a wonderful life with Tamar."

Others were about to speak, but there was too much noise. They ate, drank more wine, and some were singing. It sounds as if they had a good time.

At the palace we were singing and dancing. We had lamb that was cooked as it is done in Egypt; it was smothered in garlic and onions. We had plenty of David's wine plus cheese, bread, fruit, and cakes. The fruit included melons. The palace musicians played for us. The men were jealous when they found out about this entertainment. We did not have speeches like the men, but we did get to talk with Tamar about her plans.

We were finished eating when the men arrived. Apparently they were still hungry, because they were delighted with the lamb from our table.

Sheva and Sarah stood before us and Sheva spoke. "We have just come from Jonathan and Keziah's house, and we have sent Khety to his house. Next we will bless the bride and get ready for the procession. Every one will carry at least one item. So Tamar we hope for you and Khety many days in our midst. May your love keep you even as it frees you to build a new home and family."

With that we were off. Sheva and Sarah escorted Tamar, and we sang as we followed. It was too bad that David could not find the time to attend. When we got to the house, Khety appeared out front, and walked over to his bride. He took her by both hands and turned to the crowd. He said, "I understand that since the wedding of Jonathan and Keziah there is a new tradition in this land. It is a good tradition, and it allows the groom to know that he has the right woman."

Then he lifted Tamar's veil and gave her an Egyptian kiss, nose to nose, and next she gave a kiss, lips to lips. After that Khety carried her over the threshold, protecting her from threshold demons. Khety waved as he shut the door. The rest of us went over to our house. We had some more wine, and Noah said, "Khety not only shut the door, but he bolted it." Everyone soon departed, and that was for the best. Now things were quiet.

As Jonathan and I were getting ready for bed, I said, "Let's try a nose to nose."

"Among other things."

Chapter Twenty-Three

Three More Entries

After the wedding, I managed to get some time to write two more entries and to look at what Jonathan had written on royal editing. My first one was short.

Entry Eleven

The Treatment of Enemies

We have a proverb that says:

> Do not say, "As he did to me so I will do to him;
> I will pay back the man for what he has done."
> (Proverbs 24:29)

The majority would say, "pay him back," but we agree with the proverb.

Magon gave me a Babylonian text that is similar:

> Do not return evil to your enemy;
> Pay with kindness your evildoer,
> Preserve justice for your enemy,
> Be pleasant to your adversary.
> (For this text see "Afterword")

This is certainly a minority opinion. Even if there is a minority that would agree with these words, *could they practice them?* I make no claims in this area. We have enemies, and it is difficult to be pleasant to them. However it is probably wise to think on these words.

The results of not paying your enemy back could be far-reaching. It is possible that your enemy would be so confused by your unexpected actions or lack of action that the confusion could lead to conversation. The conversation could address past misunderstandings. Perhaps not, but it is worth a try.

This morning Jonathan handed me his work on "Royal Editing." I will read it and probably do a little editing myself, because I touched on some of these issues in *Entry Eight,* "Free and Eloquent Speech."

Entry Twelve

Royal Editing

When we published our *Royal Epic,* Part I, Jonathan knew that sooner or later a royal priest would alter some of its most important parts. In fact, Abiathar warned him that he would change the seven-day creation story to a six-day story. He did it, and he created confusion. After he changed the "seven" to "six," he left the line "Elohim finished on the seventh day his work that he had been doing." Abiathar changed the story in order to allow Elohim to keep the Sabbath. If he felt that he had to change it, he should have been careful; he changed order into chaos.

In our recent past, there is a tragic example of royal editing. David ordered the removal of the writings of Ahban from our library, and whenever he was mentioned in our chronicles, his name was to be changed to Ahithophel. Ahban was the sage in our school, a "brother of understanding," yet the administration saw him as a "brother of reproach." The majority opinion of these kinds of changes goes along with the royal view. The minority opinion has not been able to change matters, but in recent years we have won a few converts.

The royal editing of Jonathan's poem on Job has been subtle. David has allowed him to speak on this subject, to read it in public, and helped in arranging the debate, but he published it with royal editing. The editors were careful not to change the text that they published, but they did leave out some things. Then they buried Jonathan's poem in the confused rubble of *Job I* and *The Speeches of Elihu*. David can now claim a willingness to publish Jonathan's work, but he has buried it. It will never exist in the land of the living. Anything that is published with royal editing is not an example of free speech.

Jonathan is not a prophet, but this is his prediction. In the future, priests or scribes will attempt to soften the language of the rebel Job; they will make him more like *Job I*. In some places they will be able to do this without changing the ambiguous oral text. At one point the rebel says, "So he will kill me; I have *no* hope. / Yet, I will argue my case to his face." (Job 13:15) In the first line we have the negative *lo'*. But if you read *lo* it would not be a negative but would mean "him." Both readings would sound the same but mean the opposite. Hence one could understand it as: "Though he slay me, yet will I trust *him*, / but I will maintain my own ways before him." If anyone looked at the written text, this change would be impossible. The point is this: they will try to change the rebel into one of their own.

If we are interested in publishing our minority opinions, we will have to publish them ourselves, and hope that we can get them out to many others. This will be the difficult part of our task.

I will have to show this to Jonathan to see if he agrees with my changes. Now here is my last entry for this volume.

Entry Thirteen

There Is No Justice

This has been a central theme in my entries and in our story. It is also the main thrust of Jonathan's poem concerning the rebel Job, and it is the point that makes our orthodox and fundamentalist enemies angry. At the risk of repeating myself, I would like to stress the importance of this position; though it is has fewer adherents than other minority opinions. The key lines for the rebel Job come at a low point in his argument; he seems to be close to death.

> So, I cry, "Violence," and I am not answered;
> I cry for help and there is no justice.
>
> (Job 19:7)

These are not the words of spoiled children who are whining because their feelings are hurt. Rather, the rebel Job has suffered every possible disaster, and why? There is no answer and no justice. When I lose something, it is an exasperating experience. This is true even if the lost item has little value. I look for it; I go back to the last place that I saw it or was using it. This experience can put me in a bad mood, but how much worse is the experience of looking for something that you never had and that does not exist. I am talking about justice; justice is pure fantasy. At one point in our discussions Jonathan said, "There is no justice from the God of the pious or from our leaders; they are not able to provide it. There is no justice from the powerful who oppress the poor, the orphan and the widow, and our world does not judge. Our world is a place where life is possible for a brief moment."

We know almost nothing about God. In our stories about the beginning, we seem to need one who ordered chaos, but it is clear that this God has never been all-powerful. The pious make such claims for their God, but it is obvious that what evidence we have argues against their claims. Those who are religious, that is, the ones who fear God, are not protected; they also suffer. This situation should not cause us to create some fantasy about justice at some future time. Rather it demands a reality check. I sometimes compare it to my role as a mother. Yes, I have wondered if it was right to bring my children into this world of suffering and death. I do not have the power to protect them at all times or to make them happy, but I can love them and help them. Nothing is guaranteed, but so far we have had our moments of joy. It has not been all sadness. Also the children feel that they can participate in our task of bringing a minority voice to future generations.

In this situation human beings are called to help each other. There needs to be a lot of understanding and love. When we helped the gleaners, whose children were on the verge of starvation, we did not bring them justice. They will never have that. We helped them for the present. We brought them food. We tried to practice that which exists in our legal traditions; we tried to do the right thing for these poor people, and it was not for any reward in the future or for now. If we can help others, perhaps we can build a community that can have more moments of joy. As the Egyptian Harpers say, "Make holiday."

Chapter Twenty-Four

A Unique Burial

That thirteenth entry was my last for Vol. I of *The Minority Report*. After finishing it, I was ready for some fresh air and a walk. I went to Jonathan's office to tell him that I had finished. He let out a shout. It may have not been good timing on my part, because I did not know that he had a guest from Bethlehem in his office. He introduced me to his friend, Elhanan. I said, "I am glad to meet you again. I met you at the Beth Marzeah, your 'house of mourning,' when we buried my father at Jonathan's tomb in Bethlehem."

"Right. I do remember, and Jonathan has just told me that you will be coming back for a rather strange funeral."

"I was telling Elhanan about the burial of my Job poem. I told him that we were going to have a proper burial. Elhanan suggested that we do it next week before he goes on a trip. Could we do that?"

"I think we could. It will not take long to get the word out here and invite people to join the procession to Bethlehem. The children are going to love the trip."

"If Keziah says we can do it, we can. Let's make it one week from today Elhanan. Will you inform the men of the Marzeah to get things ready?"

"Yes. I can do it. I will be returning to Bethlehem before the sun sets."

"Do you have any plans for this funeral?" I asked Jonathan after Elhanan left.

"Not yet but I will work it out. We will have a ritual here at the school before we leave. Then we will have the procession, and the ceremony in Bethlehem should start at the Beth Marzeah. Then we will go to the tombs and back to the Beth Marzeah for food and drink." He put his chin in his hands. "Right now I feel defeated. I worked so many years on that poem. I am not certain the funeral will help me, but it does mean that we will read the poem once a year when we go there to remember your father and the rebel Job."

"I am sorry," I said and kissed his head. "Let's really make this a big celebration. When we start the procession, we should leave the school and circle down around the palace. We might as well let everyone know about the death of the rebel Job."

"Good. We will have to take a donkey and pack some lunch supplies for the march."

"I will set that up. You spend your time on the rituals. I expect some fine speeches from you."

"I'll try. Let's go home," he said getting up from his desk. "I want to write notes announcing our plans, and the children can take them around to our friends and post some at the school."

The children were more than willing to deliver the notes. But as they posted them at the school, some older students came by and tore the signs down. Naam went back to put up new ones, and the students started to throw rocks at him. He told the girls to run home, and he stood his ground. Noah and Danel came along about then. Noah told the students to stop, and Danel took down their names. He told them if they wanted to continue in school they had better change their ways. As soon as the girls came home and told us what was happening we ran over to the school. We saw Naam talking with Noah and Danel. They told us that all was well and then gave Jonathan the names of the students. Jonathan thanked Noah and Danel.

"I did not intend to get you in trouble," said Jonathan

"It was all right," Naam said. "They were not dangerous. They did not hit me, but I picked up one of their stones and threw it back. I hit one of them right in his crotch."

Noah said, "That one was still yelling when we arrived."

Naam was pleased with himself, but it worried me; he could have been hurt.

During the next few days, Jonathan prepared the rituals, his speeches, and even worked on some poems. Deborah and Naomi helped me with food preparation. Magon, Sheva, Khety, and other friends dropped by several times to ask Jonathan questions, because they were also preparing some talks for the funeral. It really didn't matter any more to me if this was a wise idea, because we were all having a good time getting ready. I was convinced that the preparation was just as important as the event. I was finished with my book, and Jonathan was preparing to put his to rest.

On the day of the funeral, we all got up early to start the ritual at the school about an hour after sunrise. We would still have an early start for our procession to Bethlehem. Jonathan had made a small olive wood case for the jar, which held the scroll containing his poem. Jonathan said that he would start the procession carrying the case, but others would take their turns during the procession.

When we got to the school, a much larger crowd than we had expected greeted us. There must have been fifty people there. Jonathan took his case to the front of the room, put the case on a table, and stood behind it.

"I'm pleased to see so many who have come to mourn. When I talk about what we are doing here today, I usually give mixed signals. Sometimes I speak of my Job poem or *Job II* being buried in the administration's *Book of Job*. Other times

I personify the scroll and speak of the rebel Job being buried, because it is his minority voice that is so important in the poem. But it is really not so strange. What happens to the poem also happens to the rebel, and if the rebel is silenced the poem has nothing new to say.

"The scroll is in its jar, and the jar is neatly packed in this case made of wood that is much older than any of us in this room; it is older than our grandfathers. It is older than any of our traditions. It came from an ancient tree, which has heard again and again the old words that we read in *Job I* concerning why we suffer, but this old wood is willing to protect the rebel's voice, and listen to new ideas. I wish that our orthodox and fundamentalist neighbors were as flexible as this wood.

"I will miss the rebel Job. He has been speaking to me and with me for twenty years. He is difficult to understand at times, but I allow him to make his point again in a slightly different way. He is quite certain that his orthodox friends are wrong, because they and their all-powerful God have no interest in the innocent and their sufferings. The rebel does not know much about God, but apparently God is not all-powerful even if he did defeat chaos and order our world. Also the rebel has no way of knowing what the future will bring; he only knows that in the absence of justice the powerless need our help.

"The rebel Job has had a short life. Today belongs to him, and it becomes an important celebration. We who call forth his name can extend his influence, and his blessing will be ours. Let our procession begin."

Jonathan picked up the case, and we all followed him as he headed for the palace to circle it before leading the procession to Bethlehem. We began singing and could see onlookers wondering what was going on:

O that my words would be written!
That they would be engraved on the stela;
With an iron stylus and lead,
They would be carved in rock as a witness.

(Job 19:23-24)

On our way to Bethlehem we picked up a few people. At one point Ruth ran up to us and said, "The children of the gleaners are with us. Look! Their mothers are talking to Tamar."

"You are right," I said. "You should walk with them, and you and your sister make sure that when we stop for lunch, they feel welcome to eat with us."

It was only a few moments later when we did stop for lunch. Jonathan and Naam unloaded the donkey, and we put the baskets of food on some flat rocks near the road. We did not have a fancy meal, but there was plenty of bread, cheese, and cucumbers. Most of the people were eating in small groups of six to ten. I moved around to each group to find out about their interest in the rebel Job. Jonathan was doing the same thing. Most of the people with whom I talked were interested in free speech. One old man said, "The rebel Job had the right to oppose the priests. They tell us to fear God and bring them our produce, but they know nothing of our labor and our suffering. We are oppressed by the landlords; it is that simple."

All of our friends were entertaining small groups. The children chased each other, eating on the run. The weather was wonderful, and I was getting sleepy. It was a good thing that we only brought water.

As we got ready to move on, a few turned back to Jerusalem. Some of them were old and did not want to go to Bethlehem, and others may have just come for the lunch. But that was fine. We were glad to have them. Just before we started on our way Jonathan said to the entire group:

"I have traveled this road many times, and when I get to this area, I always think about the story of Jacob. It has to do with another funeral. Here he buried his wife, Rachel. She died just after giving birth to Benjamin. As she was dying Rachel named her son Ben-oni, 'son of my suffering,' but Jacob called him Ben-jamin, 'son of the right-hand.' I have always liked the name that Rachel gave her son. 'Jacob set up a sacred pillar on her grave.'" (Genesis 35:20a) I don't know where the pillar is, but the story places it in this area. We have lost the tomb of Rachel, but I trust that we will always know the place of the rebel Job's tomb."

It did not take long to reach Bethlehem. We would have most of the afternoon for the funeral. As we were approaching from the north, Elhanan and his friends from Bethlehem met us. He informed Jonathan that all was ready at the Beth Marzeah. We went there first for some refreshments, and then went to the tombs. It was difficult for me, as usual, to go to this tomb where we buried my father, but today we would remember father and try to do something significant for the rebel Job. I was now sure that this was the right move. Jonathan took the case and stood before the tomb, saying:

"We have arrived at this tomb where we buried Gad, Keziah's father. Today we bring him a friend for his tomb; we bring him this scroll and its 'man of renown.' Gad knew the rebel Job quite well, and in fact they regularly inspired each other. The rebel Job was in part responsible for Gad's rejection by David as a royal prophet.

"I have referred to the rebel Job as a 'man of renown,' but he achieved this status without the benefit of a divine parent. He was courageous in the midst of his suffering and loss; he was unbending before the gales of his righteous enemies; and his complaints against the cruel God of his 'friends' were not selfish but they were made in order to help all of us.

"It has been said that I wrote about myself when I gave the rebel Job his voice. There is a bit of truth in this but not much. When I began to write about the rebel, I was in control, but soon he escaped from my pen. After that, my pen could not keep up with him, and I did not know what his final words would be. Also I have never possessed his courage. His voice utters rare words that teach us to be human, and he was impatient for our cause. Note these words:

> Am I for humans in my complaint?
> And if so, why should I not be impatient?
>
> (Job 21:4)

I consider Gad and the rebel to be my teachers.

"As we started our procession, we sang, 'O that my words would be written! / That they would be engraved on the stela; . . . . ' Today we can fulfill his wish. We will bury this scroll, and we will set up 'the stela' at his tomb."

Then Elhanan and two others stepped forward carrying a stela, which they slipped into its base. Now I understood why we needed to follow Elhanan's schedule for this event. He had prepared the stela for Jonathan.

Jonathan read from the stone:

> "You who stand before my tomb
> Stand as avengers for my cause.
> Stand as witnesses and friends.
> Seek not justice, but help the poor.

"Before we return to the Beth Marzeah, we will listen once again to the rebel. He says, 'All the men of my association have abhorred me.' (Job 19:19a) Here he is speaking about the men of his Marzeah or association. His close friends have turned against him. Here in Bethlehem the men of this Marzeah remain faithful to him and to us. Now we will hear our friends from Jerusalem and from Bethlehem."

Elhanan, who was standing beside the stela, spoke first. "Jonathan and I have been friends since we were small boys. I think Jonathan has a lot of courage, but we never know how much we have until it's demanded of us. Jonathan is not Job, because he has not suffered as much as Job. So it is true: Job is our teacher. I look at this funeral as an important event in my life, and because of it, I intend to visit here every year to read Job's words and to become more human because of them."

Magon was next. "Most of you know that I am from Tyre. In Tyre we live by the sea. The world seems bigger, because it opens to the west and disappears into the horizon. That is an advantage, but in our large world, we do not pay enough attention to our fellow creatures, to humans, and to the other animals. We have been helped by our contacts with Egyptian and Babylonian literature, but no one has a teacher like the rebel Job. It is an honor to be here today and to join in this event. Everyone who stands at this tomb will have a more meaningful future. I am thankful that my family is here."

Sheva made a confession. "I too have learned from Job. For a few years in our recent past, I was not at all like Job. I did not stand with Ahban or Gad when I was needed. But the debate between Job and the fundamentalists convinced me that I had been supporting the wrong side of this important question. One of our problems is that we learn too late that we are standing in the wrong place. But I agree with Magon that this day will make a difference in our lives."

Tamar and Khety walked to the front together. Tamar said, "You, who have been sitting at the feet of Job for several years, have helped me and have helped others. Khety and I had lunch with some children who are better as a result of your caring. I do not have to wonder if Job has a word for me; he has already given me the help that I needed."

Khety continued, "Even though I come from the land that celebrates the immortality of humans, we also have our skeptics, and I am one of them. We stand here today, because Job is mortal just like the rest of us. In fact he did not have a long life. Jonathan told us that he had known him for twenty years. A young person's funeral is always sad, but it appears to me that even though an attempt was made to bury him without a celebration, it failed. Today we have done the right thing, and it seems that he will have an impact on many lives for many years. In Egypt we have a school text that relates to this occasion. It maintains that writers in one sense are immortal. Many build tombs where their heirs pronounce or call forth their names, but these tombs crumble and are lost as is the corpse. It is different with writers; their names are called forth because of their books. It is their writing that makes them remembered and allows us to call forth their names."

I can't remember all of the speeches of that day from people I did not know. I do know that they were all important and the day was special. When it seemed that most of the speakers were finished Naam and I went forward. I said, "I have been moved and encouraged by all these speeches. As you could guess, we have seen a lot of Job at our house. At times, he has even had a place at our table. Those who subscribe to the teaching of the ancient story of Job have resented the rebel's visits to our home, but after today, I am not going to worry about what they think. This day will become one of my best memories."

"I want to add to my mother's remarks," said Naam. "I cannot add much, but I want to make a pledge. I will remember the rebel Job each time I remember my grandfather, who was the rebel prophet. Also I want to spend part of my life making this scroll available to many readers; I will do the same for my mother's book, *The Minority Report.*"

Jonathan thanked all of the speakers. "We will now return to the Beth Marzeah. When we get there you will notice that there are two empty chairs: one for Gad and one for the rebel Job. Their chairs are empty, because they will be

with every group enjoying the conversation. Also they want
to thank you for your kind words and to give you their
blessing:

> *Shalom*!
> *Shalom* to our friends!
> *Shalom* to all who call forth our names and tell our
>   stories!
> *Shalom* to those who hear the cries of the innocent!
> *Shalom* to the children who will continue this
>   witness!
> *Shalom* to the Jerusalem Academy!
> *Shalom*!

So let's have a good evening together. There will be plenty
of food and wine plus some good music. We will return to
Jerusalem in the morning."

We had a large crowd at the Beth Marzeah. We were all
hungry, and we took a long time eating our evening meal.
We had an ample supply of lamb stew, which was requested
by Jonathan, Naam, and Khety. They had enjoyed it at Beth-
Shan. It was made with small pieces of lamb and lentils,
seasoned to perfection. And we also had our usual bread,
cheese and fruit. We went back and forth from the table to
the small groups with their interesting conversations. When
the musicians arrived, the singer Hanani, son of Heman,
was well known to Jonathan, and he was a friend of Elhanan.
He sang beautiful songs backed up with a flute and a harp.
One song was a lament from the words of the rebel Job:

> Yes, there is hope for the tree;
> If it is cut down, it will grow again,
> And its young shoots will not cease.
> Or, if its root grows old in the earth,

And in the dirt its stump dies,
At the scent of water, it will sprout,
And make branches like a plant.
When a hero dies, he has collapsed;
A human has expired, and where is he?
Waters from the sea have disappeared.
And a river dries up and is parched,
And a mortal has lain down, and he does not rise.
They wake not until there are no heavens,
And they rouse not from their sleep.

(Job 14:7-12)

I asked Jonathan where everyone would sleep, and he said, "They will all find a spot. There are benches, and there is plenty of floor space. Some of the people from Bethlehem will go to their homes. Some of them will take a few guests home with them. I don't worry about it, but I was thankful that the men of the Marzeah said that they would be here early to fix us something to eat before we left for Jerusalem."

"They have been good to us. Have you seen the children lately?"

"Yes I have. They are all outside, and Khety is telling them one of his great stories. However, I also noticed that Naam and Rachel were walking hand in hand over to the olive orchard. For once they do not have to entertain the other children. Khety is really a helpful person."

"There is do doubt about it. Khety is one of the great things that has happened to the academy this year."

"I agree. I am going to start a bit of clean up before it gets completely dark."

I went over to see my friends, and Naomi said, "We were all saying that this has been an important event for us, and the children are all having lots of fun thanks to Khety."

Tamar said, "Khety loves the children. He is going to make a wonderful father."

"I'm sure that he will," I said.

Deborah asked, "How are you handling the emotions, the speeches, and this busy day?"

"This is one of the best days of my life. There is some sadness, because I remember my mother and my father. Also I know that Jonathan had great hopes for his poem, but this will do. The rebel Job has brought us here for a fine day, and my hope is that he will be remembered. If he is not remembered, the future generations will have to live in the fear of a God who will punish them for their sins, test them for their purity, and leave unanswered the reason for their sufferings."

We did not get much sleep that night. The wine made us sleepy, but the children were having too much fun. I had found some cushions in a storeroom and made a nice bed. Later the girls came to me, and Ruth asked, "Could we sleep with you?"

"Of course you can."

"Mother," Elissa said, "I did not really understand how we could bury Job who only lives in father's poem. I know that we buried a scroll, but we have other copies."

"It is difficult, but perhaps this will help. Yes, we buried a scroll, and the copies will help us to remember and will be here for us to read. Perhaps it is similar to the burial of my father in that we kept some of father's writing, which we read as we remember him. The difference is that we did not bury a corpse. I don't want to say that we only pretended to bury Job. Your father helped to create Job, and that person is not only real but also helpful. This is our way of saying no to the priests who have tried to erase him from our minds. We have given him a proper funeral, and he will remain with us. Does that help?"

"I guess it does but not much."

"Well, I will try to think of a better explanation tomorrow."

When I looked at the girls again, they were both asleep. Things were getting quiet, and Jonathan and Naam soon joined us.

In the morning we awoke to the sounds of breakfast preparations. We had a hearty breakfast, and Jonathan had the last word. "We were glad that you took the time to be with us for this event. The world and its future generations have lost a true friend, unless we can continue to call forth his name. Yesterday we took up this task; we will not be silenced by the religious. As many of you walk back to Jerusalem, the rebel Job has a suggestion for you. We not only need to care for our fellow creatures, but we need to take the time to learn from them. Job says:

> But indeed, ask please the domestic animals,
> And they will teach you;
> And the birds of the heavens, they will tell you.
> Or speak to the earth, it will teach you.
> And the fish of the sea will recount to you.
>
> (Job 12:7-8)

The Minority Report

Introduction

Most minority opinions will remain so. Some of them may become important to subsequent generations if they meet the needs of the people and the people can organize to support them. But members of the majority may never try minority opinions. We sometimes say that we can live in the future today, but we should not expect others to join us as we try to create a place for these opinions in our lives. For us this has been fun, but we will not always put into practice our opinions because of the chaos it would cause in our daily lives.

One

The Equality of the Human and His Mate

Our Royal Epic contains two creation stories. The first one says little about the humans. In the second, Yahweh-Elohim forms the human or "living being" from the clay of the ground. Then he says, "It is not good for the human to be alone; / I will make for him a helper just like him." (Gen 2:18) So from the ground he formed the rest of the animals or "living beings," and they were brought to the human, who named them. But the human did not find a helper just like him. In order to produce such a being, Yahweh-Elohim had to take some bone and flesh from the human and build that into a woman. Then he brought the woman to the human, and the human said:

> "This one, at last, is bone of my bones
> And flesh of my flesh.
> This one shall be called woman (*'ishshah*),
> For from man (*'ish*) this one was taken."
>
> (Gen 2:23)

In this story the human finally has a mate "just like him." They are equal; they are of the same substance, and this is why "They become one flesh." (Gen 2:24c) This emphasis on the equality of the man and the woman was a minority opinion, and it was never practiced among our people and had no place in our laws and traditions.

We know that this is an important opinion. In Jonathan's poem against the ancient Job, one of the so-called "righteous friends" of Job, Bildad, says, "And how can one born of woman be pure?" (Job 25:4b) This view is typical.

When David's palace was dedicated and our Royal Epic was performed, I was shocked by the story of Lot and the destruction of Sodom. Each evening after the day's performance a discussion group of family and friends met in our home for good food and good talk. On the evening after the story of Lot was performed, the women in our group were angry. We asked why that story was included in our epic. It contained one scene in which a mob gathered outside of Lot's house; the mob wanted to rape the two men who were Lot's guests. According to the rules of hospitality, Lot was obligated to keep his guests from harm. In this situation Lot offered the mob his two virgin daughters to spare his guests. The laws of hospitality, which were also observed by the ancient Job, were more important than Lot's daughters.

"The minstrels say that the people love the story and its sequel about Mrs. Lot, and why she became a pillar of salt," said Jonathan. Elishama was quick to agree with him.

I said, "We know that in an epic you must deal with the people's stories, but with a little more thought on your part concerning your views on the equality of men and women, you could have excluded this story. You should have excluded it even if the minstrels threatened to put it in their performance. After all you have read the second creation story."

And Jonathan answered, "Even when one knows better that knowledge does not always attend the decision-making process. I regret our hurried decision."

The equality of men and women, which we see in the second creation story, is a minority opinion that we live by in our home, but for most this idea does not exist. The majority is conservative and orthodox, and they will guard their opinion and keep women "in their place."

Two

The Question of Prayer

Among our people prayer is thought to be important and helpful. Based on a belief that God is personal, it may be helpful for some people. However as we look around and notice the poor and the homeless, it seems that their prayers are never answered. Jonathan has addressed this problem in one part of his poem on Job:

> From the city the dying groan,
> And a person with wounds cries out,
> Yet Eloah does not pay attention to prayer.
> (Job 24:12)

Granted, this is a minority opinion, but we consider it to be valid, born out by observation. Further, we think the poor deserve to be heard.

There is prayer that is hideous in comparison to the cries of the poor. The "righteous" among us, who tell us to pray, exhibit their humility. "We are mere worms and maggots," they say, while at the same time they stress their importance by calling on the creator to pay attention to their personal needs. The "righteous" become the center of the ordered world. We have one suggestion to stop such prayer. Do not speak to God unless he speaks to you.

Note the silence.

Three

Divine Parents

When the human beings began to multiply,
upon the face of the ground,
and daughters were born to them,
the sons of the gods saw that the daughters
of the human beings were beautiful,
they took for themselves wives from any of those they chose.
Yahweh said:
 "My spirit can not be bottled up in human beings forever,
 In as much as, they are flesh.
 Their days will be a hundred and twenty years."
The Nephilim were on earth in those days, and afterwards,
for the sons of the gods did mate with the daughters of the humans;
they bore [children] to them—
they were the heroes of old,
the men of renown.

(Gen 6:1-4)

Jonathan and I have always appreciated this text, because it says that even the heroes are mortal. This is also the case with the Babylonian hero, Gilgamesh, who was two-thirds divine but mortal (the math escapes me). However, we do not agree with the majority opinion that says if you are a hero, one of your parents was divine. The majority also makes this claim for Isaac:

> Yahweh visited Sarah as he had said;
> Yahweh did to Sarah as he had spoken.
> Sarah became pregnant; . . .
>
> (Gen 21:1-2a)

In our world, the majority believes that the mother is the only obvious parent. The father does not want to claim the below average or deformed child; perhaps the mother was impregnated by some evil god. This being the case, he cannot claim the hero or the renown, who was surely fathered by a god. I suppose the father could claim the average child. This view does not make any sense to us.

Our minority opinion would suggest that education, character, time and circumstance have much to do with shaping a hero's life. People can learn and think. We do not have to give human achievement to the gods. And what of the handicapped among us? Why should one say that one parent was an evil god? Magon has told us that there is a Sumerian story supporting such a view, but the same story makes a place in society for such people to live and perform a service. One interesting example concerns the one who is born blind. The Sumerian god Enki said that this one should excel in music. It is interesting that scribes have thought about such problems, but in our opinion, we are the ones, not Enki, who should make a place for the handicapped among us, and we should admit that we do not know why such things happen.

Four

No Surrogates

I remember the evening when father, Jonathan, and I planned our wedding. We were sitting around our table, and Jonathan with a serious look on his face told father that he would need a marriage contract. He wanted the marriage contract to name the surrogate who would have our babies if I were barren. He added that Jacob had such a contract from Laban. Leah's surrogate was Zilpah and Rachel's surrogate was Bilhah. He said that this was all according to our traditions. Also he told us that other countries had the same legal traditions, for example, the city-state of Nuzu.

In response, I said: "You had better be joking, because I'm not living in the past. As members of the minority, we will be living in the future. I come without dowry, and I'll have the babies, if there are babies. I'm starting new traditions."

We laughed and had a good time. By the end of the evening we had decided that there would be no marriage contract. Instead Jonathan would write a love song for me. We were having fun, but there is an important issue here. Most families in Jerusalem would not joke about such things. We are aware that the more important minority opinion in this case has to do with our view of tradition. Tradition is helpful, because from it we gain a sense of our identity. But if one part of our identity has to do with openness to change then tradition must not be allowed to stifle our freedom.

Five

The Fear of the Lord

Among the majority of the scribes, the fear of God, the Lord, or Yahweh is the beginning of wisdom or can be equated with wisdom. The ancient Job is described as "one who feared Elohim and avoided evil." This majority view is not difficult to hold. After all when David took Bathsheba and had her husband, Uriah, killed, the prophet Nathan said that their child should die. Also in the story of Judah, Yahweh killed Judah's first two sons. If Yahweh is like that, he is a God to fear. Likewise the God in the ancient story of Job is to be feared. On this last point Jonathan has recently found a poem by one who supports the ancient story of Job. Jonathan has created a poem denying any truth in the story of the old Job, and now this new poet has written one to uphold the old Job. It summarizes the old story and its basic teaching. The point of view is not good, but the poetry is actually rather nice. Here is the poem that Jonathan calls, "Where Can Wisdom Be Found?"

> Yes, there is a smelter for silver,
> And a place where they refine gold.
> Iron is taken from ore,
> And stone produces copper.
>
> [Man] made an end to darkness,
> And to every end he searches
> [For] dark and gloomy rock.
> Foreign people broke shafts,
> [Shafts] forgotten by pathways,
> They hung; [far] from men they swayed.
> Earth, food comes from her,
> And under her, it was changed by fire.
> Her stones are [the] source of sapphire,
> And particles of gold are in them.
> [The] path no raptor has known,
> And [the] falcon's eye has not seen it.
> [The] proud beasts have not used it;
> [The] lion has not come upon it.
>
> [Man] put his hand into the flint;
> He overturned mountains from [the] root.
> In the rocks he hewed out channels,
> And his eye saw every precious thing.
> [The] sources of the rivers he stopped,
> And hidden things he brought to light.
>
> And wisdom, where can she be found?
> And where is [the] place of understanding?

Man does not know her dwelling,
And she cannot be found in the land of the living.
[The] Deep said, "She is not with me,"
And [the] Sea said, "Not with me."
Fine gold cannot be given for her,
And silver cannot be weighed out [as] her price.
She cannot be purchased with the gold of Ophir,
With precious onyx or sapphire.
Gold and glass cannot equal her,
Nor vessels of fine gold be her exchange.
Coral or crystal will not be mentioned;
[The] endurance of wisdom surpasses rubies.
The topaz of Ethiopia cannot equal her;
She cannot be purchased with pure gold.

And wisdom, from where does she come?
And where is [the] place of understanding?
She is concealed from [the] eyes of all living;
From the birds of the heavens she is hidden.
Abbadon and Death said,
"With our ears we have heard a rumor of her."
Elohim has understood her way,
And he has known her place.
For he looks to the ends of the earth;
He sees everything under the heavens:
Giving weight to the wind
He measured the waters with a measure.
When he made a channel for the rain
And a path for the thundershower,
Then he saw her, and he evaluated her;
He established her, and he tested her.
He said to Adam,
"See, the fear of the Lord that is wisdom,
And to turn from evil is understanding."

(Job 28:1-28)

This poem makes wisdom so remote and unobtainable that a mere human does not have a chance of finding it. Certainly, human skill has nothing to do with wisdom, and of course it cannot be purchased. It is only God who knows wisdom, and the human who fears god is also "wise" or at least smart and religious.

My father, Jonathan and I have always had a different opinion concerning the nature of God. We don't know much about him. Perhaps he ordered this not-so-perfect world and made life possible for us, but there is no need to fear such a God and to do so hardly would seem to be the beginning of wisdom. For us wisdom is born of understanding based on observation. Note one of our favorite accounts of the birth of a proverb:

> I passed by the field of a lazy man,
> And by the vineyard of a senseless man.
> Here, thorns climbed up all over them.
> Its surface was covered with weeds,
> And its stone wall was broken down.
> I observed; I took it to heart.
> I saw; I studied [this] lesson:
> A few naps, a few drowsy times,
> A few times of folding the hands to rest,
> And your poverty will come marching on,
> Even as a [charging] warrior your dire straits.
>   (Proverbs 24:30-34)

Here the sage has learned something about "poverty" or "dire straits." The lazy farmer will have nothing. But the important thing to note is the method of the sage. The sage observes and studies. We suggest that the conclusion is exaggerated, because the sages also talk about the need to enjoy one's work and to rest (this is true for all of us, the humans and the other animals as well). In fact we have another proverb that says:

> The fool is one who folds his hands
> And the one who devours his flesh.
> Better is one handful of rest
> Than two handfuls of labor and [the] pursuit of
>   wind.

(Eccl 4:5-6)

Once again our view is that wisdom is the result of observation and study. It does not come from the fear of the Lord.

Six

The Word of God

In our stories and ancient traditions God speaks to many of our ancestors, such as Abraham and of course Moses. But I remember from many conversations with my father, Jonathan, and Ahban comments like: why is it that God always speaks to the ancients but never to us? Ahban gave a short poem to father, and it made the same point.

> To the ancients, came God's word;
> In the present, there's no word.
> Yes. He spoke to Samuel,
> But then only a few words,
> And to King Saul, not a word.

Ahban and father were talking about how easily we ascribe greatness to the past while making the present rather dull. We forget that the present is our opportunity to make a real difference. After reading Ahban's verse Jonathan said, "We must give the past its due, but we must also rethink everything in the present if our thought is going to make a difference. Most of us are not bold enough or certain enough to stand by our best thinking."

Father said, "It empowers a prophet to claim that his 'best thinking' is a word from God, but after David dismissed me, I decided to never make such a claim. I like to solve problems, and if the solutions are helpful, that is enough. We will always have people who claim that God spoke to them. I cannot say that their claim is false, but my best thinking says to me, 'Don't believe it.'"

In light of several years of such conversation and thinking, we have decided that "the word of God" should remain in the past. It certainly is not a part of our experience. Many of our fellow human beings know all about God, and they know exactly what he wants them to do. But we do not know such things, and we have a suspicion that their God does not exist. Nevertheless, we think it is important to love and to care for others. We need to do those things that a loving father would want us to do if he spoke to us. I would like to use one of Ahban's stories to make this point.

When he was young, he journeyed to Egypt and was gone for about two years. His father had built for his family a wonderful house, and he had well kept vines and olive trees. But after many years his health was bad. Just before Ahban left on his trip his father said, "If I am not alive when you return, I want you to know that you have my blessing."

Ahban said, "Though I did not know it, my father died a few weeks after I left for Egypt. During my stay in Egypt, I encountered many problems, but I knew what to do. Why? Because I had my father's blessing, and I knew how he cared for us, for his fields, and for others. He was no longer alive, but I did not need a new word."

Humans have always wished for a clear word; many have claimed it. For us it is more important and interesting to attempt the creation of a better future. True, our world is not perfect and suffering is all around us, but it is our home. According to our story of the first human, we are here to guard it and care for it. That is the word we hold dear.

Seven

Humans and Beasts

We have already discussed the equality of men and women as human beings. We also believe that some of those same traditions emphasize the relationship between the humans and the beasts; they are all classified under one term: *nephesh hayyah* ("living being"). This does not mean that we cannot distinguish between the various types of animals. The human is different in many ways from the horse, but they are both valuable as separate parts of creation; they are both called *living beings*. Our views on this subject are derived, once again, from our second creation story in the *Royal Epic*. Note the following:

> Yahweh-Elohim formed the human [from] the
>   clay of the ground;
> He blew into his nostrils the breath of life;
> The human became a *living being*.
>
> > (Genesis 2:7)
>
> Yahweh-Elohim formed from the ground all the
>   wild animals
> And all the birds of the heavens.
> He brought [them] to the human to see what he
>   called them,
> And whatever the human called each of the *living*
>   *beings*,
> That was its name.
>
> > (Genesis 2:19)

In this section of our epic it is clear that the human can see the differences among the creatures. It is also clear that the human cannot find one exactly like him for a mate. Therefore there has to be a special formation of the woman from the same substance as the man. Nevertheless, the humans (male and female) function within the framework of creation and with all living beings. This is important for us to remember, and this opinion has found a place in some of our traditions. The commandments that Moses gave include a commandment for the Sabbath. In that law the domestic animals are given rest just as the humans. The Sabbath is for all the *living beings*; it is for *all flesh*, to use a term from the flood story. After the flood Elohim says that the rainbow is a sign of his covenant. Then he says:

> I will remember my covenant that is between me
> And between you and between every *living being*
> among *all flesh*,
> And never again shall the waters become a flood
> to destroy *all flesh*.
> When the bow is in the clouds, I will see it,
> Remembering the eternal covenant between
> Elohim
> And between every *living being* among *all flesh* that
> is upon the earth.
>   (Genesis 9:15-16)

I like this entry, but not many people pay any attention to such things. They don't really consider the livestock as a part of our community; they would rather listen to one of our psalms, which makes the majority opinion:

> What is man that you remember him,
> And [the] son of man that you visit him?
> You have made him a little less than [the] gods,
> And [with] glory and honor you crown him.
> You make him ruler over the works of your hands;
> You put all things under his feet:

Small and large cattle, all of them, and even [the]
    wild beast,
[The] birds of [the] heavens, and the fish of the
    sea,
That travels [the] paths of [the] seas.

(Psalm 8:5-9)

Eight

Free and Eloquent Speech

Khety inspired this minority opinion. After the public debate about Jonathan's Job poem, we were at Sheva and Sarah's party. Khety urged Jonathan to publish his poem even with all of the opposition. He was speaking to Jonathan, but soon everyone was listening to what he said about free and eloquent speech. He spent most of his time talking about *The Eloquent Peasant.* This story was written about one thousand years ago, and it shows the importance of fine speech and points out the equality of a peasant with a lord or an official; both had the right to defend their interests with bold and effective speech. Khety added that this was a great moment for the people of Egypt, but later, Egypt was only interested in expanding its empire. Orderly conduct and devotion to the state became more important than the rights of individuals, and people were advised to be silent. Then he said, "This is a tragic story."

In *The Eloquent Peasant,* a poor man was robbed of the labor of his hands and imprisoned illegally. Since his wife and children were also in dire straits, he pleaded with the chief steward for the return of his goods. He needed to market them, and return to his family. After prolonging his prison stay in order to hear his great speeches, the peasant's goods were returned to him. Even the poor could speak up for their rights by means of true and perfect speech. It is important to have eloquent speech, but it even more important to have the freedom to express your thoughts in such speech. It appears that the majority of the ruling class and their officers, priests, and royal prophets are always ready to take away this freedom, which is so vital.

This is a different sort of minority opinion than we have discussed earlier. In other words, most minority opinions never become important in our lifetime, but here is an important majority opinion that soon became a minority opinion. At one time in Egypt, good speech and the freedom to use it equaled a great moment in its history. But soon the rulers took it away. Free speech became a minority position that only a few among the oppressed people dared to practice.

In our Royal Epic, it is said that Joseph had perfect speech:

> His brothers saw that their father loved him more
> than any of his brothers. They hated him, and
> they could not overcome his perfect speech.
>
> (Gen 37:4)

Joseph needed such speech when he was in prison. He used it again when he became a ruler in Egypt. I wonder if the Joseph story was told as if the days of the eloquent peasant were still in tact during Joseph's time? Or was Joseph rewarded not for his speech but for his skill in dealing with dreams?

It is interesting that David has allowed Jonathan to speak, but he did not like it when, Gad, my father, spoke his mind. David dismissed father from his position as a prophet in the administration. The freedom of speech must be guarded at all times. We do not want to lose it and be forced to say what Khety had to say, "This is a tragic story."

Nine

On Being Mortal

Most of the great literature in our part of the world teaches that human beings are mortal. Death is real. This is certainly the case for the Babylonians. Gilgamesh searches for eternal life but he does not find it. Also Adapa gives up any chance for eternal life. At Ugarit Aqhat, son of Danel, rejects an offer of eternal life from the goddess Anat. In our own Royal Epic, our first humans elected to be mortal in order to have all knowledge, and our flood hero or Noah remains mortal unlike the Babylonian flood hero, Utnapishtim and his wife. So in our literature this seems to be the majority opinion: humans are mortal.

As I have said in my prologue, this is not the case in Egypt. In Egyptian texts it is clear that death is not real. Death is a door to a better life in the land of the "West." There you will have good food and a wonderful life. However in the Harpers' Songs we find a minority opinion; in these songs there is grave doubt and uncertainty concerning immortality. These Harpers are skeptical and suggest that that you should have a good time now. "Make holiday" is the word. We are also interested in *this* minority opinion coming from a land that celebrates immortality. Also it is interesting that some of these skeptical songs were carved on the tombs.

When Naam asked me why we called forth the names of our dead at the tombs if we believed that humans were mortal, I did not have a ready answer. In our stories we do talk about Sheol, the Pit, the Netherworld, and other such places where our dead reside. Does such talk also point to a kind of immortality even though it is dark and slimy? It is certainly different from the Egyptian "Land of the West." It is possible that many people think that when we call forth the names of the dead we are thinking in literal terms. But is this the case? In our funeral rituals when we "call forth" the names of our dead, our main purpose is to tell their stories. We do ask for blessings, but is it the dead who bless or is it God who blesses those who remember? Our actions have nothing in common with necromancy and the work of the witches. The witches, for a fee, bring up the spirits of the dead or the dead, and with their magic they ask about the future. The fact that king Saul had forbidden such activity is proof that there are people who visit the witches. In fact there is the persistent rumor that Saul visited the witch of En-dor shortly before his death.

Jonathan suggests that those who visit the witches and practice other forms of magic do not believe that human beings are mortal; they are close to the majority in Egypt. We stress that human beings are mortal and do not understand our tomb rituals to argue against mortality. We find that we agree with the minority opinion of the Harpers in Egypt. Mortals who accept death have a deep desire to enjoy life.

I close with this poem:

Life: A Precious Moment

Death is a destructive reality.
We mourn the loss of a beautiful mind,
Of wisdom and friendship of every kind.
Even for happy souls there is a cloud,
A dark reminder of our brevity.

Our world will not miss us; perhaps our kin?
But we'll miss out on the future of all.
The human and Eve wanted all knowledge;
They gave up immortality to know,
And what they gave us was freedom to know.

Their gift makes our moment interesting.
But can we enjoy a precious moment?

It cannot be detained or extended;
It can be savored but note: not for long.
It is "swifter than a weaver's shuttle."

A popular fantasy says, "Fear God!
Fear God and live," but death is all around.
The rebel Job said, "There is no justice."
We must face this to enjoy our moment
And with love share our small accomplishments.

Our youth is our prologue that seems so long,
But soon enough our story takes its shape.
Joy, work, love, and suffering find their place.
Then we need to set our house in order.
Our epilogue seems long, our final song.

Ten

Storing up Punishment for Children

In Jonathan's Job poem, he argues against the three righteous 'friends,' who claim that God will punish the wicked. Jonathan's Job says that this is not the case, and he asks:

Why do the wicked live on?
They have grown old;
They have even become wealthy.
Their seed has been established in their presence
    with them
And their offspring before their eyes.
Their houses are safe from fear,
And the rod of Eloah is not upon them.
His bull has bred and never fails;
His cow calves and never aborts.
They send out their young ones as a flock,
And their children dance about.
They take up the timbrel and harp,

And they rejoice at [the] sound of [the] flute.
They finish their days with good times,
And in a moment they go down to Sheol.
They said to El, 'Depart from us;
The knowledge of your ways, we have not desired.
What is Shaddai that we should serve him,
And what do we profit when we encounter him?'

. . .

[You say,] 'Eloah stores up punishment for his
    children;'
He should pay him that he might know.
Let his eyes see his destruction,
And let him drink the wrath of Shaddai.
For what does he care about his house after him,
When the number of his months has been cut off?
(Job 21:7-21)

Here the wicked are portrayed as doing just fine. But the righteous answer in the last section of this quote, "Eloah stores up punishment for his children." Job's answer is that God should pay the sinner; he should "drink the wrath of Shaddai!" Job knows that the wicked are not punished by God, and their answer is an evasion based on one of our old legal traditions. In this tradition God is warning the people not to worship images. Then he says:

You shall not bow down to them or serve them,
For I, Yahweh your God, am a jealous God.
One who visits [the] sins of the ancestors upon
    [the] children,
Upon the third and upon the fourth [generations]
Of those who reject me,
And one who keeps covenant love with thousands,
Who love me and keep my commandments.
(Exodus 20:5-6)

This old legal tradition is the majority opinion and resides in the tradition of Moses, but that does not make it correct in the eyes of Job. He asked, "Why do the wicked live on," and prosper? He was expecting the answer, "Eloah stores up punishment for his children," and he got it. Anything to delay the truth!

The minority opinion in this case would emphasize that the wicked live on, because they are powerful. Of course we all have to live with the consequences of some of our actions, but it does not follow that there is any justice. God cannot manage it; the God of the righteous "friends' is helpless and absent, and if he plans to punish the children for the sins of their parents, he is cruel. When we say that there is no justice, we are not just saying that things are unfair. Rather we are saying that our leaders and their God cannot provide justice, and our world is not a person who rewards or brings punishment.

Eleven

The Treatment of Enemies

We have a proverb that says:

> Do not say, "As he did to me so I will do to him;
> I will pay back the man for what he has done."
> (Proverbs 24:29)

The majority would say, "pay him back," but we agree with the proverb.

Magon gave me a Babylonian text that is similar:

> Do not return evil to your enemy;
> Pay with kindness your evildoer,
> Preserve justice for your enemy,
> Be pleasant to your adversary.
> (For this text see "Afterword")

This is certainly a minority opinion. Even if there is a minority that would agree with these words, *could they practice them?* I make no claims in this area. We have enemies, and it is difficult to be pleasant to them. However it is probably wise to think on these words.

The results of not paying your enemy back could be far-reaching. It is possible that your enemy would be so confused by your unexpected actions or lack of action that the confusion could lead to conversation. The conversation could address past misunderstandings. Perhaps not, but it is worth a try.

Twelve

Royal Editing

When we published our *Royal Epic*, Part I, Jonathan knew that sooner or later a royal priest would alter some of its most important parts. In fact, Abiathar warned him that he would change the seven-day creation story to a six-day story. He did it, and he created confusion. After he changed the "seven" to "six," he left the line "Elohim finished on the seventh day his work that he had been doing." Abiathar changed the story in order to allow Elohim to keep the Sabbath. If he felt that he had to change it, he should have been careful; he changed order into chaos.

In our recent past, there is a tragic example of royal editing. David ordered the removal of the writings of Ahban from our library, and whenever he was mentioned in our chronicles, his name was to be changed to Ahithophel. Ahban was the sage in our school, a "brother of understanding," yet the administration saw him as a "brother of reproach." The majority opinion of these kinds of changes goes along with the royal view. The minority opinion has not been able to change matters, but in recent years we have won a few converts.

The royal editing of Jonathan's poem on Job has been subtle. David has allowed him to speak on this subject, to read it in public, and helped in arranging the debate, but he published it with royal editing. The editors were careful not to change the text that they published, but they did leave out some things. Then they buried Jonathan's poem in the confused rubble of *Job I* and *The Speeches of Elihu*. David can now claim a willingness to publish Jonathan's work, but he has buried it. It will never exist in the land of the living. Anything that is published with royal editing is not an example of free speech.

Jonathan is not a prophet, but this is his prediction. In the future, priests or scribes will attempt to soften the language of the rebel Job; they will make him more like *Job I*. In some places they will be able to do this without changing the ambiguous oral text. At one point the rebel says, "So he will kill me; I have *no* hope. / Yet, I will argue my case to his face." (Job 13:15) In the first line we have the negative *lo'*. But if you read *lo* it would not be a negative but would mean "him." Both readings would sound the same but mean the opposite. Hence one could understand it as: "Though he slay me, yet will I trust *him*, / but I will maintain my own ways before him." If anyone looked at the written text, this change would be impossible. The point is this: they will try to change the rebel into one of their own.

If we are interested in publishing our minority opinions, we will have to publish them ourselves, and hope that we can get them out to many others. This will be the difficult part of our task.

Thirteen

There Is No Justice

This has been a central theme in my entries and in our story. It is also the main thrust of Jonathan's poem concerning the rebel Job, and it is the point that makes our orthodox and fundamentalist enemies angry. At the risk of repeating myself, I would like to stress the importance of this position; though it is has fewer adherents than other minority opinions. The key lines for the rebel Job come at a low point in his argument; he seems to be close to death.

> So, I cry, "Violence," and I am not answered;
> I cry for help and there is no justice.
>
> (Job 19:7)

These are not the words of spoiled children who are whining because their feelings are hurt. Rather, the rebel Job has suffered every possible disaster, and why? There is no answer and no justice. When I lose something, it is an exasperating experience. This is true even if the lost item has little value. I look for it; I go back to the last place that I saw it or was using it. This experience can put me in a bad mood, but how much worse is the experience of looking for something that you never had and that does not exist. I am talking about justice; justice is pure fantasy. At one point in our discussions Jonathan said, "There is no justice from the God of the pious or from our leaders; they are not able to provide it. There is no justice from the powerful who oppress the poor, the orphan and the widow, and our world does not judge. Our world is a place where life is possible for a brief moment."

We know almost nothing about God. In our stories about the beginning, we seem to need one who ordered chaos, but it is clear that this God has never been all-powerful. The pious make such claims for their God, but it is obvious that what evidence we have argues against their claims. Those who are religious, that is, the ones who fear God, are not protected; they also suffer. This situation should not cause us to create some fantasy about justice at some future time. Rather it demands a reality check. I sometimes compare it to my role as a mother. Yes, I have wondered if it was right to bring my children into this world of suffering and death. I do not have the power to protect them at all times or to make them happy, but I can love them and help them. Nothing is guaranteed, but so far we have had our moments of joy. It has not been all sadness. Also the children feel that they can participate in our task of bringing a minority voice to future generations.

In this situation human beings are called to help each other. There needs to be a lot of understanding and love. When we helped the gleaners, whose children were on the verge of starvation, we did not bring them justice. They will never have that. We helped them for the present. We brought them food. We tried to practice that which exists in our legal traditions; we tried to do the right thing for these poor people, and it was not for any reward in the future or for now. If we can help others, perhaps we can build a community that can have more moments of joy. As the Egyptian Harpers say, "Make holiday."

Fourteen

Jonathan's Job Poem or Job II
A Debate between the Rebel and the Righteous
(Job 3-26)

Introduction

I am a scribe and a poet. For many years, I have disliked and argued against the ancient story of Job. The idea that the righteous are rewarded and that sinners are punished is not true. The question of suffering has been important in Babylonian and Egyptian texts, but it seems that this question is never solved or answered. Our ancient story is no better, in fact it is worse. At least in the Babylonian traditions there was some argument against the traditional answers. This being the case, I want to write a poem in the form of a debate, and I hope to show that our old story of Job is false. The old story informs the reader why Job suffered; God was testing Job, but Job does not know.

The righteous in my poem think they know why Job suffers, but my Job does not know why and neither do my readers.

Prologue

There was a man in the land of Uz; his name was Job. He was wealthy; he had a good wife, seven sons, and three daughters. One day a messenger brought the following message: The Sabeans took your oxen and donkeys; they killed your plowmen. Lightning burned your flocks and shepherds. The Chaldeans took your camels; they killed your servants. And a great wind destroyed your house and killed your children. This was not enough. After Job had lost everything, Job was afflicted with horrible sores from the sole of his foot to his head.

His wife said to him:

> "Curse God, and we will hold a funeral for our children.

Job said to her:

> "You speak as one of the wise women might talk. Should we, indeed, accept all of the evil with no explanation? In any case we must bury the children. We will bury them, call forth their names, and tell their stories."

"The three friends of Job heard of all this evil that had come upon him. They came each from his place, Eliphaz the Temanite, Bildad the Shuhite, and Zophar the Naamathite. They arranged together to go to console him and to comfort him. They lifted up their eyes from afar; they did not recognize him; they lifted up their voices; they wept. Each one tore his robe. They threw dust heavenward upon their heads. They sat with him on the earth, seven days and seven nights. No one spoke a word for they saw that the suffering was very great." (Job 2:11-13)

During these seven days Job and his wife did hold the funeral ritual for their children. The three friends said nothing, but they were confused. They were confused, because they could tell that Job and his wife were so angry; they did not fear God. When Job began to speak, their confusion turned to shock.

Afterward Job opened his mouth; he cursed his day.

Job answered; he said:
"Perish the day on which I was born;
The night that said, 'A hero is conceived.'
That day, let it be pitch-black.
May Eloah from above not find it,
And light not shine upon it.
May darkness and the shadow of Mot claim it;
May a cloud settle over it.
May the deep glooms of day terrify it.
That night, may gloom take it.
Do not count it among the days of the year;
Within the number of months, it shall not enter.
As for that night, may it be barren,
A joyful sound shall not enter in it.
Let those who curse Yamm, damn it,
Those skilled in arousing Leviathan.
May its twilight stars be dark,
Let it hope for light [where] there is none
And not see the eyes of dawn,
For it did not close the doors of my [mother's]
    womb,
Nor hide trouble from my eyes.

Why did I not die from [the] womb,
Or expire [when] I came out from [the] belly?

Why did knees receive me,
Or why breasts that I could nurse?
For by now, I would have lain down; I would be quiet;
I would have been asleep; then I would be at rest,
With kings and counselors of the netherworld,
The ones who built for themselves ruins,
Or with princes who had gold,
The ones who filled their houses [with] silver.
Or [why] was I not like a buried stillborn infant,
Like babies who never saw light?

There rascals cease turmoil,
And there, the weary are at rest.
Together, prisoners are at ease;
They do not hear the voice of the taskmaster.
There small and great are the same,
And a slave is free from his master.

Why does he give light to [the] overworked
And life to those bitter to the core of being;
The ones who wait for Mot, but he is not [there];
They dig for him more than for treasure;
The ones who would rejoice [with] the gods of a
     grave;
They would gladly discover a tomb,
For a hero whose way is hidden,
Whom Eloah has protected?

In place of my food comes my sighs;
My groans are poured out as water.
That dread that I dreaded has come upon me,
And that which I feared comes to me.
I was not at ease,
And I had no quiet,
And I had no rest;
Turmoil engulfed [me]."

(Job 3)

Eliphaz the Temanite answered; he said:
"If one attempts a word with you, could you
handle it?
But who is able to restrain words?
Note! You have instructed many,
And you have strengthened fistless hands.
Your words have given support to one who
stumbles,
And you have strengthened failing knees.
Now, when it comes to you, you are impatient.
It touches you; you are terrified.
Is not your fear your confidence
And the integrity of your ways your hope?
Remember now, who of the innocent has ever
perished,
Or where have the righteous been destroyed?
As I have seen, those who plow evil
And who sow trouble, they will reap the same.
From the breath of Eloah they perish,
And from the wind of his nostrils they are
destroyed.
A roar of a lion and a growl of an angry lion,
And teeth of young lions were broken.
A lion perishes without prey,
And cubs of a lioness are scattered.

A word came to me as a thief [in the night];
My ear caught a whisper of it.
From wild thoughts, from visions of [the] night,
When deep sleep falls upon humans,
Fear fell upon me and trembling,
And most of my bones were filled with dread,
And a wind was blowing over my face;
The hair of my body was standing up.
It was standing still, but I could not discern its
appearance.

A form before my eyes, a whisper, and I heard a
   voice:
'Can a man be made righteous by Eloah?
Or can a hero be made pure by his Maker?
If he cannot trust his servants
And charges his angels with error,
How much the less those who dwell in houses of
   clay,
Whose foundation is in the dust,
Who are crushed before a moth.
From morning to evening they are crushed;
Without accomplishment they perish forever.
Is not their tent cord pulled up with them?
They die and not with wisdom.'

(Job 4)

Please call out. Is there anyone to answer you?
To whom of the holy ones will you turn?
For anger kills a fool;
And passion slays a simpleton.
I myself have observed a fool taking root;
Suddenly I cursed his home:
May his children be far from prosperity;
May they be oppressed in the gate with no one to
   help;
May the hungry consume his harvest,
Taking it from the thorns,
And [the] thirsty gasp for their strength.
Yes! Evil does not come up from dirt,
And trouble does not sprout from the ground.
Yes! Humanity is born for trouble,
And the sons of Resheph go flying high.

But, I myself, I would seek El,
And before Elohim, I would place my case,
Who does great deeds and none can be fathomed,

Wonders beyond number;
Who gives rain upon the face of the earth,
And sends water upon the face of the land;
Who raises the lowly on high,
And mourners are lifted to safety;
Who thwarts the plots of [the] crafty,
And their hands cannot achieve success;
Who catches [the] wise in their craftiness,
And the counsel of twisted minds evaporates?
By day, they meet darkness,
And as in the night, they grope at noon.
He saved the needy from the sword of their mouth
And from the hand of the strong;
There was hope for the poor,
And injustice shut its mouth.

Indeed, fortunate is the man whom Eloah corrects;
Do not reject the discipline of Shaddai.
Yes, he injures, and he treats;
He wounds, and his hands heal.
From six troubles he shall rescue you,
And in seven, evil shall not touch you.
In famine, he saves you from death,
In war, from the wielders of the sword.
From [the] scourge of [the] tongue, you shall be
    hidden,
And you shall have no fear of destruction that
    comes.
At destruction and at famine you shall laugh,
And from the beasts of the earth, you shall not fear.
For with the stones of the field is your covenant,
And the wild beasts shall be at peace with you.
You shall know that your tent is safe;
You shall visit your fold and miss nothing.
You shall know that your descendants are many;
Your progeny are like the grass of the earth.

You shall come in full vigor to [the] grave,
As a shock of grain is brought up in its time.
Here it is! We have investigated it; it is so!
Listen and you shall know it for yourself."

(Job 5)

Job answered; he said:
"O that my anger could be weighed
And together with my misery be put on the
     balances,
Right now, it would be heavier than the sand of
     the sea.
Therefore my words cry out vehemently.
For the arrows of Shaddai are within me,
Whose venom my spirit drinks;
The terrors of Eloah are arrayed against me.
Does a wild ass bray over grass?
Does a bull bellow over his fodder?
Can insipid [food] be eaten without salt?
Or is there flavor in slimy cheese?
My being has refused to touch [such things];
They are like the pollutions of my food.
Who will grant that my request will be fulfilled,
And will Eloah give [me] my hope?
May Eloah be pleased; may he crush me;
May he free his hand and cut me off.
That would be my comfort;
I would revel in unsparing pain,
For I did not conceal my words [against] the Holy
     One.
What is my strength that I should wait?
What end that I should prolong my being?
Or, is my strength [the] strength of stones?
Or, is my flesh bronze?
Or, has my help vanished within me,
And has success deserted me?

For the sick [there should be] loyalty from his
     friend,
Though he forsakes the fear of Shaddai.
My friends have been treacherous like a torrent,
Like a wadi of torrents, they pass away.
[Torrents] are dark with ice;
Snow covers them.
When they should flow, they are dried up;
When its hot, they disappear from their place.
Stream beds wind their way;
They go out in the waste, and they perish.
The caravans of Tema look;
The travelers of Sheba hope for them.
They are ashamed because of overconfidence;
They reached the place; they were confounded.
Thus you have become nothing.
You see terror; you are afraid.
Have I said, 'Give to me,
From your wealth, pay a bribe for me,
Rescue me from [the] hand of an enemy,
From [the] hand of evil men, redeem me'?
Teach me, and I will be silent;
Where am I wrong? Bring understanding to me.
How trenchant are [the] words of the upright!
How does reproof from you reprove?
You think to reprove [with] words,
But of wind are words of one who despairs.
Even over an orphan you would cast lots,
And you would bargain over you friend.
And now be pleased to face me;
I will not lie to your face.
Relent! Let there be no injustice!
Relent! My justification is in this.
Is there injustice on my tongue?
Can my palate not distinguish words?

                                        (Job 6)

Is not warfare [the lot] for man upon earth?
Are not his days like those of a hireling?
Like a slave who pants for shade,
And like a hireling who hopes for his wage,
So I have inherited for myself months of
    emptiness,
And miserable nights have been apportioned to
    me.
Whenever I lie down, I always think,
'When can I get up?'
But an evening always drags on,
And I am sated with tossing until dawn.
My flesh is now covered with maggots and lumps
    of dirt;
My skin has cracked; it is dripping [pus].
My days are swifter than a weaver's shuttle;
They are finished without hope.

Remember! My life is as wind;
My eye will not again see good.
The eye that looks for me will not see me;
Your eye will be on me, but I shall not be there.
A cloud is finished; it is gone.
So is the one who descends to Sheol;
That one will not ascend;
He does not return again to his house;
Nor will his place know him again.
I, moreover, will not restrain my mouth;
I will speak in the anguish of my spirit;
I will complain from the bitterness of my being.
Am I Yamm or Tannin,
That you set a guard over me?
Whenever I thought, 'My bed will comfort me;
My couch will ease my complaint,'
You would dismay me with dreams,
Terrify me with visions.

My being preferred suffocation,
Death more than my bones.
I despised [my life]; I will not live forever.
Let me be, for my days are a breath.
What are human beings that you make them so
    great,
Or that you pay attention to them?
You have visited them every morning;
Every moment you test them.
How long will you not turn your gaze from me?
Will you not let me alone till I swallow my spit?
Have I sinned? What am I doing to you, O watcher
    of humanity?
Why have you made me your target?
Am I, myself, a burden?
Why don't you lift my transgression,
And make my iniquity pass away?
For now, I shall lie down in dust,
And you will search for me, but I shall not be there."

                                                    (Job 7)

Bildad the Shuhite answered; he said:
"How long will you utter these [things]?
The words of your mouth are a mighty wind.
Does El pervert justice?
Does Shaddai pervert [the] right?
If your children have sinned against him,
He has sent them into the power of their
    transgression.
If you will search for El,
And from Shaddai seek mercy,
If you are pure and upright,
Now he will rouse himself for you;
He will restore your righteous dwelling.
Your beginning will seem a small thing;

Your end will be very prosperous.
So, ask an ancient generation,
And consider what their fathers discovered.
For we are of yesterday and do not know;
For our days on earth are a shadow.
Will they not teach you, tell you,
And bring forth words from their minds?

Does papyrus grow without a marsh,
Or a reed thrive without water?
While it is still green, not yet cut,
Before any other grass, it will wither.
Such is the way of all who forget El,
And [the] hope of [the] impious shall perish:
Whose confidence snaps,
Whose basis of trust is a spider's house.
He leans on his house, and it does not stand.
He grasps it, but it will not stay up.

He is moist before Shamesh,
And over his garden, his root spreads out.
His roots are interwoven over a pile of rocks;
A house of stones he visions.
If he is swallowed up from his place,
It will deny him: 'I have never seen you!'
Such are the joy[s] of his way,
And from another clod, they will grow.

So, El does not reject a perfect person,
Nor take the hand of evildoers.
He will yet fill your mouth with laughter,
And your lips with shouts of joy.
Your enemies will be dressed in shame,
And [the] tent of the wicked will be no more."

(Job 8)

Job answered; he said:

"Indeed I know that [the following] is so:

What human can be acquitted before El?

If one wanted to file a lawsuit with him,

He could not answer him once in a thousand.

[Of the] wise of mind and mighty in strength,

Who has provoked him? [Who] has remained
   healthy?

The one who overturns mountains,

And they do not know that in his anger he
   overturned them;

The one who shakes [the] earth from its place,

And her pillars tremble;

The one who commands the sun, and it does not
   rise;

He seals up [the] stars.

Who stretched out [the] heavens by himself,

And who trod on the back of Yamm.

Who made [the] Bear, Orion,

Pleiades, and the Chambers of Teman.

Who does great deeds which cannot be
   understood,

And wonders without number.

So, he passes me by, and I do not see [him];

He goes on, and I cannot perceive him.

Thus he despoils; who can stop him?

Who can say to him, 'What are you doing?'

Eloah will not turn back his anger;

The helpers of Rahab were prostrated beneath
   him.

Indeed, could I answer him,

Could I choose my words against him?

Him, though I am innocent, I could not answer;

I would be pleading for mercy from my judge.

If I summoned, [if] he answered me,

I do not believe that he would hear my voice.
He who would crush me with a storm,
He multiplies my wounds gratuitously.
He does not allow me to catch my breath,
But he stuffs me with bitterness.
If for strength, a mighty one is here;
If for judgment, who will summon me?
If I am right, my mouth would condemn me;
[Though] I am innocent; he has [already]
    declared me crooked.
I am innocent;
I do not know myself;
I loathe my life.
It is one. Therefore I said,
'He destroys [both] innocent and guilty.'
If a scourge suddenly kills,
He mocks [the] despair of the innocent.
Earth has been placed in [the] hand of [the]
    wicked;
The faces of her judges he covers.
If not, then who is he?

My days have been swifter than a runner;
They fled; they saw nothing good.
They have raced by like reed boats,
Like an eagle dives on prey.
If I say, 'I will forget my complaint;
I will change my face, and I will look cheerful,'
I remain in fear of all my pain;
I know that you will not acquit me.
I will be guilty.
Why should I work in vain?
If I washed myself with soap,
And I purified my palms with lye,
Then you would dip me in the pit [of slime],
And my clothes would abhor me.

For he is not a man, like me, whom I could answer,
'Let us come together in the trial.'
There is no arbiter between us
To lay his hand on us both.
Let him turn away his club from me,
Let his dread not terrify me,
[Then] I would speak, and I would not fear him.
But I am not so with him.

(Job 9)

My being is disgusted with my life;
I will give free rein to my complaint;
I will speak from the bitterness of my being.
I will say to Eloah, 'Do not condemn me;
Let me know for what you are charging me.
Does it seem good to you that you oppress,
That you despise the labor of your hands,
And on the counsel of [the] wicked you have
    beamed?
Do you have eyes of flesh?
Or do you see as a human sees?
Are your days like [the] days of a human?
Or are your years like [the] days of a hero?
That you seek out my iniquity,
And you search for my sin.
You know that I am not guilty,
And there is no one who can escape from your
    hand.

Your hands shaped me; they made me,
[Then] a complete turnaround, you have
    destroyed me.
Remember that you formed me as clay;
And you will return me to mud.
Did you not pour me out as milk,
And curdle me as cheese,

Clothe me [with] skin and flesh,
Knit me with bones and sinews?
Life and kindness you gave me;
And your visitations guarded my being.
These [things] you hid in your mind;
I knew that this was your way.
If I sinned, you were watching me;
From my iniquity, you would not clear me.
If I were guilty, woe is me;
If I were innocent, I could not lift my head,
Sated with shame and seeing my misery.
As a lion is bold, you stalk me;
You return; you show yourself wondrous against
    me.
You renew your witnesses against me;
You multiply your anger against me;
[Always] changes, but hardship [remains] with
    me.

Why did you bring me from the womb?
I would have expired;
Not an eye would have seen me.
That which I was not, I would have been;
From womb to tomb, I would have been carried.
Are not my days few? Desist!
Stand away from me, and let me smile a little
Before I go (and I will never return)
To the netherworld of darkness, to the shadow of
    Mot,
A netherworld of darkness like gloom,
The shadow of Mot and chaos;
[The netherworld] was brightened with gloom.'"
                    (Job 10)

Zophar the Naamathite answered; he said:
"Should a multitude of words not be answered?

Or should an articulate man be acquitted?
Should your idle talk silence men?
When you have mocked should no one be
    humiliated?
You have said, 'My doctrine is pure,
And I am clean in your eyes.'
But would that Eloah might speak,
Might open his lips against you.
He would tell you [the] secrets of wisdom,
For there are two sides to sound wisdom.
Know that Eloah forgets, for you, some of your
    iniquity.

Can you discover the hidden nature of Eloah,
Or can you discover the limits of Shaddai?
[The] heights of [the] heavens, what can you do?
Deeper than Sheol, how can you know?
Longer than [the] earth is its measure
And broader than Yamm.
If he should pass on, or imprison,
Or call an assembly, who can turn him back?
For he has known worthless men;
He has seen iniquity, and will he not understand?
An empty headed man will get understanding,
When the wild ass of the steppe is born domesticated.

If you had [only] redirected your mind,
If you had spread out your palms to him,
If you have iniquity in your hand, remove it,
And do not allow wrongdoing to dwell in your
    tents.
Then you will lift up your face without defect;
You will be firm, and you will not fear.
For you will forget trouble,
You will remember [it] as water that has flowed by.
Life will be brighter than noon;

Darkness will be like morning.
You will trust, because there is hope;
You will search for security [and] sleep well.
You will bed down, and no one will disturb.
Many will seek your favor.
[The] eyes of [the] wicked will fail;
A way of escape has been taken from them;
Their hope is the last breath of life."

(Job 11)

Job answered; he said:
"Indeed, you are [educated] people,
And with you wisdom will die.
But I have a mind even as you;
I am not less than you.
Who does not know such things as these?
A laughingstock to his friends, that is me.
He who called to Eloah; he answered him;
[He is] a perfect and righteous laughingstock.
For disaster is contemptuous in [the] thought of
    those at ease,
Prepared for those whose feet slip.
The tents of the violent are at ease,
And security belongs to those who enrage El,
Whom Eloah carried in his hand.
But indeed, ask please the domestic animals,
And they will teach you;
And the birds of the heavens, they will tell you.
Or speak to the earth, it will teach you.
And the fish of the sea will recount to you.
Who does not know among all of these,
That the hand of Eloah has done this?
[He] in whose hand are all living beings
And the spirit of all human flesh.
Does not [the] ear test words,
And the palate tastes its food?

Among [the] aged is there wisdom,
Or is there understanding in length of days?
With him is wisdom and might;
His are counsel and understanding.
If he tears down, it cannot be rebuilt.
He imprisons a person, and he cannot be set free.
If he withholds the waters, they dry up;
If he lets them go, they devastate [the] earth.
With him are strength and insight;
To him belong the deceived and the deceiver.
He makes counselors walk about disrobed,
And judges he drives mad.
[The] belt of kings he has loosened;
He bound a cloth on their loins.
He makes priests walk about disrobed,
And the well established he overturns.
He deprives [the] faithful of speech,
And [the] judgment of elders he takes away.
He has poured contempt on princes,
And has loosened [the] belt[s] of nobles.

He has revealed [the] mysteries from darkness;
He has brought to the light the shadow of Mot.
He has made the states great; he has destroyed
    them.
He has scattered the states; he has led them [away].
He has deprived the minds of the leaders of the
    people of the earth;
He has made them wander in chaos [with] no path.
They grope in darkness with no light;
He has made them stagger like the drunk.

(Job 12)

There, my eye has seen everything;
My ear has heard; it has understood.
I, even I, know that which you know;

I am not less than you.
Indeed, I want to speak to Shaddai;
I will be pleased to argue with El.
And indeed, you are the ones who cover up lies;
You all are worthless healers.
Who will insure that you are totally silent?
If [someone could], that would be wisdom for
    you.
Hear, now, my argument,
And attend the accusations of my lips.
Is it for El that you speak unjustly?
And for him will you speak deceitfully?
Will you declare El's innocence?
Or for El will you plead?
Will it be well when he examines you?
Or as one deceives a person, can you deceive him?
He will surely rebuke you,
If in secret you declare [him] innocent.
Will not his fear terrify you,
And his dread fall upon you?
Your arguments are slimy proverbs;
Your defenses are defenses of clay.

Be silent before me, and I will speak.
Let come upon me whatever.
I will take my flesh in my teeth,
And my being I will place in my palm.
So, he will kill me; I have no hope.
Yet, I will argue my case to his face.
Also, he could be my salvation,
For no impious one would come to his face.

Listen closely to my words,
And my declaration be in your ears.
There, now, I have arranged a just case.
I know that I am innocent.

Who is he who will contend with me?
For then I would keep silent and expire.

O El, do only two things for me,
Then from your face I will not hide.
Remove your palm from me,
And let your dread not fall upon me.
Summon me and I will answer,
Or let me speak, and you reply to me.
How many are my iniquities and sins?
Make known to me my transgression and my sin.
Why do you hide your face,
And count me as your enemy?
Will you terrify a driven leaf,
Or will you pursue dried up chaff?
For you write bitter things against me,
And you cause me to inherit the iniquities of my
    youth.
You put my feet in the stocks,
And you watch all my ways;
You put your mark on the soles of my feet.

He wastes away like a rotten thing,
Like a moth-eaten garment,

                                        (Job 13)

A human, born of woman,
Is of few days and sated with strife.
Like a flower that came forth; he withered;
Like a shadow, he fled, and he does not endure.
Indeed, on such a one you opened your eye;
And me, you bring into judgment with you.
Who can make a clean thing out of an unclean one?
Not one!
If his days are determined,

The number of his months with you,
You have set his limits, and he cannot exceed.
Turn from upon him, and he may rest,
Until he enjoys, as a hireling, his day.

Yes, there is hope for the tree;
If it is cut down, it will grow again,
And its young shoots will not cease.
Or, if its root grows old in the earth,
And in the dirt its stump dies,
At the scent of water, it will sprout,
And make branches like a plant.
When a hero dies, he has collapsed;
A human has expired, and where is he?
Waters from the sea have disappeared.
And a river dries up and is parched,
And a mortal has lain down, and he does not rise.
They wake not until there are no heavens,
And they rouse not from their sleep.

O that you would hide me in Sheol,
Conceal me until your anger passes,
Set for me a time, and remember me.
If a hero dies, will he live again?
All the days of my service, I will endure,
Until my relief comes.
You would call and I, I would answer,
For the work of your hands, you would long.
But now you number my steps;
You should not watch over my sins.
My transgression would be sealed in a parcel;
You would plaster over my iniquity.

But if a mountain falls, it collapses,
And a rock moves from its place.
Water has worn away stones,

Its torrents wash away earth's soil,
And you have destroyed man's hope.
You overpower him forever; he has gone.
You change his face; you have dismissed him.
His children receive honor, and he does not
  know,
And they become insignificant,
And he does not perceive them.
Only his own flesh pains him;
His own being mourns him."

                                        (Job 14)

Eliphaz the Temanite answered; he said:
"Does a wise one answer windy knowledge,
And does he fill his belly with an east wind?
Should he argue with speech that is not
  profitable,
And words in which there is no value?
Indeed you destroy religion,
And you do away with meditation before El.
For your iniquity instructs your mouth,
And you choose a crafty tongue.
Your mouth condemns you, not I,
And your lips testify against you.

Were you [the] first human born,
And were you brought forth before the hills?
Do you listen in the council of Eloah,
And do you limit wisdom to yourself?
What do you know that we do not know?
[What] do you understand that is not with us?
Even gray headed and aged are with us,
Older in days than your father.
Are the consolations of El too little for you,
And a gentle word with you?
What takes from you your mind,

And why are your eyes failing,
That you turn your wind against El;
You throw out a word from your mouth?
What is man that he can be pure,
And that he can be righteous, one born of woman?
Even his holy ones, he distrusts,
And the heavens are not pure in his eyes.
How then one who is abhorred and foul,
Man who drinks iniquity like water?

I will tell you, listen to me,
And what I have seen, I will declare,
What sages make known,
And their fathers did not conceal,
To whom alone the land was given,
And no alien passed among them.
[The] wicked writhes in pain all his days,
And few years have been stored up for the
    ruthless.
Dreadful sounds are in his ears;
When all is well, the enemy falls upon him.
He does not believe in returning from darkness,
And he is destined for the sword.
He wanders for food; where is it?
He has known that fixed in his hand is a day of
    darkness.
Distress and anguish terrifies him,
[Anguish] overpowers him
Like a king ready for attack,
Because he lifted his hand against El,
And against Shaddai he acts as a hero.
He charges at him with neck chains,
With the thick bosses of his shields,
For he has covered his face with his fat;
He has gained great muscle on [his] loins.
He has dwelt in ruined cities,

[In] houses, no one lives in them,
Which are ready for heaps of rubble.
He will not be rich, nor will his wealth endure,
Nor [his] possessions reach the netherworld.
He will not escape from darkness,
A flame will wither his shoot,
And he will depart from the breath of his mouth.
He should not trust in vanity, being misled;
For vanity will be his reward.
Before his time is complete,
His branch did not grow green.
He will ruin, like a vine, his unripe grapes;
And he will cast, like an olive tree, his blossom.
For an irreligious band is desolate,
And fire devours tents of bribery;
Pregnant with pain and giving birth to evil,
Their womb has produced deceit."

(Job 15)

Job answered; he said:
"I have heard many things like these;
Painful comforters are you all.
Is there a limit to windy words?
Or what afflicts you that you answer?
I too could speak like you,
If you were in my place.
I could string words together against you,
And I could shake my head at you.
[Or] I could strengthen you with my mouth;
The quivering of my lips would bring relief.
If I speak, my pain will not be relieved;
And if I desist, what departs from me?
But now he has exhausted me;
You have destroyed my entire community.
You have compressed me;
It has become a witness.

My leanness has risen against me;
It testifies to my face.
His anger has torn and assaulted me;
He has gnashed his teeth against me.
My enemy narrows his eyes at me.
They have opened wide their mouths against me;
They have slapped my cheeks with scorn;
Together they mass themselves against me.
El hands me over to [the] vicious,
And into the hands of the wicked he throws me.
I was at ease; he shattered me,
And he grabbed me by the neck; he broke me in
    pieces.
He set me up as his target.
His archers surround me;
He splits my kidneys; he shows no compassion;
He pours out my gall on the earth.
He slices me, slice upon slice;
He rushes against me like a warrior.
I have sewed sackcloth over my skin,
And I have thrust my horn in slime.
My face is reddened with weeping;
Upon my eyes is the shadow of Mot,
Although there is no violence on my palms,
And my prayer is pure.
O earth, cover not my blood,
And let there be no tomb for my outcry.
Even now, my witness is in the heavens;
And my witness is in the heights.
My interpreters, my friends,
To Eloah my eyes have cried,
And let him plead for a hero with Eloah,
[Like] a human for his friend.
For a number of years will come,
And the way of no return, I will go

                          (Job 16).

My spirit is broken;
My days are finished;
[The] tombs are for me.
Surely, the mounds are before me,
And in their slimy pits, my eye fixes its gaze.

Make a pledge for me with you!
Who is he who will strike my hand?
Since you have closed their mind from reason,
Therefore you must not exalt them.
He [who] informs on his friends for a reward,
The eyes of his children will fail.
He has made me a byword of the peoples,
And I exist for spitting in my face.
My eye was dimmed because of anguish,
And my body parts were all like a shadow.

[The] upright are astonished at this,
And [the] innocent are aroused against the
    impious,
And [the] righteous holds to his way,
And [the] clean-handed grows in strength.
But all of you return and come now,
And I will not find a wise one among you!

My days have passed,
My plans have been broken,
My mind's possessions.
They make night into day;
Light is near to the face of darkness.
If I wait for Sheol [as] my home,
In the dark I have covered my bed,
To the pit I have called forth, 'You are my father,'
To the maggot, 'My mother and my sister,'
Then where, where is my hope?
My hope, who can see it?

It will descend into the power of Sheol;
We shall rest in the slime together."
(Job 17)

Bildad the Shuhite answered; he said:
"How long will you set snares of words?
You should [all] be sensible, and afterward we
  could speak.
Why are we considered as domestic animals?
Deemed dull in your eyes?
One who tears himself in his anger,
Will earth be abandoned on your account,
[Or] a rock be moved from its place?

Indeed, [the] light of the wicked is extinguished,
And the flame of his fire does not shine.
[The] light in his tent became dark,
And his lamp above him is extinguished.
His strong strides are shortened,
And his own plan throws him down.
For he has been thrown by his feet into the net,
And he walks on a pit-fall.
A trap seizes [his] heel;
A snare lays hold on him.
His noose is hid on the earth,
And his trap is on [the] path.
On all sides terrors have fallen upon him;
They drive him to his feet.
Let his strength be famished,
And calamity is ready at his side.
He devours his skin with two hands,
The first-born of Mot with both his hands.
He is torn form his tent, his security,
And he is marched to the King of Terrors.
In his tent is set fire;
On his abode is scattered brimstone.

From below his roots dry up,
And from above his branch withers.
Memory of him has perished from [the] earth,
And he has no name upon the face of the land.
He shall drive him from light into darkness,
And he shall chase him from [this] world.
He has no offspring and no posterity among his
    people,
And there is no survivor in his old haunts.
On his [last] day, westerners were appalled,
And Easterners were seized with horror.
Surely these were the dwellings of [the] wicked,
And this is [the] place of one who did not know El."

                            (Job 18)

Job answered; he said:
"How long will you torment me
And crush me with words?
You humiliate me, this is ten times;
You are not ashamed; you abuse me.
And even if, truly, I have erred,
My error remains with me.
Though, truly, you are overbearing against me,
And you argue my disgrace against me.
Know then that Eloah has perverted me,
And he has thrown his net over me.
So, I cry, 'Violence,' and I am not answered;
I cry for help, and there is no justice.
He has blocked my way, and I cannot pass;
He has set darkness upon my paths.
He has stripped my honor from me;
He has removed the crown from my head.
He breaks me completely down; I am gone.
He has uprooted my hope like a tree.
He has kindled his anger against me;
He considers me as one of his foes.

His troops come in together;
They have built seigeworks against me;
They camped around my tent.
He has sent my confederates far from me,
And he has estranged my friends from me.
My relatives and intimates have gone;
The guests of my house have forgotten me,
And my maids consider me as a stranger;
I have become a foreigner in their eyes.
I summoned my slave, but he does not respond.
With my mouth I implore him.
My breath was offensive to my wife,
And I was loathsome to my own children.
Even urchins despised me;
If I would rise up, they spoke against me.
All the men of my association have abhorred me,
And those whom I have loved have turned against
        me.
My bones have stuck through my skin and my flesh;
I, myself, have escaped by the skin of my teeth.
Have pity on me, have pity on me, O you my
        friends,
For the hand of Eloah has struck me.
Why do you pursue me like El?
Are you not satisfied with my flesh?
O that my words would be written!
That they would be engraved on the stela;
With an iron stylus and lead,
They would be carved in rock as a witness.
But as for me, I know that my avenger lives;
And a guarantor by [my] grave will stand.
This, even after my skin has been peeled off,
And without my flesh, shall I see Eloah?
Whom shall I see who is for me?
My eyes saw no stranger.
My heart is destroyed in my bosom.

Because you say, 'How will we pursue him?'
(And [the] root of the matter is found in me.)
Fear for yourselves before the edge of the sword,
For these things are crimes [deserving the] sword,
So that you may know Shaddayan."

(Job 19)

Zophar the Naamathite answered; he said:
"Surely, my disquieting thoughts cause me to answer,
And because of my inner turmoil,
I listen to the rebuke that [creates] my shame,
So the spirit of my understanding replies to me.

Have you not known this from old,
Since a human was placed on earth,
That [the] triumph of [the] wicked is brief,
And [the] joy of [the] impious is for a moment?
If his pride reaches up to the heavens,
And his head touches the clouds,
He will perish forever like his own dung;
They who saw him will say, 'Where is he?'
Like a dream he will fly away, and they will not
    find him,
And he will flee like a vision of [the] night.
An eye that saw him will do so no more;
His place will not see him again.
His children will seek the favor of [the] poor,
And his hands return his wealth.
His skeleton was full of his youthfulness,
And with him it will lie down in the slime.
When evil is sweet in his mouth,
He hides it under his tongue,
He savors it, and he will not let it go,
And he retains it under his palate;
His food in his guts has been changed;
The venom of vipers is within him.

Wealth he swallowed; he disgorged it.
El expels it from his belly.
[The] venom of asps he shall suck;
[The] tongue of a viper shall slay him.
He shall see no streams:
Rivers [and] wadies of honey and yogurt.
He is the one who shall return his gain not consumed,
That is, the wealth of his trading, and he shall not
    rejoice.
Because he has he has crushed [and] forsook
    [the] poor,
[And] he has seized a house that he did not build,
Because he has not known ease in his belly,
In his greed, he does not allow [any] to escape.
There is nothing left for his meal,
Therefore his good times will not endure.
In the fullness of his plenty, he shall know distress;
Every powerful misery will come upon him.
He shall have his belly filled.
He shall send on him his burning anger,
And it shall rain down into his bowels.
He will flee from an iron weapon;
A bronze bow will pierce him.
He pulled; it came out from his back,
Lightning from his gall.
Terrors come upon him.
Complete darkness awaits his treasured ones,
An unfanned fire will consume him.
Who survives in his tent will be injured.
[The] heavens shall reveal his iniquity,
And the earth will rise up against him.
A flood shall roll away his house,
Torrents on the day of his wrath.
This is [the] lot of a wicked human from Elohim,
And [the] inheritance appointed him from El."

(Job 20)

Job answered; he said:
"Listen closely to my words,
And let this be your consolation.
Bear with me, and I will speak.
And after my speech, mock on.

Am I for humans [in] my complaint?
And if so, why should I not be impatient?
Look at me and be appalled,
And lay [your] hand upon [your] mouth.
Whenever I have remembered, I have been
    terrified;
My flesh is seized with shuddering.

Why do the wicked live on?
They have grown old;
They have even become wealthy.
Their seed has been established in their presence
    with them
And their offspring before their eyes.
Their houses are safe from fear,
And the rod of Eloah is not upon them.
His bull has bred and never fails;
His cow calves and never aborts.
They send out their young ones as a flock,
And their children dance about.
They take up the timbrel and harp,
And they rejoice at [the] sound of [the] flute.
They finish their days with good times,
And in a moment they go down to Sheol.
They said to El, 'Depart from us;
The knowledge of your ways, we have not desired.
What is Shaddai that we should serve him,
And what do we profit when we encounter him?'
So, is not their well being in their hand?
[The] counsel of [the] wicked is far from me.

How often is [the] lamp of [the] wicked put out,
Or does their calamity come upon them,
Or does he apportion pain in his anger?
Are they as stubble before the wind,
And as chaff [the] storm wind carried away?
[You say,] 'Eloah stores up punishment for his
    children;'
He should pay him that he might know.
Let his eyes see his destruction,
And let him drink the wrath of Shaddai.
For what does he care about his house after him,
When the number of his months has been cut off?
Does he teach knowledge to El,
Does he judge [the] highest?

One dies with perfect bones,
Wholly at ease and tranquil.
His vessels are full of milk,
And the marrow of his bones is moist.
And another dies a bitter person,
And he never tasted the good [life].
They lie together on the slime,
And worm[s] cover them.

Look, I have known your plans
And devices you are plotting against me.
For you say, 'Where is the royal house,
And where are [the] dwellings of [the] wicked?'
Have you not asked those who travel [the] road[s],
And do you not acknowledge their evidence,
That on the day of disaster [the] wicked is spared,
From the day of fury they are led forth?
Who will tell [him] to his face his way?
And who will pay him [for what] he has done?
So he is carried to the graves,
And upon [the] mound [one] guards.

[The] clods of [the] wadi were sweet to him,
And after him all humans will follow,
And before him [they are] innumerable.

So how can you comfort me with air?
And your answers have remained fraudulent."

                                        (Job 21)

Eliphaz the Temanite answered; he said:
"Can a man be of service to El,
Or a sage benefit him?
Is Shaddai pleased if you are righteous,
Or does he gain if you are perfect in your conduct?
Is it because of your piety he reproves you,
Enters into judgment with you?
Is not your wickedness great,
And your iniquities have no end?
Because you have taken a pledge from your
     brother unjustly,
And the clothing of the naked you have stripped.
You do not give the weary water to drink,
You withhold food from the hungry.
So a strong man owns the land,
And as one forgiven he dwells in it.
Widows you sent away empty,
And the arms of orphans are broken.
Therefore snares surround you,
And sudden dread frightens you.
Or darkness you will not see,
And a flood of waters covers you.

Is not Eloah [in the] height of [the] heavens?
And see [the] top of stars, for they have [always]
     been high.
You say, 'What does El know?
Can he judge through the dark cloud?

Clouds hide him, and he does not see,
And he walks around [the] circle of [the] heavens.'
Do you watch the perpetual path
That worthless men have walked
Who were snatched before [their] time,
A river washed away their foundation?
The ones who said to El, 'Depart from us,
What can Shaddai do for us?'
Yet he filled their houses [with] good!
So [the] counsel of [the] wicked is far from me.
[The] righteous see, and they rejoice,
And [the] innocent deride them:
'Surely their substance was destroyed,
And a fire consumed their surplus.'

Serve him and be complete;
In this, good will come to you.
Take instruction from his mouth,
And put his words in you mind.
If you return to Shaddai you will be restored;
You shall put iniquity far from your tent.
So, set on the mud [your] gold,
And on the rocks of the stream [your] Ophir.
Shaddai will be your gold
And a mountain of silver for you.
When you delight in Shaddai,
And lift up your face to Eloah,
You shall pray to him, and he will hear you,
And you shall fulfill your vows.
And you will decide something, and it will stand,
And on your path, light has shone.
When some sank down, you said, 'pride,'
For [the] humble, he will save.
He will deliver the guilty,
Who will be delivered by your clean hands."

(Job 22)

Job answered; he said:
"Even today my complaint is bitter,
[His] hand is heavy on account of my sighing.
O that I knew where to find him,
That I might come to his dwelling.
I would set [my] case before him,
And I would fill my mouth with arguments.
I would [like] to know [the] words he would
    answer me,
And I would understand what he would say to
    me.
Through an attorney would he prosecute me?
Surely not! He would charge me.
There [the] upright could reason with him;
I could bring forth my case to an enduring life.
Lo, I go east, and he is not there,
And west, and I cannot discern him.
North, in his work place, and I do not behold
    [him].
He hides in the south, and I do not see [him].
But he knew [the] way to me;
He tested me; I will emerge as gold.
My foot stays in his path;
His way I have kept, and I will not stray.
I will not depart from the command of his lips;
In my bosom I have treasured the words of his
    mouth.
But he is one; who can change him?
And his being has desired [something]; he has
    done it.
So, he will execute my sentence,
And many such things are with him.
Therefore I am dismayed before him;
I consider, and I am afraid of him.
El weakened my heart,
And Shaddai has terrified me.

For surely, I am annihilated by [the] faces of
    darkness,
And my face covered by dark gloom.

(Job 23)

Why are [the] times not treasured by Shaddai,
And [why] do those who know him not perceive
    his days?
They remove boundaries;
They have stolen flocks; they have pastured
    [them].
They drive away [the] donkey of [the] orphan;
They take the widow's ox for a pledge.
They push the needy from [the] road;
[The] poor of [the] land hide themselves together.
Like wild asses in the steppe,
They go out to their work,
Seeking hopefully for food;
Surely, [the] desert [yields] food for the young.
They harvest fodder in the field,
And they glean [the] vineyard of [the] wicked.
Naked they pass the night without clothing,
And they have no covering from the cold.
They are wet from [the] mountain rain,
And without shelter, they stay close to [the] rocks.

They snatch the orphan from the breast,
And they take the suckling of the poor as security.
Naked they go without clothing,
And hungry, they carry [the] sheaves.
Between their rows they press oil;
They have stomped [the] wine-vats;
They were thirsty.
From [the] city [the] dying groan,
And a person with wounds cries out.
Yet Eloah does not pay attention to prayer.

They, yes they, have been among those,
Who rebel [against the] light;
They have never known its ways,
And they have never dwelt in its paths.
At daylight [the] murderer arises;
He kills [the] poor and [the] needy,
And in the night he becomes like the thief.
[The] eye of the adulterer watches for twilight,
Saying, 'No eye will see me,'
And he puts a cover over [his] face.
In the dark such a one has dug into houses;
By day they shut themselves up;
They do not know [the] light.
Yes, it is the same for them, morning and deep
    darkness,
Yes, they are acquainted with the terrors of the
    shadow of Mot.

'Swift is he on the surface of the water;
Cursed is their portion in the earth,
He does not turn on [the] way to [the] vineyards.
Drought and heat steal [the] water of [the] snow,
[As does] Sheol those who have sinned.
[The] womb forgets him;
His sweetness is [the] worm;
He is remembered no more;
Injustice has been broken like a tree.'

He is the one, who feeds on the barren woman
    with no child,
And he does no good for [the] widow.
He has prolonged [the life of the] mighty with
    his power.
He arises but cannot believe in life.
He gives him security,
And he is sustained.

'But his eyes are on their ways.
They were exalted for a moment, but it is gone.
And like the head of grain, they wither.'

If it is not so, who will prove me a liar,
And make as nothing my words?"

(Job24)

Bildad the Shuhite answered; he said:
"Dominion and dread are with him;
He is the one who makes well being in his heights.
Is there a number to his troops,
And upon whom does his light not rise?
How can a man be righteous before El,
And how can one born of woman be pure?
Even [the] moon does not shine,
And [the] stars have not been pure in his eyes.
How much less a man, a worm.
And the son of Adam, a maggot."

(Job 25)

Job answered; he said:
"How have you helped [the] powerless?
Have you aided a weak arm?
How have you counseled [the] unwise,
Or made known wisdom to a multitude?
With whom have you uttered words,
Whose breath came forth from you?
The Raphaim writhe
Under the waters and their inhabitants.
Naked is Sheol before him,
And Abaddon has no covering.
He is the one who stretched out Zaphon over
    chaos;
He is the one who suspended the earth on
    nothing.

He is the one, who bound the waters in his clouds,
And a cloud does not break because of them.
He is the one who obscured [the] face of [the]
    full moon;
He spread over it his cloud.
He made a circle on the surface of [the] waters
As a boundary of light with darkness.
[The] pillars of [the] heavens tremble,
And they are astounded from his rebuke.
By his power he stilled the Sea;
By his cunning he smashed Rahab.
By his wind the heavens were cleared;
[By] his hand he pierced the fleeing Serpent.
Lo, these are just traces of his rule;
What a whisper of a word we hear from him;
Who can understand the thunder of his might?"

(Job 26)

Epilogue

Job expected Zophar to respond, but he did not say a word. Job had made his case; he was tired; he went back to the tomb where they had buried their children. His wife was there, and he sat down beside her. "So what do we do now?" Job asked his wife. "We have buried our children; we have lost everything. What do we do now?"

She answered; she said: "I have been thinking about what we should do, but first what happened in your long talk with your pious 'friends'?"

He answered; he said: "The whole thing was a heated debate. They thought that our loss was a sign of our sin. I said no! I told them that I would like to go to court with their God, even though I knew I would be defeated. Why? Because their God does not care about the cries of those who suffer. There is no justice in his court or any place, and in fact their God does not exist. Where is he? He is not to be found. They finally just quit; they could not answer. This does not mean that I could ever convince them. Their ears are filled with righteous wax, and they are probably praying for us. In my last words I did suggest that the one who conquered chaos did give us an ordered world, but 'What a whisper of a word we hear from him.'"

"She answered; she said: "What you have just said helps me, just a bit. Earlier you asked, 'What do we do now?' Well, we can moan; we can cry out; we can wish for death. But we can also remember our children, call forth their names at this tomb, and try to build new lives out of these ruins. I think we must avoid the night terrors when the God of the pious creeps into our dreams and marvel at the wonders of this world though it is also full of suffering. I am certain of one thing: it will take more than 'a whisper of a word;' there has to be between us a shout and a hopeful song of love and support."

(For this translation of *Job II* with Introduction and Notes [plus a translation of *Job I*] see Loren Fisher, *Who Hears the Cries of the Innocent*, Willits, CA: Fisher Publications, 2002 [available from Xlibris])

The Speeches of Elihu

(Job 32-37)

(These speeches are attributed to Elihu [perhaps the brother of David?], but they are based on the arguments of those who challenged Jonathan and his poem on Job. Thus they represent the 'majority opinion' with which we are surrounded. They represent an unfair, unreliable, dull, and senseless commentary on Jonathan's poem, but they help us to understand the nature of our opposition.)

Introduction

"These three men ceased answering Job, because from his viewpoint, he was right. The anger of Elihu, son of Barachel the Buzite of the clan of Ram, burned against Job; his anger burned, because [Job] made himself more right than Elohim. And against his three friends his anger burned, because they did not find an answer, they made [Elohim] guilty. So Elihu waited for Job with words for they were older than he. Elihu saw that there was no answer in the mouth of the three men; his anger burned." (Job 32:1-5)

Elihu, son of Barachel the Buzite, answered; he said:
"I am young in days, and you are old.

Therefore I feared; I was afraid
To make known my knowledge to you.
I said, 'Days should speak,
And many years ought to make known wisdom.
But it is [the] spirit in man,
And the breath of Shaddai that gives understanding.
[The] great ones do not give wisdom,
Nor do [the] elderly understand justice.'
Therefore I said, 'Listen to me.
I will make known my knowledge, even I.'

Here I have waited for your responses,
So that I could weigh your understandings,
Until you could search [for] words,
And until I could understand you.
But it was clear; Job did not have a judge;
Not one of you could answer his words.
You cannot say, 'We have found wisdom.
El will defeat him, not man,'
And he did not arrange words against me,
And with your words I will not refute him.

They have been broken; they cannot answer again.
Words have fled from them.
And I waited, because they did not speak,
For they stood; they did not answer again.
I will answer, even I, my portion;
I will make known my knowledge, even I.
For I am full of words.
The wind in my belly pushed me.
Therefore my belly is like unopened wine,
Like new [wine] skins it will break.
I will speak, and it will break wind from me.
I will open my lips, and I will answer.
Please note: I will not forgive a man,

And to a human I will not give a title.
For I do not know how I could give a title;
My maker would quickly carry me off."

(Job 32)

Elihu's First Speech

"So now, Job, hear my utterances,
And give ear to every one of my words.
Please note, I have opened my mouth;
My tongue has spoken from my palate.
My words are [from] an upright heart,
And my lips have spoken pure knowledge.
The wind of El made me,
And the breath of Shaddai gives me life.
If you are able, answer me.
Prepare! Take your position before me.
See, I am like El's vessel;
I, too, was nipped from clay.
So, my terror should not frighten you,
Nor should my pressure on you be heavy.

Indeed, you have said in my ears,
And [the] sound of [the] words I hear,
'I am pure without transgression;
I am clean and without guilt.
Yet, he finds reasons to oppose me;
He considers me his enemy.
He puts my feet in stocks;
He watches all my ways.'

On this, you are not right; I will answer you,
For Eloah is greater than man.
Why have you accused him,
[Is it] that he does not fulfill any of his words?

For El speaks in one [way],
And in two, [yet] no one perceives it.
In a dream, a vision of the night,
When deep sleep falls upon men,
In slumbers upon [the] bed,
Then he uncovers [the] ear of men,
And he seals their discipline
To turn a human [from] work,
And pride from a hero he covers up.
He holds back his being from [the] Pit
And his life from crossing the Channel.
He is chastened by pain upon his bed
And the strife of his bones is constant;
His life makes food loathsome to him,
And his being [loathes] fine meals.
His flesh disappears from view;
His bones, [which] were not seen, appear.
His being drew near the Pit
And his life to [the] Angels of Death.
If there is by him an angel,
An interpreter, one from a thousand,
To declare to a human his right,
Who favored him; who said:
'Deliver him from going down into the Pit;
I have found a ransom.'
Healthier is his flesh than a boy's;
He returns to the days of his youth.
He prays to Eloah; he accepted him.
He saw his face with joy.
He returned to [the] man his righteousness.
He sings before men; he said:
'I sinned, and I perverted the right,
And he did not pay me back.
He saved my being from passing into the Pit,
And my life sees the light.'

So, all these things El does,
Twice, three times with a man,
To turn back his being from [the] Pit,
To light [him] with the light of life.

Heed, Job; listen to me.
Be silent, and I will speak.
If there are words, answer me;
Speak, for I have desired your righteousness.
If you have nothing, listen to me;
Keep silent! I will teach you wisdom."

(Job 33)

Elihu's Second Speech

Elihu answered; he said:
"Hear, O wise ones, my words,
And those who have knowledge, give ear to me.
For the ear tests words,
As [the] palate tastes food.
Justice we will choose for ourselves;
We will know among us what is good.
For Job has said, 'I am righteous,
And El has taken away my justice.
Concerning my justice will I lie?
I am wounded [by] my arrow [though] sinless.'

What man is like Job?
He drinks mockery like water,
And goes with wicked men.
For he said, 'A man gains nothing,
From his favor with Elohim.'

Therefore, men of understanding, hear me.
Far be it from El to do evil,

And from Shaddai to do wrong.
For [the] work of a human he pays him,
And according to [the] way of man he causes him
    to attain.
Surely El would not cause evil,
And Shaddai would not pervert justice.
Who appointed him over [the] earth,
And who ordered [the] entire world?
If he sets his mind to it,
He can take back his spirit and his breath.
All flesh would expire together,
And humankind would return to slime.

If [you] have understanding, hear this;
Give ear to the sound of my words.
Can one who hates justice clothe [you]?
Or will you condemn [the] great Righteous One?
Him who calls a king 'scoundrel'?
[Or] nobles 'wicked,'
Who has not forgiven princes,
Nor favored [the] rich over the poor?
They are all the work of his hands.
[In] a moment they die, and [in the] middle of
    the night;
People are shaken and pass away;
[The] mighty are removed without a hand.

For his eyes are on a man's conduct,
And he sees all his steps.
There is no darkness, no shadow of Mot,
Where evildoers can hide.
For he does not set a time for man
To go to El in judgment.
He shatters the mighty without a search,
And he sets others in their place.

Therefore he knows their deeds;
He overturns night, and they are crushed.
With [the] wicked he struck them down
In a public place.
Because they turned away from following him,
And they did not heed any of his ways
To bring before him [the] cry of the poor,
And he might hear [the] cry of the afflicted.
If he is silent, who can condemn?
If he hide his face, who can see him,
Other than a group or an individual alike?
From [the] reign of an impious human,
[There is] more than snares for [the] people.
For has he said to El, 'I have asked forgiveness,
I will not act corruptly;
What I cannot see you teach me;
If I have done evil, I will not do [it] again?'
Shall he repay it from what you have
Since you despise [him]?
So you choose and not I,
And whatever you know, speak.
Intelligent men will say to me,
And a wise man who hears me:
'Job speaks without knowledge,
And his words are unintelligible.
Job ought to be tried until the end
On account of answers from evil men.
For he adds to his sin rebellion;
He strikes out among us,
And he multiplies his words against El.'"

(Job 34)

Elihu's Third Speech

Elihu answered; he said:
"Do you consider this justice,

Do you say, 'My righteousness is greater than El's'?
That you say, 'What does it profit you,
What do I gain from my sin'?
I will answer you [with] words,
And your friends with you.
Look to the heavens and see,
And behold [the] clouds; they are higher than you.
If you have sinned, what are you doing against him?
If your transgressions have multiplied, what are
    you doing to him?
If you have become righteous, what are you giving
    to him?
Or what does he take from your hand?
Your wickedness belongs to a man like yourself
And your righteousness to a human being.

From great oppression they cry out;
They call for help from the arm of the mighty.
And nobody has said, 'Where is Eloah my Maker?
Who gives strength in the night,
Who teaches us by the beasts of the earth,
[And] he makes us wise by the birds of the
    heavens.'
There they cry out, but he does not answer
Before [the] pride of [the] evil men.

Surely, El does not listen to deceit,
And Shaddai does not look at it.
Indeed you say [that] you cannot see him.
[The] case is before him; you should wait for him.
And now, there is nothing that his anger has
    punished,
And he has not known much folly.
And Job? In vain he opens his mouth;
He multiplies words without knowledge."

                                        (Job 35)

Elihu's Fourth Speech

Elihu continued; he said:
"Wait for me a little, and I will show you
That for Eloah there are still [more] words.
I will bring my knowledge from afar,
And I will grant righteousness to my maker.
For truly my words are not false;
Perfect knowledge is with you.

So, El is mighty, and he does not hate;
[He] is mighty [and] strong of heart.
He will not let the wicked live;
And justice he gives to [the] oppressed.
He does not withdraw his eyes from the righteous,
And with kings on the throne,
He has enthroned them forever;
They have been exalted.
And when they are bound in fetters,
[Or] should they be caught in cords of distress,
He has always told them what they have done,
And their transgressions that they magnify.
He has opened their ear to discipline;
He has said that they should turn from evil.
If they listen and serve [him],
They will end their days in the good,
And their years with the pleasures [of life].
And if they do not listen, they cross the Channel,
And they expire without knowledge.
[The] impious of heart display anger;
They do not cry out when he has chastised them.
Their being dies when young
And their life among the male prostitutes.
He rescues [the] afflicted by his affliction,
And he opens their ear by the oppression.
Indeed, he has lured you from [the] mouth of distress,

Instead, an unopened vessel [of wine]
And the comfort of your table full of rich food.
But you are full of judgment of [the] wicked;
Judgment and justice will be upheld.
But beware, lest he allure you by riches,
And let not a great bribe mislead you.
Will he compare your cry when there is no distress
With all your powers of strength?
Do not long for the night,
[When] people go up [from] their place.

Lo, El is exalted in his power;
Who is a teacher like him?
Who has reproached him [for] his conduct?
Or who has said, 'You have done wrong'?
Remember to extol his work,
Of which men have sung.
Every human has seen it;
Mankind sees [it] from afar.

Lo, El is great,
And we do not know the number of his years,
And [they] cannot be counted.
When he draws up drops of water,
They form rain for his flood,
Which [the] clouds trickle down;
They pour on the ground showers.
Can anyone understand [the] spreading of a cloud,
The thundering [from] his booth.

Lo, he spread his lightning over it,
And he covered the roots of the sea.
For with these things he judges peoples;
He gives food in abundance.
Lightning covered [his] palms;
He commanded it to attack.

His thunder speaks concerning him,
[As] cattle snorting against evil.

(Job 36)

Also at this my heart trembles
And leaps from its place.
Pay attention to the raging of his voice
And [the] rumbling that comes from his mouth.
Beneath the whole heavens he flashes it,
His lightning to the corners of the earth.
After it a voice roars;
He thunders with his majestic voice,
And he does not delay them when his voice is heard.
El thunders marvels with his voice;
He does great things we cannot comprehend.
For he commands to the snow, 'Fall to earth,'
And [to the] shower, 'Rain,'
And [there is] a shower of his mighty rains.
He seals up every human,
As all mankind of his making knows.
[The] living has entered [its] lair,
And in its den it lies down.
From the chamber comes the tempest
And from [the] storehouses [the] cold.
From the breath of El comes ice,
And [the] wide water is frozen.
Also with moisture he loads [the] clouds;
He scatters his lightning [among the] clouds.
And it flashes about in every way with his
    guidance,
Doing all that he commands,
Upon the surface of the world [and] its earth.
Whether for discipline, or for his earth,
Or for kindness, he makes it find [its mark].

Give ear to this, O Job;
Stand and consider the wonders of El.
Do you know how Eloah commands them,
How he flashes lightning [from] his clouds?
Do you know concerning [the] movements of
    clouds,
The wonders of perfect knowledge?
You whose clothes are hot,
When [the] earth is becalmed from [the] south,
Can you beat out the skies with him,
Strong as a mirror of cast metal?

Tell us what we should say to him;
We cannot arrange it in the presence of darkness.
Should it be told to him that I will speak?
Does a man ask that he be swallowed up?

And now, they have not seen [the] light;
It was bright in the skies,
And the wind has passed; it cleared them.
From Zaphon comes gold;
Over Eloah is awe-inspiring splendor.
We cannot find Shaddai,
Great [in] strength and justice,
And abundant righteousness, he will not oppress.
Therefore mankind should fear him;
He does not pay attention to any who are wise of
    mind."

                                        (Job 37)

Afterword

There are many interesting minority opinions that surfaced later than the time of David and hence the time of this story. Usually these opinions are not included in this book. But in the interest of this story, I have included some minority opinions that are later than this story, for example, the final and published form of Jonathan's poem (*Job II*) against the ancient story of Job or *Job I*. I have also attached a still later majority opinion, namely, the speeches of Elihu, which are directed against Jonathan's poem. I thought that it was important to make these speeches available in this context. The content of the Elihu speeches and the critical remarks against *Job II* were certainly alive and well during the time of this story as was Jonathan's criticism of *Job I*. In other words, Jonathan's debate was possible with those who stood with *Job I*. Also it is possible that their arguments in an abbreviated form once stood where the Elihu speeches now stand (or perhaps just after the end of *Job II*, [Job 3-26]). These arguments, and the later Elihu speeches, were meant to neutralize *Job II*.

In Chapter Eight Khety's story is from about 1800 B.C.E. My son, John Fisher, and I have published this story (*The Story of the Shipwrecked Sailor*) in a picture book for older children. John painted twenty-two illustrations for our book. The last illustration appears on the cover of *The Minority Report*. For the Hieroglyphic text used for my translation see, A. De Buck, *Egyptian Reading Book*, Vol. I, pp 100-106. Such Egyptian stories are forerunners of the great stories of Homer.

Cyrus Gordon has said, "Indeed, the whole *Tale of the Shipwrecked Sailor* is to be compared with the episode of the wondrous land of the Phaeacians on which Odysseus was shipwrecked" (*The Common Background of Greek and Hebrew Civilizations,* New York: Norton, 1965, p 111).

In *Entry Seven*, Keziah's minority opinion ("Humans and Beasts") on the relationship between the humans and the other animals comes from ancient traditions (Genesis 2:7 and 19). In this case, a later text, Ecclesiastes 3:16-22, was not included in the discussion, but I would like to include it here as an example of how a minority opinion can continue:

> And again I saw under the sun, [everywhere]:
> [In] the place of justice there was wickedness;
> And [in] the place of righteousness there was
>   wickedness.
> I said, I from my reasoning:
> "The Gods will judge the righteous and the
>   wicked,
> For [there is] a time for every pleasure
> And in addition for all their work."
> I said, I from my reasoning:
> "Regarding human beings, the Gods test them
> And disclose that they are animals; they belong
>   to them.
> For as to [the] fate of human beings and the fate
>   of beasts,
> [The] fate is the same for them:
> As dies this one thus dies the other,
> And [there is the] same spirit for all.
> And the superiority of the human over the beast
> Does not exist for all is vanity.
> All go to one place; all came from the clay, and all
>   return to the clay.
> Who knows if the spirit of human beings goes up
>   above,

And the spirit of the beasts goes down to a place
in the netherworld?"
And I saw that nothing is better than that the
human receives joy,
From his work, for that is his portion;
For who can bring him to see what will be after
him?

For a modern treatment of this topic see Charles Birch
and John Cobb, Jr, *The Liberation of Life,* Cambridge:
Cambridge University Press, 1981.

In *Entry Ten,* Keziah is dealing with a difficult problem
concerning visiting the sins of the ancestors upon the
children. Children may indeed suffer because of what their
parents have done, but this is not because God saves up the
parent's punishments for the children. The position of *Job
II* and Keziah is partially taken up by two later prophets.
This can be noted in Jeremiah 31:29-30 and Ezekiel 18:19-
20. They do not venture as far as *Job II,* or Jonathan and
Keziah, in saying that there is no justice, but they do make
the point that each person must bear the consequences of
his/her own sin. Why punish the innocent?

In Chapter Seventeen, Khety mentions a letter sent from
Egypt to Ugarit. This letter deals with a monument that
Marniptah will install in the temple of Ba'al at Ugarit. There is
such a letter, and it can be found in *Études Ougaritiques,* I (Ras
Shamra-Ougarit XIV), Paris: Éditions Recherche sur les
Civilisations, 2001, pp 239-248, text 2, "Une Lettre D'Égypt"
with translation and notes by Sylvie Lackenbacher. This should
be compared to the stela or monument of Seti I and the stela
of Rameses II from Beth-Shan. These two are the ones that
Khety saw copies of at Tamar's estate, and later Khety, Jonathan,
and Naam saw them when they went to Beth-shan. In 1928 an
expedition by the University of Pennsylvania actually discovered
these two stelae. See A. Rowe, *The Topography and History of
Beth-Shan,* (Philadelphia, 1930).

In Chapter Twenty-Three, *Entry Eleven*, Magon's text can be found in W. G. Lambert, Babylonian Wisdom Literature, Oxford: At the Clarendon Press, 1960. Page 101, lines 41-44.

In Chapter Twenty-four, when Khety speaks at the funeral, he is referring to a text, which is available in *Ancient Egyptian Literature*, Vol. II, p 175 and in *Ancient Near Eastern Texts*, pp 431 & 432. See "Acknowledgements" for more publication details.